The Fall into Ruin

THE FALL INTO RUIN

A DAUGHTERS OF DISGRACE
HISTORICAL ROMANCE

BRONWYN STUART

TULE
PUBLISHING

DEDICATION

Only you can live your best life.

Don't wait another moment for it to start…

CHAPTER ONE

IT SEEMED A perfectly innocent night when Rose Clairmont discovered the truly shocking nature of London's inhabitants and how quickly one could fall from grace. If one was at a place of grace to start with that is.

The sweet smell of spring lay heavy in the air, damp and intoxicating. She couldn't help but breathe it all in as she waited in the dark behind a dense shrub in her parents' garden. Nights like these weren't meant for nefarious activities. It should have been pitch-black and stormy; the skirts of her ridiculous gown should have blown all about and perhaps rain would dampen her hair to cling, wet and cold to her cheeks.

Instead, the warm evening made for an even warmer ballroom crush. Despite the fact her very overdue come-out shouldn't have even been at the bottom of the ton's entertainments that night, her mother knew how to throw a party and it seemed all of London had turned out to sample the champagne, delicate pastries and fashionable sweet cakes.

The gown Rose had been stuffed into was suffocating and heavy, with layers and layers of white skirts trimmed with pale yellow ribbons and yards of puffy lace. Her mother's attempts at hiding her youngest daughter's ungainly figure resulted in an evening gown that very closely resembled the dramatically high meringue atop the lemon tarts on the refreshment table. She had heard mumbles of delight and groans of rapture over those tarts. Only groans of a painful nature and titters about the Earl of Clairmont's poor, fat daughter had reached her ears even though she looked like one of those sweet dessert treats.

Society was, for the most part, an arsehole, she decided, not in the least bit ladylike in her mind.

But Rose did certainly appear to have sampled all of the sweet treats life had to offer. She felt so incredibly ridiculous. She felt hindered and closed-in. The only reason she had acquiesced to the ball at all was because her best friend was in trouble and had asked her to go to London to meet a secret contact. To pass along a note of the utmost importance.

All very exciting and very dangerous. Her heart soared.

Rose's parents pressuring her to come to the capital where they spent most of the year had actually been well timed. Her brothers and sisters were there as well as most of the household staff. So many bodies under the one roof guaranteed she was ignored here as well. Rose's figure, along with her inability to play the pianoforte or carry a tune, made her father wince each time he laid eyes upon her, which meant she had been able to remain at the estate in Dover with a handful of faithful retainers for years. After all, when one had four much older siblings, one could take pride in them and forget the youngest existed at all. She had thought she'd been forgotten entirely until that first summons came from her mother. By the time the third arrived, along with a threat from her father, she and her friend had come up with a plan of action but one of them had to travel to London to deliver the blasted note.

She wished she had stayed forgotten as she tried for the hundredth time to press down the layers of skirts so they didn't appear so full. Her partner in crime had insisted the danger would be too high for a lady and that he should be the one to make the journey. But as a mere stable lad, he would be missed from the Ashmoor estate and the large village in between. Michael could hardly travel with her. He would be turned out without thought if her father or the Duke of Ashmoor suspected they were more than lady and servant. Far too many questions would be asked. Many more lies would need to be told.

Rose almost snorted. She was hardly a lady anyway. Not on the inside. Not even on the outside despite the gown and the party.

The breaking of a twig nearby and the crunch of gravel gave her hope that her part in the charade was almost upon her but then a door opened on the terrace above her hiding place. Light fell on the shrubs and flowers before her. The lilting sounds of a waltz met her ears, followed by the slamming of the door and then the quiet descended once again. But only for a moment.

She continued to hold her breath as heavy footfalls sounded a furious pacing. A curse was muttered only a short distance from her head but she couldn't duck down any further, nor could she exit the area without being noticed. A sigh, another oath, more footsteps as the stranger seemed to head back towards the ballroom.

Rose wasn't as terrified of being seen as she was of missing the contact she was to pass the letter to. Michael had told her the man was a member of the ton, a man not to ever be fully trusted, a man he sought to help them from the trouble that had found them back in Dover.

Breathing as quietly as she could, Rose peered into the darkness beyond the gravel path but whoever was there had been frightened away by the newcomer on the terrace above. Blast it all. She'd had only one chance and now it was gone. How could she go home to Hell's Gate and explain to Michael that she had failed him? That she had also failed her people and practically opened the door for a wolf to stride on in without resistance. There was nothing else for it, she would have to go after the contact and run him to ground. Michael had trusted her and she was letting him down.

Climbing from beneath where the terrace jutted out from the main building, Rose had taken only one determined step when all at once her world came crashing down around her.

Literally.

Figuratively.

Painfully.

ANTHONY GERMAINE YOWLED in agony as he half hit the ground and half landed on something soft. He reached out for purchase, to stop from falling face first into the gravel even as he felt the bone in his foot crunch and give way beneath him.

The next sound to rent the still air was a tearing of fabric followed by feminine shrieks both from under and from above. He closed his eyes against the pain and rolled onto his back on the damp ground.

"Damn it all to hell," he howled, unable to hold it in any longer.

Light reached his closed lids and at the sounds of the masses emerging onto the terrace where he'd sought refuge, he opened his eyes and groaned again.

Lady Ulverston stared down at him in horror, her brows high and her fan dangling from fingers held in front of her open mouth. Only, she didn't really stare at him, more right above him.

Anthony tilted his head back, careless of his perfectly arranged hair, of his expensive tailored suit and highly shined boots. The sight that met his narrowed gaze made him want to howl again. All he could see were legs and skirts. Two slender legs encased in white hose disappearing beneath a mountain of pale, frothy skirts.

Like a turtle on her back, the unfortunate matron he'd knocked over in his haste to escape the ballroom, attempted to regain her feet but failed miserably. A blistering curse emerged from the pile of silks and ribbons.

Actual minutes passed before a few gentlemen ran down the stairs to assist the matron back to the standing position she'd been in before he'd so inelegantly crashed into her. All the assembled gentry seemed to be in a state of shock. But then the whispers began, turning into a torrent of fast-moving gossip intermingled with barely smothered laughter.

Anthony couldn't move. Pain gripped him so even breathing became difficult. When the crowd fell silent with a collective gasp, Anthony had to tilt his head back again to see what held the group transfixed. The matron had regained her standing but what captured his attention was the fact that the woman he'd jumped on in the dark was no middle-ager. She couldn't have been more than eighteen years old. What caused the instantaneous hush was that she held her pale gown together over her chest, her breasts pushing up and over the fabric as she tried to hold on and not come spilling out. Her chestnut hair was loose and sticking out in every direction possible, her spectacles were askew and her lower lip and chin shone bright red in the light of the ballroom.

She turned away from their growing audience but not quickly enough.

How would he talk his way out of this one? He had snuck into the ball to confront the Earl of Clairmont regarding a position with the Bow Street Runners. A position he had been continually rejected for even though he had the right skill set for the job. The earl had threatened to have him tossed out before telling him what he really thought of him.

"*I'm going to be completely honest with you now so that you might leave me the hell alone,*" he'd said.

Anthony had gulped, his cheeks burning with anger, with despair. "Please do."

"*You may have saved the prince's life. You may even have*

the best set of investigative skills England has ever known, but you will never get this position while I am in charge of the Runners. I don't trust you. I don't like you. Your father is a murderous pirate and your sister a wild hoyden, barely a woman and never a lady."

Anthony had opened his mouth to dispute the charges as they were but found there wasn't much to say to a man who, like so many before him, had already made his mind up about the son of a pirate first, a baron's daughter second.

The earl wasn't done. "I have been charged with the great honour of organising these men, of restoring some amount of law and dignity back to this city by apprehending criminals and seeing they hang for their crimes. You, sir, amount to a criminal. Your unfortunate start to life has tarred you with the same brush as every other villain in this city, and I will not besmirch the institution I am trying to build by naming you a Runner. Not today. Not ever."

His dreams of rising above his birth, of making a difference, had been shattered by those cruel words. He was on his way out of the ballroom when he'd noticed the earl's two eldest sons shadowing him. He'd bumped into a woman, which had sent her stumbling into a circle of yet more bejewelled viragos, all shooting glares at him. *The commoner. The klutz.* He'd heard their whispers.

Anthony had fled out onto the terrace and vaulted over the balustrade to escape what was surely going to be a beating from the brothers and a flaying from the grand-dames. He'd hide for a moment and then be on his way.

He hadn't counted on anyone being below.

He hadn't had enough time to think about it one way or another.

Who the bloody hell dithered in the garden at a ball, amongst the rosebushes of all places?

Anthony came to the wrong conclusions at the exact time the assembled guests did. They were partially hidden from anyone wandering the path and to make matters so much worse, the poor girl looked thoroughly ravished.

He was doomed.

CHAPTER TWO

A N ODD WAILING reached Rose as if from a great distance away. Her ears rang, her head ached and her chin felt the size of a child's ball toy. Her hands hurt from the effort to hold her dress together over her chest where it had been torn when the oaf had fallen on her. She and he both knew it had been an accident. He'd fallen over the balustrade of the terrace at the exact moment she'd emerged from her hiding place. He'd tried to stay on his feet but his hand had shot out and gripped the first thing in its path, which happened to be her hideous gown. Unfortunately for her, she was very well endowed and now every inch of her bosom threatened to spill forth.

Not one gentleman offered her a coat or a lady her shawl. Did anyone even breathe? She willed someone to break the oppressive silence and save her. But no. Even the wailing had ceased.

"What the hell?" Finally, someone spoke above a gossiping whisper. Her father. He pushed through the crowd and she felt a spark of relief. Her father would save her.

"Rose Elmira Clairmont, what have you done?"

A sob threatened to escape her, which was ridiculous because she wasn't a watering pot. She certainly wasn't prone to sobbing. But she was very definitely in trouble. The last time her father had used all of her names in that tone she'd been ten years old with a penchant for hiding slimy frogs in chamber pots.

"Papa, there was an accident. Please let me explain."

Her father turned away from her without even looking her in the eye. His attention lay on the groaning man who had ruined everything. "Germaine? What the hell is going on here?"

"I...I fell... She was in the wrong place," he tried to tell the earl.

For a moment Rose almost felt sorry for the man. He was clearly in a lot of pain.

Lady Ulverston, Rose's godmother and her mother's oldest friend and mentor, harrumphed and then interrupted. "I think it is obvious what was going on, Henry. The poor girl has been sheltered for far too long and had her eye turned by the first beau to walk her way."

Her father turned an impossible shade of purple while the crowd muttered and nodded as if it were the only explanation.

Rose surged forward to appeal to her father. "It isn't like that at all. I don't even know this man. I was taking a breath of air—"

"All the way down there?" Lady Ulverston enquired, cutting her off.

Rose threw her a glare but ignored her words and addressed her father again. Why wasn't he listening to her? "It was warm inside; he fell on me. This isn't what it looks like."

Lady Ulverston tsked with her tongue. "It never is, m'dear; it never is."

Why wasn't she helping? Why did she make matters worse?

Her father motioned to her two brothers to pick up the injured man. "Perhaps we should take these discussions inside?"

The man suddenly became animated and tried to shake off her brothers' hands. "I'll leave of my own accord. Just give me a moment."

Her father knelt before the stranger and spoke quietly in his ear but Rose was able to make out the words. "If you don't come inside now, I'm going to call you out and put a bullet in you at dawn. Your choice, bastard."

Rose's gasp was loud enough to draw both men's attention but she didn't care. Just because she had lived in Dover practically on her own for years, didn't mean she didn't know where this situation was about to lead. She stamped her foot with growing frustration and then had to readjust her tenuous grip on her gown. "This was nothing more than an unfortunate accident. Let him go on his way and let us be done with it."

No one seemed to be able to hear her words at all despite this particular tone of her voice working on almost everyone back at Hell's Gate. Their audience returned to the ballroom with an excited hum in their conversations, ready to begin the spread of gossip the second their coaches could be called, perhaps even before that.

Anger finally began to make way through the cloud of confusion, but Rose bit down on it and instead watched as the stranger sat up on the dewy grass. He sent her a look that said he was sorry. Or perhaps he was sorry for himself to have fallen on her and not someone prettier or richer. She was no great heiress and right then, she must have looked an absolute fright.

He surprised her when he shrugged out of his evening coat and offered it to her. He was the only one there who had thought about her discomfort so far. She mumbled her thanks as she took it and turned her back to shrug it on without further shame. To her horror, it barely covered her chest and only just hid the ruined gown. Tears filled her eyes but she drew several deep breaths and willed them away. *Stay strong*, she told herself.

"Rose, go upstairs and change your gown while I deal with this…this…piece of pond scum."

Her father couldn't seriously think she wasn't going to be present while they discussed her future, could he? For the last month she had appeared biddable, silent and perhaps a little slow to her family so they would forget her again and let her go back to the estate to fade into the background of their lives. How was she to make her point *and* keep up the charade?

The truth was, she couldn't. As soon as her father noticed she had a brain, she would be offloaded all the quicker to the highest bidder and then she would lose everything: her home, her freedom, her choices. The Earl of Clairmont didn't like his daughters having a say in anything. Her two older sisters had been married off by the end of their first seasons after having exhibited 'smarts'.

In the end, Rose didn't bother arguing. Her father wouldn't hear her anyway. "Yes, Papa," she murmured, eyes downcast.

Behind her she heard the groans and curses of the stranger and hoped like hell he could talk her father into forgetting the whole mess. She had agreed to a season on the town knowing full well no one would offer for her. At the end of those months, she figured her parents would have despaired of ever getting rid of her and sent her back to the country estate. She would have delivered Michael's message, along with some ill-gotten goods exchanged for coin, and they would be assisted with the pirate problem plaguing their part of the Channel. It was to have been a simple mission. It certainly wasn't to end in marriage.

It would never do for Rose to wind up tied to a stranger who would curtail her adventurous nature. From the cut of his coat and the cologne on his lapel, Rose knew for sure the strait-laced man who had fallen on her would treat her as any other gentleman of the ton would. As property. As a breeding mare and mother to his children.

Not only were her days of freedom threatened, the life she had built for herself would be at risk and the lives of others also. Her father might think her useless but the people of Hell's Gate—the tenants and villagers—relied upon her.

She wouldn't let it happen. She couldn't.

ANTHONY RETURNED THE glares of the earl and his sons as he faced them over the very same desk where he'd been humiliated earlier in the evening.

I don't trust you; I don't like you, rang in his head over and over. His ankle hurt like the devil's own dog had chewed on the bone and then spat it back out. Every time he moved, darkness encroached and he thought he would faint from the agony.

He drew a breath and then exhaled slowly before addressing the earl. "It was an accident," he bit out, not for the first time and probably not for the last.

"Did you come here tonight to do this to me?" Clairmont demanded.

What?

"Do what to you?"

"You came to beg for the position and then when I turned you down, you got it into your head to force my hand? I tell you it won't work!" The statement was punctuated with both hands slamming down on the mahogany.

"I didn't even know she was your daughter. How could I have orchestrated anything?"

"Everyone knows she is my daughter! You cannot miss her!"

Anthony cringed as though he had been slapped by the man at the crude description of his own child. Before he could defend or reply, one of the brothers stepped in and added, "I say we let him have her. It would serve them both right to be stuck with one another. What was she doing out there on her own anyway? Everyone is thinking the worst.

Let him have her, Father."

Clairmont looked about three seconds away from cuffing the one who'd spoken but then turned his fury back to Anthony. "Is it blackmail then? Are you threatening to marry my daughter if I *don't* give you the position?"

There were too many questions and too much pain. "I don't want to marry anyone. I don't even know the chit."

"So revenge then? You thought to create a scandal beneath my own roof to discredit me? Perhaps you thought if I was replaced, you would have a better chance of a position?"

Anthony kept wondering what any of it had to do with the earl and his reputation. It was all about the girl, Rose? Or was it Elmira? He couldn't remember but this was her future and his. Not the earl's. "Why can we not just explain it all as the accident it was?" he suggested. "Nothing happened between us. We didn't even exchange words for God's sake."

The eldest of the sons said, "The damage to her virtue has been done now. The girl was already going to have the devil's own time trying to land a man this side of fifty years with good eyesight. Now it will be impossible to pass her off as a virgin."

Anthony wished he'd got a better look at her. Was she so awful beneath the yards of fabric and lace? All he could recall were two slender legs poking from the layers of yellow petticoats and terrified eyes as big as saucers.

They kept their discussion going as though Anthony wasn't even in the room.

The earl said, "I don't care if she stays on the shelf for eternity. She will not be marrying the spawn of a pirate. No daughter of mine will be touched by a criminal."

Rage took over as the pain seemed to momentarily subside. Anthony rose to one foot, wobbling slightly, and leaned over the desk. "If I have ruined her, I will marry her. Honour demands it."

Clairmont met him nose to nose. "You will keep your filthy hands away from my girl."

"Half the ton think we have been intimate. You won't be able to change their minds." He knew his words would provoke rather than assure but he was already sick to death of the subject and wanted to go home or to a doctor.

"I'll kill you before I let you have any daughter of mine."

"Father," the eldest son warned. "There were too many witnesses tonight. They are engaged whether we like it or not."

Clairmont digested the information while Anthony fell back into his chair with a roar of agony. He'd never felt pain like it before. He just wanted it all to stop. The humiliation, the agony, the voices. This was not how he'd intended the night to go. He just wanted to be a Runner. He only wanted to help stamp out illegal activities in the city and keep London's citizens safe from being attacked in their own homes. He wanted an honourable purpose.

His aspirations faded to black, eclipsed by the agony. He'd need a jug of laudanum to get through the next hour, let alone the night. He'd give his other leg to swim in a bathtub of the stuff if they would just let him leave.

A glass was pushed into his hand as the younger of the brothers gave him a drink. He tipped it straight down his throat and asked for another. Anything to numb his body he would readily accept. He would even drink poison if it gave him peace for a time.

Confusion, anger, bewilderment—all were emotions crashing into each other in his chest, making it hard to breathe. He couldn't *not* marry the girl. He was a man of honour. No matter what had been thrown at him—the names he'd been called, the taunting he'd endured—he'd nearly always behaved as a gentleman of honour and high morals.

There was a time when he'd lashed out against society but for three years he'd been good. He'd played the part well and had earned a few friends along the way. With one mistake, he'd ruined his own life and that of an innocent young lady.

Dread should have filled him but instead he suddenly felt light, like a floating feather on the breeze as the pain lessened a degree. The glass fell from his fingertips, empty. He tried to raise his head but he couldn't move. The darkness from earlier gathered at the edges of the room. The earl and his sons blurred and their voices dimmed. Then everything went black.

For a second in time, he actually hoped he was dead.

ROSE SHRANK BACK from the door to her father's study and tucked herself flat against the wall in the next room, hidden in the shadows.

There was a commotion in the corridor as footmen were

called. She heard some curse words from her brothers, heard a pained groan, her father's angry voice as he shouted orders for Germaine to be returned to his townhouse. Who was he? she wondered. She would have her maid begin discreetly questioning the staff immediately.

They had been discussing her as though she were property. She shouldn't have been all that surprised really. The men in her family were still discussing her as they walked down the corridor towards the stairs that would take them to their bedchambers. "I don't care what it takes, Rose isn't marrying him," her father said.

"You could offer him the Runner position if he breaks the betrothal?" her brother suggested.

"We're going to have to kill him," came her father's muttered reply.

She almost gasped. Kill him? It was barely his fault at all. She was about to reveal her presence when Josiah spoke. "You can't kill him straight away. Everyone will know you had a hand in it. Why don't you wait for a time? Let him court Rose and let her decide. No one's going to marry her now and we all know it. Her dowry isn't big enough to entice a man to her size and...and...her appearance. I say we wait and see what happens. We can have him killed in a few months if we have to. Make it look like an accident rather than an outright murder."

Rose had known full well what her 'size' would mean to her father. The smuggling suit she wore beneath her gowns was a necessity to her plans and when her father had reacted so negatively to what he perceived to be her weight, she'd decided to continue wearing it just to annoy him further. Add to that her spectacles and the way her maid frizzed her hair, the freckles they drew on her skin, and she made for an interesting sight; she knew that. She felt sorry for these men who couldn't look past appearance to the person beneath but she hadn't realised her brothers thought so ill of her behind her back as well. Then again, she had never been close to Samuel or Josiah. They had been away at school and she had been at the estate. She found it actually hurt that they could be so shallow.

Her father spoke again. "I should have never let her stay at Hell's Gate. I should have had her brought here, starved and stuffed into corsets and put on the market."

"It's not your fault she's like she is, Father."

"It's all my fault. I should never have let your mother talk me into a debut for her. Society had all but forgotten about her anyway. We could have left her where she was."

A tear rolled down Rose's cheek as her chin dropped to her chest. She was thinking exactly the same thing. If they'd left her where she was, forgotten about the ugly duckling of the Clairmont family once and for all, none of it would have happened.

As quietly as she'd come, Rose took the servants' passage back to the upper family floors and tiptoed into her bedroom. She knew she shouldn't feel hurt. They were society men. They were London's men. Men who liked a woman to have curves but not the fat they thought she had, not the spectacles or the wild frizzy hair. Everyone looked down on her. Michael had told her for years, society men couldn't and shouldn't be trusted. That class and title and face were all that mattered to them.

The note!

Removing the nuisance spectacles from her nose, Rose dashed away her tears and admonished herself for being silly. She then sat down to pen a letter to Michael. He had to know she'd failed to make contact and pass the note along. She had to remember she had bigger worries than the man who'd accidentally compromised her virtue. She had bigger worries than what her brothers thought of their ugly sister. Michael was the only man in her life who had earned her respect and loyalty and he was in trouble. They were all in trouble. Her people were relying on her. The only important task at hand was to fix that bind first. The rest could wait.

If their crew of smugglers were dead and the estate at Hell's Gate and the village beyond burned to the ground as the pirate Mr Smith had threatened, Rose wouldn't have to worry about dessert gowns or wedding breakfasts. She wouldn't have to worry about much at all…

CHAPTER THREE

Three months later

IT HAD TO *be a trap.*

Unfolding the invitation and reading it again made no more sense to Anthony now than it had when it had first been presented to him on a silver tray along with his other missives. He hadn't been able to find an excuse plausible enough to decline. He'd asked his sister, Daniella, if he could use her confinement as a reason to stay in the city. The vixen had laughed and wished him happy travels.

Now that his ankle had healed, he once again had reason to leave his townhouse. He'd visited his club—it wasn't *White's* but it wasn't a slum den in The Dials either—and found the betting on his impending nuptials had reached epic proportions. Commiserations had been offered by those who'd witnessed the incident. Snickers of cruel laughter had been offered by those who'd heard of Rose Clairmont's…physique.

Anthony himself couldn't remember much of the night's events after he'd fallen on the girl. He'd been informed that he'd fainted like a delicate woman and smelling salts hadn't worked on him—the pirate spawn already familiar with the sulphuric smell of hell. He'd actually smiled and perhaps chuckled when he'd received that information in the first note from the Earl of Clairmont. It certainly was creative.

In the second note a week later, Anthony had been informed he wouldn't be able to see nor talk to Rose Clairmont until he was able to call on her at the estate, Hell's Gate, in Dover, where she had been rushed off to right after that fateful night. Obviously Clairmont knew nothing about the handling of a scandal. You needed to stay and meet the gossipmongers head-on, not run and hide, confirming the awful words being said behind your back. Anthony had dealt with scandal his entire life so he knew a thing or two about it.

He read the words again on the parchment in his hands. He was being summoned to a house party. Clairmont's handwriting was messy and lacked anything remotely resembling warmth but the words were there. He just didn't understand any of them. The man didn't want his daughter married to the son of a pirate first, a baron's daughter second. So why was he clearing the way for Anthony to be in the same house with said daughter?

It had to be a trap.

Anthony had run out of excuses and had little left to lose. If he didn't find employment soon, he would run out of his own funds and be forced to turn to his father for assistance. If he did find employment, he would be a laughingstock amongst the families of the peers who considered him their friend. He had nothing to offer Rose Clairmont and hoped like hell the earl had found a way out for them both. The idea that Anthony could indeed blackmail his way into a Runner position, Clairmont's idea, had some merit. If he was actually the pirate spawn his future father-in-law believed him to be. No, he would behave with honour. He would behave with decorum and pay the price for his actions. That's the man he was.

"I don't understand why I have to come along to some boring house party," Zachery Charles complained from across the carriage. "I don't know any of these people well enough to spend a week with them."

Anthony had dragged his cousin, now a minor baron and Anthony's closest relative after his sister, from his club at dawn and forced him to come along. If it was the Earl of Clairmont's intention to kill him the moment he alighted from his carriage, his blood and brains splattered all over the gravelled drive, then Anthony would have a witness. A witness who could not so easily be dispatched and then dropped from a cliff into the roiling sea. That's how every scenario had played out in his nightmares so far.

His stomach pitched like he was already on the ocean and his mouth watered for a calming brandy or five. He had a feeling even showing up with an army of barons wouldn't help him once he stood before Clairmont and his sons. Though having at least one person on his side couldn't do any harm.

"Perhaps you will find your true love there?" Anthony suggested with a raise of one brow.

Zach looked at him for all of three breaths and then began to guffaw and slap his hand against his thigh. "I cannot believe you just made a jest, cousin. And a good one at that. True love indeed. I have years until I need to shore up the succession. Years to bed anyone and anything my prick desires."

"You mean years until you catch a nasty disease and your prick falls off?"

"We can't all transform into monks overnight like you have. Damned waste if you ask me. You used to be all sorts of fun. What happened?"

He'd nearly had his throat cut. That's what had happened. He'd spent too long carousing and not enough time thinking of the damages it did to his mind and his body. After finally facing the fact that his father's reputation would forever taint his every second on this earth, Anthony had grasped the notoriety and flung himself into the pits of sin. He'd thought himself invincible because of his father, the dreaded Captain Richard Germaine. He'd been wrong about that too. Wrong about everything. "For too long I've lived off my father's reputation and his blunt. I'm nine and twenty and it's high time I began to stand on my own two feet. I don't want to be Richard Germaine's rotten son for eternity. I don't want to be the pirate spawn. I want to earn my own reputation and I'd rather it be for good deeds than debauchery."

Zach made a pfft sound with his lips and began to rummage in a bag at his side. "I say why stop now? Your father will send more money. You can remind everyone now and then how mean and fearsome he is, or was, and we carry on like we always have. There's nothing wrong with the fear that comes with being who *you* are. It's time we enjoy ourselves again."

Regrets about bringing the other man niggled. He would have far preferred his best friend Darcy's company than his cousin's. "You'd better not be thinking of causing trouble, Zach. You will keep your hands and thoughts to yourself while I find a way out of this marriage."

"I could bed the chit? You claim you haven't touched her and no one else would. If I bed her, you won't have to marry her."

His teeth clenched in his mouth so hard he almost couldn't reply. Anthony had yet to decide on his next course. Honour demanded he do right by Lady Rose and marry her, even if her father didn't approve. His true yearning lay in a position with the Bow Street Runners. For three years it was all he'd worked hard at. Now he was firmly stuck between doing what was right and doing what he wanted. He'd nearly always leaned towards the path of the right. "You will also have a care as to whom you are speaking of. This was not Rose Clairmont's fault, and I will not have her suffer any more than she already has. There will be no bedding and no more scandal."

"You really are no fun at all. I was only playing about. From what I hear, even to lay eyes on the Lady Rose takes one's manhood three whole months to rise again."

Even worse than the cruel words his cousin spoke was the fact that Anthony couldn't remember anything but a slender set of stockinged legs and tiny slippered feet. He couldn't associate the picture with anything he'd heard since. If she was so hideous, why hadn't the earl postponed her come-out until it was too late? It's not like he needed to marry her to a rich man to swell his own coffers. Nothing about the situation made any sense and the entire puzzle gave him a headache.

"Here, drink some of this." Zach offered him a swig from a bottle. "You've gone all pale."

"You brought your own liquor?" He tried to inject some admonishment into the question but his brain had other plans. Taking the bottle from his cousin with greedy hands, Anthony didn't take just one swig, he tipped the glass high and drank like a man denied water for a month.

He'd promised himself no alcohol until the mess was sorted. Wiping his mouth with the back of his hand, he almost snorted. The liquid burned its way down his throat and settled like an old friend in his stomach. The roiling ceased immediately. Even the carriage seemed to stop swaying like a leaf in the wind. He sighed. God, but it was good.

"You were supposed to save some for me," Zach complained, tipping the last of the drops into his own mouth with a scowl. As the carriage jolted one last time, he smiled. "Oh well, perhaps Clairmont will have a glass or two waiting as a welcome?"

When the nondescript carriage door was opened and the steps folded down, Anthony leaped out with a smile of his own when he saw the wide entryway to the imposing castle stood empty. No pistols or bullets or angry fathers. He did have to suppress a shiver when he finally tipped his head all the way back to take in the facade of what had been named Hell's Gate over a century earlier. Dark stone dripped moisture from moss growing in places that likely never saw warmth or even respite from the inhospitable coastal weather. Ancient turrets jutting into the overcast sky bespoke just how long the castle had been guarding the Dover coastline. He imagined battles being fought and won by those on the other side of the walls. Anyone caught on this side would be doomed.

The wind howled through the trees and the horses shifted restlessly as the sun dropped below the horizon and daylight faded. He wrenched his thoughts away from broken bodies and bloodstained paths. He was always on the side that lost. *So many mistakes*, his mind called. He hoped this wasn't to be another.

ROSE ALWAYS FELT like a Nordic conqueror when she stood at the highest point of Hell's Gate. The parapets shielded her from most of the wind and she could see for miles around. From this side of the castle, there was mostly only forest and ocean but the view was spectacular. Nothing like hell at all. Unless you counted the wind that never stopped blowing and the deadly cliffs where the waves crashed like the boulders of old thrown from the catapults of giants.

She smiled to herself and shook her head. This is what worry did to a soul. In the three months since she had been back at the country seat that her father rarely visited, she had done nothing but worry. Perhaps if she'd spent some time with Anthony Germaine, she could have measured his character and would already know his answer to the question she had to put to him.

Would he laugh at her? Would he admire her tenacity? Or would he run to her father and tell him what his daughter really got up to when there was no family around to bear witness? When it was only the servants to tell her no. Not that they ever did.

What good fortune that she had been ruined by the son of a pirate, she thought with a private smile.

As the wind changed direction and her hair was whipped higher into the air, Rose heard the sound of a carriage approaching. It was now or never. She climbed back down the steep stair and took the servants' corridors all the way to the room her mother had had made up for her fiancé. There were to be twenty guests in all for the house party. Some were lords and ladies of affluence, others misters and their wives from smaller neighbouring estates. Her father thought it prudent to begin to win their friends over to their side first and then London after. Rose kept telling him there were no sides and he could have put it all to rest then and there had he but listened to her. Those words only earned her glares and sermons about virtue and the realities of lightskirts living on the streets of London.

Michael had been the one to assure her it would all work out for the best. After failing to get his note to the gentleman that awful night, they'd had to devise another plan to get the pirate, Mr Smith, off their backs once and for all. His goons had been intercepting the ships destined for the sheltered jetty behind Hell's Gate for months. Men had lost their lives and Michael and Rose had lost their blunt. It was almost to the stage where they were unable to smuggle anything across the Channel and Rose would not have it.

If she couldn't sail and smuggle, she would become as useless as her father thought her. There would be no reason to live. There would be no *her*. The last ten years of her life would have been for nothing. The lengths she had gone to, to hide her real self, would have been for nought and her people would starve. Her father would sell her to a distant lord and all would be lost. *She* would be lost. Rose Clairmont would become a wife and blend into the background of some man's more important existence. She would never again be more than a housekeeper and breeder.

Firming her resolve, Rose pushed the door open to the chambers Germaine would spend the next week in. A thrill shot through her and she welcomed the rush of it in her veins. It had been too long since she had felt that lightness right to her soul. She was definitely doing the right thing.

Turning to the tiny dressing room, Rose walked straight in and closed the doors behind her until the dark was absolute. She felt with her fingers the edges of the great cape hanging in the corner. She'd had Foster, the head butler, hang it there that morning so she could remain undiscovered if Anthony Germaine brought a valet with him. If her plan was to work, she would need the element of surprise. It could have waited for the next day, she supposed, but she had already waited three long months to confront her would-be husband. She would not waste another minute to learn of her fate and that of Michael and their crew of ragtag smugglers.

CHAPTER FOUR

T HE INSULT WAS clear as Anthony made his way behind
the housekeeper to his room for the week, Zach mumbling about the lack of a welcome drink right behind him on
the carpeted stair.

Not one member of the Clairmont family had met them
at the door or the antechamber. Instead there had been a
formidable-looking woman of around sixty years, a large set
of keys in her hand and a frown on her face with not one
word of greeting waiting for them. "Follow me," she had
commanded and then turned for the huge staircase against a
wall hung with archaic tapestries. Though modern touches
had been added to the entryway to Hell's Gate, it still had
the smell and aesthetics of a Gothic, medieval castle. Anthony actually shivered when the wind howled even inside.

"Won't Lord Clairmont wish to see me?" he asked of the
housekeeper's wide back.

The woman actually sniggered and then threw over her
shoulder, "He's out polishing his skills with a rifle at the
moment. I suspect he'll see you when the house convenes for
supper."

Was that meant to worry him? "And Rose Clairmont? Is

she about the house?"

The housekeeper stopped dead and finally turned to face him with more than a frown this time. "The lady herself will decide if and when she sees the likes of you. I'll not be telling where she is or where she isn't to ravishers of young misses."

He stood taller but didn't argue, only inclined his head. "I see."

The housekeeper nodded. "See that you do. We'll not stand to see our Rose upset."

Interesting. *Our Rose*, was it? Anthony had done some investigating of his future bride and had come up with nothing more than her age and her whereabouts for the last decade. The elder Clairmonts spent their time in the capital, rarely returning to Dover every few years, but they hadn't set eyes on Hell's Gate for at least five. He hadn't been able to learn if Rose travelled to the city or if her parents had been set on forgetting their youngest daughter's existence altogether. As he'd dug deeper, the stories had become more and more unbelievable and worrying. Besides the rumours of her appearance, he wondered what else was wrong with the chit. There had to be something. Perhaps she was cracked?

He was filled with apprehension but fuelled by curiosity. His inquisitive mind had conjured up all manner of answers but each had been either ridiculous or impossible. Perhaps she hid a deformity beneath her petticoats and that's why she had been all but hidden from the world? Perhaps she had disgraced her family in some way and it had been kept from society? But he'd discounted that notion. Before she was even ten years old, she had been left in the care of others.

Not a thing explained why she had been recalled to the capital and then put on display. In some groups, a price tag had been hinted at for the gentleman who offered for the girl. In others it was whispered that Clairmont was in a financial bind and needed to sell his virginal beast of a girl. Anthony had cringed upon learning that piece of news although it would explain why the earl was so vehemently opposed to a match between a veritable pauper and his daughter. If the pirate thing hadn't been there. Which it was. And besides, all the smart men pushed away the idea that the earl was in need of coin.

Jittery nerves skated along his arms and made him clench his fists against the urge to demand to see Rose Clairmont immediately. It wouldn't do to get the staff offside right from the get-go. He was still mulling over the *our Rose* comment when the housekeeper finally came to a stop in front of a huge timber and iron door. He hadn't paid the least amount of attention to the way from which they'd come. He hoped Zach had.

The woman spoke, her voice harsh in the silence, her disapproval high. "This room is for Sir Anthony and the one to the right is for Lord Damer. A footman will come for you when it is time to convene before supper."

He nodded and smiled despite the frost beginning to accumulate from her tone and demeanour. "Thank you, Mrs…?"

"Good day to you," came her sniffed reply and then she was gone.

Zach laughed and rapped his thigh again. "Well, I never," he said.

"I have," Anthony sighed. He'd received receptions like that one all over England. Some better, some worse. He was quite used to it from the lowliest servant right up to the lord of the house. "I need time to freshen up before I'm summoned." Time to prepare himself for battle with Clairmont.

Anthony was probably going to marry his daughter, and he definitely wasn't going to like it. Neither the earl nor the intended husband. But he had his honour and he'd made a mistake. The earl himself had said he would never give Anthony a position as a Runner. He had to accept that fact just as much as the earl would have to accept his new son-in-law. God, it was going to be the longest week of his life. Right after the longest three months already endured. He wasn't even going to yet think of the lifetime to come.

When he stood in the darkened room, the door closed behind him with a slam of finality, he doubled over and heaved in great breaths of stagnant air. He could do this. He had to do this.

It was going to kill him.

When he eventually got his flailing sensibilities back under control, he turned up the wick on the lantern and surveyed the room. It matched the rest of the castle. The four-poster monstrosity was edged with blue velvet curtains. He assumed it was so the sleeper could block out the gruesome hunt depictions hanging from the walls. He wondered why Lady Clairmont hadn't redecorated the room but then thought perhaps this was Hell's Gate's version of a dungeon. It clearly wasn't a family wing. It probably hadn't been inhabited since the turn of the last century.

A writing desk sat beneath a large window overlooking a garden and further on from that, a copse of gnarled trees and then the sea. A set of drawers stood with a chair next to it, a pitcher and basin taking up the opposite corner with what appeared to be a dressing room in between. No modern amenities here. The chair and chamber pot were not even sheltered from the room if there was a husband and wife staying together. No screen for privacy, no tub for bathing, no warmth at all beyond the small fire burning in the grate and the coarse rug before it. At least they had laid a fire at all, he supposed.

Mumbling beneath his breath about being part of such a cold family, he set about removing his coat and cravat, placing them carefully over the back of the chair. He never used a valet and was perfectly able to look after his own linens. A knock at the large door signalled the footmen with his trunk and valise. It was little wonder he hadn't had to attempt to navigate the corridors and carry it all himself. He thanked the men who for some reason tarried in the doorway for longer than was necessary. All five seemed to size him up. It could have been his imagination playing havoc again but he was almost completely sure they judged him, standing there in their starched livery of maroon and gold.

"Is there something else?" he asked when they didn't make a move to leave. Was this the beating he had been expecting? His hand itched for the pistol in his valise. He wasn't brave enough to wear it when entering the earl's home but neither was he stupid enough to travel without it.

The youngest of the five, clean-shaven and baby-faced seemed to want to speak and then one of the older men nudged him in the back, pushing him forward slightly.

Anthony leaned against one of the bedposts, the house-keeper's *our Rose* ringing in his ears as an idea came to him. "Let him say what he wants, please. There'll be no repercussions from me."

The lad puffed his chest out sending the cascade of frothy lace at his neck all aquiver. "Did you do it on purpose?"

He didn't pretend not to know the rest of the question. "I did not. It was an accident. One I regret dearly."

Another man pushed forward, his clothing impeccable and identical to the others, his accent unmistakably revealing him a Scot. "Are you really a Germaine? As in Richard Germaine's bairn?"

He hesitated, swallowed, stalled for time. Were they wondering because they were for or against piracy? It was a test—that much was for sure. "Richard Germaine is my father, yes."

At least one set of eyes showed admiration. Another flickered to the dressing room and then the bed and back to Anthony.

"Come on, lads, let's leave the man in peace."

Anthony wanted to call after the men and discover why they'd asked only those two questions. Usually the first questions were the most important; the rest stemmed from the answers. The fact he was still standing and not lying in a pool of his own blood meant he might survive the house party after all. The servants of the castle obviously felt as though Rose was family rather than the master's daughter if the events of the last minutes were anything to go by. Even here his father's reputation clouded his own. They'd not asked questions about the kind of man Anthony was. The kind of character he had would make the difference between being a good husband or a terrible one. But why weren't they angry? One day soon he might take their Rose far away from Hell's Gate and probably never bring her back.

Or perhaps whatever had kept her there all alone all those years, the servants wanted to see an end to? So many questions and never enough answers! Anthony dragged his trunk to the dressing room and threw the door wide. He'd hang his clothes first and then sort the rest after he'd met with Clairmont.

Light from the lantern spilled across another threadbare rug and came to a stop at a pair of shoes tucked into the corner. A pair of shoes that were not empty. Backing slowly away, he went straight to his valise and pulled his pistol from inside.

"You may step out now, sir." He pointed the loaded pistol at chest height and waited. It seemed assassination was to be his end after all. Obvious and to the point.

What, or rather who, emerged after a brief hesitation, and Anthony swore long and loud.

"Forgive my intrusion—" the girl started. She didn't get any further.

"What the hell is going on? Did Clairmont design this trap? Throwing any old harlot at me to discredit my integrity? It won't work." He was beyond furious as he stared at the creature. Only she wasn't old and harlot wasn't the word he'd use to describe this vixen. She had wild chestnut hair falling in untamed curls as though she had just risen from her bed. Her lips were so red he wondered if she'd rouged them and dark freckles led him on a trail over her nose and cheeks. The girl looked so sure of herself, her confidence seductive in a way. She wore a dark floor-length cape, only her shoes poking from beneath.

Then she gulped and betrayed a nervousness he would never have guessed at. He followed the intriguing line of her throat at the movement but then he blinked, once, twice, a third time. After shaking himself free of carnal thoughts quick to cloud his judgement, he stepped back, his pistol still high. Here was his chance to be free. Here was a chance for Rose Clairmont to regain a little of her dignity. All Anthony had to do was accept this trap for what it was, give in, throw away his honour and pack his bags for a life on the Continent. His body liked the idea. His principles slammed a lid down on lust and howled that he had morals.

He cursed again and demanded, "Who are you?"

A SMILE CREPT its way to Rose's lips after hearing muttered oaths fall into the space between them. No gentleman would say the things he did in front of a lady. But then he was no gentleman and she wasn't much of a lady.

His fury radiated heat all around the cold room but Rose did not back down. She was a little wounded that her own fiancé didn't recognise her though. "My father didn't design any trap that I know of. I came here of my own will to beg of you a favour."

He sputtered a little, his green eyes round and large. "Your father? You are Rose Clairmont?"

She inclined her head, stayed calm and in control despite the galloping discomfort of her heart trying to escape her chest. "I am."

He took her in again from the top of her hair to the tips of her shoes and then back. She let him. What more could she do?

"I don't believe this. What are you doing here?" he exploded, confusion turning back to anger. "Are we not in enough trouble as it is?"

"Trouble doesn't even begin to describe what we are in. If you'll lower your voice though, we might discuss it like adults?"

"Discuss it? In my bedchamber? Where is your common sense?"

"Would you rather I wait until supper? At the dining table? Or over a glass of port with my family?"

He seemed distracted for a moment but then blinked. She wondered if he knew he did it. Was he nervous? She sure as hell was, especially staring down the chamber of his gun. "I didn't think so. If you'll lower your weapon, I might feel a little less…threatened."

He did as she asked but he didn't put the gun away. "Lady Rose, we can't do this here. If we are caught, your father will definitely think I have concocted this entire scheme."

She chuckled. "He already does. My reputation is in ru-ins. Thank you for that, by the way. Nothing worse can happen to me that hasn't already." She instantly regretted her words when his bright eyes took on a thoughtful shine. She rushed on. "What I have come to discuss cannot wait another moment."

Finally, Anthony Germaine seemed to relax and sat on the bed, the pistol on the blanket at his side as he leaned back on two hands. "I know what you're going to say," he told her.

"I rather doubt that," she retorted.

"You are worried about marrying a stranger. Believe me when I say I never meant for any of this to happen. I wasn't going to marry for years, if ever. But we will have time aplenty to get to know one another before the wedding."

"There isn't going to be a wedding," she blurted out. *Damn.*

"What do you mean?"

Rose took four deep breaths before replying. She honest-ly hadn't meant to deflate his male ego just like that. She had intended to let him down gently so as not to cause a shock. "You don't have to marry me. I'll find a way out for you but in return I need your help with something of a…delicate nature."

His eyes dropped to where her cloak rested against her stomach—well, the blasted smuggling suit she now had to wear all the time while her family were in residence. He groaned. "You are pregnant aren't you?"

"I beg your pardon?" she hissed. She threw the cloak

wide. Never mind it wouldn't make a tiny bit of difference since her gown wasn't fitted to her actual figure. "I most certainly am not. How dare you?"

"You were the one to suggest a delicate problem. Which other conclusion would you have me jump to? Are you in love with someone? Do you need me to look the other way while you meet your lover?"

"If you look the other way right now, I might stab you in the neck." In her fingers was a dagger, wicked and sharp and ready for the taste of blood if he kept talking about her in such a way.

Germaine had the pistol back in his hand and was on his feet in an impossibly short time. "Who are you really?"

"I am Rose Clairmont but I'm not the biddable daughter my family needs me to be. I have a proposition for you if you would like to hear it, but if you intend to turn me in to my father, then tell me now and let's be done with it. You'll still have to marry me but I'll spin a very pretty tale and my brothers will want to kill you for ever touching me."

"But I never touched you, damn it."

"That's not what I'll tell them."

For long moments of time neither spoke, and Rose wondered if she'd overplayed her hand already. Had her impulsiveness gotten her into trouble again? Should she have waited until she could have discerned his character first? *No!* There wasn't time for any of that. She needed his help. Or rather his father's help.

Anthony was the first to lower his weapon, not that Rose would have stood a chance if he was a crack shot. She pulled the dagger's sheath from her skirt pocket and with a hiss of steel, put the blade away. It was a start.

Rose spoke slowly. "I know this must be something of a shock for you."

"A shock?" he repeated as he leaned against a bedpost and ran his fingers through his short hair. "A shock would have been finding a harlot in my room. Having a bullet shatter my brains all over the drive—that would have been a shock. This has to be a dream. No, a nightmare. God, I need a drink."

She waited while he searched the room for liquor. "My father won't have provided wine if that's what you're looking for. He doesn't like you much."

"I'll need more than wine to deal with you."

She smiled again. If he was a true member of the ton, he would have shrieked about propriety and then thrown her out. If she was half the girl she should have been, he might have tried to seduce her. She moved the pitcher and basin to the floor and relaxed on the chair. Well, she tried to relax. It didn't work. At any moment they were going to be interrupted by Mrs Foster, the housekeeper, who had 'forgotten' to deliver something to his room. There wasn't time for snark or hysteria. "Would you please calm down so we may talk?"

He stopped and raised a brow in her direction. "Me calm down? It's not every day a man is accosted in his room by the woman he is to marry."

This time Rose laughed. Hysteria was exactly where Anthony Germaine was headed. "I'll bet that does happen every day, just not to you."

She could tell the exact moment her words sank in but he still didn't let down his guard or return her smile. He did stop moving about though.

Now it was her turn to become nervous again. He wasn't large or imposing but she had a feeling he saw right through her disguise. That, she could not have.

"What is so important then, Lady Rose, that you would risk so much?"

"I risk nothing. If I am discovered in your room, we marry. Right now that is already our fate."

"So how do you propose to get us out of it then? We had quite an audience that night and not one of them will forget the events in a hurry."

"I don't really care what any of them think they saw. We both know what actually happened. None of that matters anyway. I need your help with a little problem we have been having but first I'll need your promise as a gentleman, no as an honourable man, that you won't breathe a word of it to anyone else. Do we have an agreement?"

He'd raised his brows at the 'honourable man' part and for a moment Rose thought he would agree, but then he shook his head and said, "No, we do not have an agreement. You could be about to tell me anything. You could tell me your lover is going to kill your entire family while they sleep and why would I keep that a secret? If you really are pregnant, we can sort it out. I can help you to tell your father. How about you give me the extent of your problem and then I can decide if we tell Clairmont together or not?"

"For God's sake," Rose yelled, surging to her feet. "I am not pregnant, nor do I have a lover. Say it one more time, sir, and I shall cut your head off."

His green eyes widened. "You are not at all what I thought you would be."

"And neither are you if you cannot give me your word as your father's son that you will not reveal my secrets."

"What has any of this to do with my father?"

"Your word?" she said and held her hand out. "I'll not tell you anything until you give it."

"And I'll not give it until I know what I get myself into."

"Then we are at an impasse." Footsteps echoed from the corridor beyond the door and Rose's shoulders slumped in defeat. "If you change your mind, one of the servants can direct you to my chambers."

He came forward, actual concern reflected in his expression as he held out a hand to stay her. "If you are in danger, Rose, I can help you. Just tell me what the problem is."

She searched his gaze, disappointed when she didn't find what she sought. Where was the pirate's son she had been told about? Where was the man who had jumped to save the prince's life when it was in danger? That was the man she needed now and he wasn't there. This was not him. "I made a mistake coming here. Please, forget you ever saw me."

Her hand went to the door handle at the same time there came a knock.

Anthony slammed his arm against the solid timber and leaned next to where she stood. "Forget? You came here for my assistance. Just tell me what the problem is."

The knock sounded again and then Mrs Foster's voice could be heard. "I have a tray of refreshments for you, sir."

Rose met his eyes with hers and shook her head. How could she have been so wrong? "Release me or I will scream the castle down."

"Tell me what the problem is or I will tell your father you were here."

"Go ahead and tell him. What can he do? Lock me in my room until the wedding? Do what you will but remove your arm right now or I will slice you open."

The sound of her dagger being unsheathed cut the tense silence and he backed away but not before she saw the look of fury come down over his face again.

God, what had she done?

CHAPTER FIVE

ANTHONY HAD BEEN threatened by a lot of men in his life. Threatened more than once and with many weapons. Pistols, fists, horsewhips, worse. Never had the same man threatened him more than twice. Never had a woman threatened him at all. And never three times. In the one hour.

"With a bloody dagger of all things," he muttered beneath his breath as he tied his cravat and inspected his waistcoat for dust or animal hair. He had a scrappy little terrier at his house in London and always wound up with fur on his coat.

"Bloody wench needs a sound spanking."

"What are you moaning about?" Zach asked as he stepped into the room. He wore a gaudy emerald number topped off with a hat that even had a peacock feather dangling from it.

"What are you wearing?" Anthony asked his cousin, his mouth agape.

"What? This old thing?" he replied with a cheeky smile. "The ladies love it. Just the ticket for attracting attention at a house party I'm told."

"Told by whom?" he asked with a snort of disbelief. "Your current bed partner?"

"Good God, no. She wouldn't be seen dead with me in this. As it happens, I am repelling females this evening. Wouldn't want to go and find true love or anything."

"I cannot believe we are related. Take off that stupid hat and toss it on the fire. The footman will be here any minute."

"What's got you in a dither, cousin?"

Anthony stopped and stared at Zach who had removed the hat but hadn't fed it to the flames. "You didn't hear the commotion just before?"

Zach rolled his eyes. "The walls of this castle must be at least a foot thick. The silence is going to drive me to insanity. What happened?"

He debated telling his cousin everything and then nutting it all out together but the other man was a bit of a dimwit. Definitely not an investigative or discreet sort. "Nothing much, just an inquisition as to my intentions by the servants."

"The servants?" he guffawed. "You don't say."

He was saved an answer when one of the footmen, the younger one from earlier, stepped right into the room since Zach had left the door open. "I'm to take you gentlemen down to the pink salon for pre-dinner drinks."

"Thank God," Anthony muttered.

I'll need your word as your father's son, kept replaying in his head. What could a young lady of sound breeding who had been hidden away from society for years possibly know about his father? A shiver worked its way from Anthony's neck and ran down the length of his spine. The servant's two questions came back to him. One in particular: *'Are you Richard Germaine's bairn?'* There was only one way they could know. If they were involved in piracy.

He almost laughed out loud. Rose was Lord Clairmont's youngest daughter. Lord Clairmont's apparently unattractive, cow-like, hermit daughter. And besides, there were no pirates on the Channel anymore. Even smugglers had mostly ceased activity now that the waters were open for legitimate trade, providing one paid the taxes due on the approved goods.

For one, Clairmont was not involved in smuggling or any other illegal activity. His every action would be thoroughly scrutinised as the Master of the Runners. Secondly, he didn't need the money from illegal activities. The man's estates were profitable, running thousands of head of sheep in the north, watched over by many others in his stead while he was in London. His lands prospered and his sons helped him by all accounts Anthony had managed to dig up.

Anthony had done his research on the man and his family, and his business dealings. At that time, he had been hoping to find some thread of commonality with the earl before attempting to enter the Runners. It wouldn't have mattered if they'd had a thousand similarities though, the answer still would have been no for Anthony. He'd finally accepted it. Sort of. But now there was Rose. Surely if he married her, her father would have to give him a position. He couldn't have his daughter shackled to a man who held no prospects. Unless he cut them both off. Anthony still held on to the hope that if he could prove himself to the wider public, to society, perhaps he would be given a chance.

Slim hope but without it he had nothing to get out of bed for.

He tucked away his melancholy and tried to pay attention to the corridors and staircases so he could wander the castle later on his own. The footman was completely silent, as was Zach at his side, but as they descended the last flight of steep stairs, voices could be heard along with the pluckings of a harp. It sounded as though the party had started without them.

As they were passed off to the butler—a dour-looking man, also by the name of Foster—so they could be announced, Anthony felt the gaze of someone on the back of his neck. He looked around but it was too dark to see much of anything in the entryway. He scratched his nape and smoothed down his hair, adjusted the hem of his waistcoat and braced for either ridicule or cold shoulders.

Gilt-edged double doors admitted the two into a room painted the same colour as the flesh of a half-cooked piece of trout. The light from a thousand candles smarted after the darkened corridors and Anthony fought not to wince. They weren't announced, the door shutting firmly behind, even the butler himself not concerned with propriety though Zach held a minor title. A title submerged in scandal since Anthony's own mother had fled to marry a veritable pauper. Zach's great-grandfather had disowned his daughter and had never seen her alive again.

"Ah, Germaine, you made it after all," the brother, Josiah, commented with a hard clap to Anthony's back.

Samuel came to his other side and Anthony once again braced himself. This couldn't be good. The two brothers edged Zach out and then herded him across the room to a shadowy corner where they spoke in lowered tones.

"Just a word of warning, old chap," Josiah started with another clap to his back, this one a little harder and filled with more than a warning. "If you embarrass our family or our father while you are here, we'll make you wish you were dead."

I already do wish I was dead, he wanted to say. Instead he smiled and said, "I wouldn't dream of it."

"Do you want to marry our sister?" Samuel asked without further preamble.

"Despite what you might think of me, I have my honour. I will marry her."

Josiah nodded. "Yes, you will."

He was puzzled for a moment. "Your father doesn't want me to have her. Why would you?"

All were silent as a footman brought a tray of drinks and offered it around their tight circle. Anthony nearly took two glasses but had to settle for one.

"She is a blight on our family name now that she has had her ruinous debut. Father should have fished around for a private offer and been done with it, with her."

"Why didn't he?" Anthony tried to sound casual about the question but he was burning to know more of the Clairmont family history. He needed to know if the brothers were aware of the trouble Rose had mentioned or if they knew she walked about the castle hiding a dagger in her skirts.

Samuel stretched his neckcloth with his finger and peered around to make sure no one listened to their conversation. "You would have liked that, wouldn't you, Germaine? Tough. Now you're stuck with her and you better take her. You better make it believable too. We won't have her hanging about when Josiah takes the title."

His gaze snapped to Samuel at that comment. Was Clairmont sick or was Samuel talking about the distant future? Anthony couldn't be sure of anything more than this was the most bizarre family he'd ever come across. "I said I would marry her."

"No matter what Father offers you or threatens you with, you have to take her away from here. Do you understand?"

The liquor was smooth and warm and welcome. He drained the glass and motioned to the footman for another. He didn't understand at all, actually, but he nodded and gulped his drink. A commotion by the door soon had the room abuzz with murmurs leaving him no opportunity to ask. Foster announced Lady Rose Clairmont but not a one moved forward to greet her. It might have been the awful pale green dress she was gowned in that repulsed the room; either that or the huge spectacles perched on her tiny nose. Her father's bent head rose fractionally, his mouth settling into a grim line. The Clairmont brothers watched Anthony with intent stares.

Anger burned through him on Rose's behalf. How dare

they treat her like that in her own home? Aware she still may have been armed and unwilling to talk to him, he approached her anyway. She watched him like a hawk does a mouse but then forced a smile to her lips, if not all the way to sharp eyes hidden behind thick glass. It occurred to him that she hadn't been wearing them earlier in his room but he tucked the information away for later.

"Sir Anthony," she said with a little curtsy.

He bowed over her hand and placed a kiss on the back of her glove, adding in a low voice, "You do not have to curtsy to me."

A blush pinkened her cheeks. He straightened, squeezed her fingers and then wrapped her arm around his to take her further into the room, away from the door and the curious looks they were attracting. The footman with the tray walked over and it appeared Rose was about to lift a scotch glass to her lips but he squeezed her fingers again. "Take the champagne, Rose."

Irritation flashed in her gaze but she took the other glass instead. Anthony picked up his third drink and twirled the cup in his fingers. At least they both knew enough about the ton to know keeping up appearances was the most important part of the game.

"You have set the tongues to wagging with that gallant bow over my hand," she said quietly once they had found a sheltered corner.

"You did it when you curtsied to a social pariah."

She shook her head and sipped her champagne. "I forget which rules are which most of the time."

She should have looked down her nose and dismissed him with a sharp gaze rather than admit her shortcomings. Luckily the rest of the room largely ignored the two, even though the night was about them. About making Clairmont's friends and neighbours believe their match wasn't the outcome of a scandalous garden assignation.

"One of the important rules is leaving your weapon in your bedroom rather than bringing it to supper with your family."

She didn't blush this time, merely grinned and then hid the action behind a delicate cough. "How did you know?"

He'd seen her lime skirts stiffen as she'd curtsied. Something was in her pocket. She'd moved with such grace, he'd almost missed it. "Since when do ladies have pockets sewn into their evening gowns?"

"The pocket is beneath the gown." She pushed the spectacles up her nose and gazed up at him before speaking again. "Have you had time to consider our discussion from earlier?"

He ignored her words and a shocking revelation came to mind, something he hadn't previously considered. "Do you think one of your family members is going to attack you?"

Rose laughed. She attempted to keep it to a quiet, musical chuckle. "Not at all. Why would you say that?"

"This is only our third meeting and you have been armed for two of them. I wonder what you are protecting yourself from, or rather, whom."

With another forced smile, Rose began to stroll the edges of the room. She already disliked that he knew the most pertinent questions to ask. Despite all the nasty things her father had said about Germaine, he was obviously very perceptive. That was dangerous. "I was armed the first time too but couldn't get to my blade quick enough to slice your throat."

"You've done that before, have you?"

Her only answer was a half-shrug to feign confidence. Of course she had never slit a man's throat. She was sure she could if she had to though. If her own life depended on it.

Dinner was announced and her mother told the room in a high-pitched voice that they were forgetting tradition for the night and had changed the seating arrangements. They were to search out their name on a card for this meal.

Anthony offered his arm once again and Rose took it. She had little choice since they were being watched by a dozen sets of eyes, her father's included. Her heart gave a loud thump in her chest but then she plastered on her practised smile and pushed the spectacles up her nose again.

"Do you wear those all of the time?" he asked, his tone barely above a whisper as they walked, the last to leave the salon.

"I am quite blind without them."

"You seemed to do well enough in my chambers earlier."

Blast it, she'd hoped he hadn't noticed. Her nerves had been so frayed, she'd forgotten to put them on. The last few months with her family at the estate had been most trying. She was used to running free, not keeping up the appearance that she was most undesirable. It began to take the shine off of the years she'd spent being in charge and in control.

Frustration tinged her lie. "They were misplaced this afternoon. Thankfully my maid located them in time for dinner."

He raised a brow but didn't comment again. When he pulled her chair out for her to be seated, her cheeks heated again. He was chivalrous and despite her propensity for independence and control, she sort of liked it. When he snapped her linen straight and then placed it over her lap, she held her breath. He was too close. Too large. Too much. But then he frowned and took his own seat.

The hours went on while Rose drowned her apprehension and anticipation in wine. No matter who spoke to Anthony, he barely lifted his gaze from her. They were right down the opposite end of the table from her mother and father and two brothers. Everyone would see it for the snub it was but she cared very little what anyone else there thought of her. She was, however, almost dying to know how Anthony Germaine judged her. She could see it there in the depths of his green eyes, flat yet curious. He didn't give much away with the stare he fixed on her, only that she retained his interest for all to see.

Vicar Campbell and his wife sat to her right and the vicar's brother to the left of Anthony. Campbell said very little other than questions about Rose's impending nuptials and that he would perform the ceremony himself if they wished to be married there at the castle. She nodded and replied where necessary, making the appropriate noises when the man began to talk about his own wedding day. His wife said not much at all, only a nod here and there. The holy couple didn't need to know there would be no wedding vows said between her and Germaine. Rose still hadn't figured all the details but she had a bit of a plan forming. She hoped her intended could be bribed or at least cajoled to forget her existence and return to London.

Anthony regaled the other Mr Campbell with stories of the capital. His cousin Zachery was seated in the middle of the table next to the Morcum sisters from a neighbouring estate. Their father was at her brothers' end of the table. Her mother had definitely set the seating arrangement to distraction. No one was where they should have been but not too many appeared uncomfortable with the change.

Rose, however, was more than uncomfortable. Sweat trickled down her back and if she wasn't careful, it would drip from her brow. Her gowns were thick and horrible out of necessity and she damned them to the deepest pits of hell. In her mind she sent everyone else there too.

Finally the seventh course was cleared away, not that Rose had eaten much of anything. Her stomach was unsettled from nerves and the glasses of wine with each plate had done nothing to help her at all. Her head was oddly light, her body predictably heavy.

The gentlemen's port was waved off and it was decided to move back to the pink salon for a game or two. It was a house party after all. She needed the household to retire for the evening. She needed the household to pack and up and go back to the bloody city.

Rose wasn't quick to rise from the table, it being awkward for her to push her chair back and wobble her way to her feet. Anthony met her gaze over the rim of his wine glass, his brows high. "Are you any good at charades, Lady Rose?" It was the first he'd spoken directly to her in two hours.

She began to stand, intending to plead a headache and disappear. "I'm afraid parlour games are not quite my forte, Sir Anthony."

But then he was at her side, helping her from the chair, talking in her ear. "Perhaps we might take a stroll on the balcony?"

Oh God, his breath was hot against her neck. Her slipper caught on the hem of her gown and Rose overbalanced. With a barely muffled shriek she fell right into his arms. Before any of the other guests noticed, he had her back on her feet and his fisted hands at his sides but his touch had burned. It wasn't humiliation warming her as he stared her right in the eye through the blurred glass of the spectacles. It was something else entirely and Rose didn't like it at all. "I'm afraid I may have had too many glasses of wine and should retire for the evening."

The edges of Anthony's lips lifted in a grin that told her he saw right through her lies. Right through her. "Running away, Rose?" he murmured.

There was no one there to hear his words but she blushed nevertheless. Why did he have to purr her name like that? She needed some air. Cool air. Distance would help too. "I'm not running. Merely regrouping."

"Coward," he countered as he stepped closer.

She tried to retreat but the chair was at her side, the table behind her. "It wouldn't be proper for us to be alone together."

Anthony gestured to the now empty dining room. "We're alone now. We were alone this afternoon in my room."

"That is beside the point," she snapped, her cheeks hotter than the embers in the grate. Sweat still slicked her beneath the dress and her breath came in short pants. It was too hot. She was too hot.

"I would very much like to pick up our conversation from this afternoon," he offered.

"Have you reconsidered my terms?"

He held his arm out for her to take and raised a brow. "Shall we?"

Blast it all. She had no choice but to be led from the room. Again. How Rose would have loved to have played it coy and left him hanging. There just wasn't any time for that though.

THE THOUGHT FOREMOST in Anthony's mind as he and Rose walked across the small terrace and down the three steps to the garden was that the lady on his arm was dangerous. In too many ways to count. How many secrets did Rose Clairmont have? he wondered.

The lady spoke first, wasting very little time. "Have you?"

"Have I what?"

"Have you decided if you will help me?"

He should simply say yes. She hadn't reiterated her terms on the particular help he was to provide. Lying for a greater cause was not beneath him no matter where his honour or pride sat. Instead he said, "No."

It was too dark to see her reaction but he certainly felt it. The drop in her shoulders, the way her fingers gripped his coat sleeve before loosening and falling away completely. She stopped walking, turned on her silk-clad heel and started back towards the house, the wind catching her gown and a few tendrils of hair that had slipped free. Anthony shot out a hand and reached for her elbow. "Wait."

"For what?" she replied, her anger clear, her fear more obvious.

"Rose, we don't know one another at all. I don't expect you to tell me all of your secrets but you have to give me something on which to go by. I can't blindly offer assistance in what could very well be a mad scheme to murder or steal."

Rose scoffed but in this new light, facing the house, Anthony recognised the fear in her honey eyes flecked with gold. He saw the trepidation there. She was scared of something. Or someone. "Is it your brothers you fear? Your father? I've already agreed to marry you, to take you from here."

When his bride-to-be crossed her arms over her chest, he realised he may have spoken wrong. "What bad luck for you, milord. Come to court your beastly bride and carry her away over your sack horse's saddle at pistol point."

"That is not what I meant and you know it."

"I don't know anything anymore," she admitted.

"You're in trouble, Rose. You are armed and waiting for a fight in your own home. If I don't know who it is you're fighting, how am I supposed to help you?"

"I won't tell you anything until you agree not to discuss the matter with my father or my brothers."

"What about your mother? Is she outside of the problem? Is she the problem?"

Rose scowled and twisted her arm from the grip he still had on her elbow. "You couldn't be any further from the truth of it, milord. And you'll never be able to guess. I suggest you pack your things and make your way back to the capital while I sort the mess on my own."

"You think I can't work it out, Rose?" Anthony's temper began to fray. "You think I don't know it has something to do with piracy? Something to do with your footmen and your housekeeper? Are your butler and cook in on it also? I cannot be a party to lawbreaking."

Her mouth had formed a little *oh* by the time he'd poured forth his thoughts. But which particular nerve had he hit?

"You have no idea. No idea at all. You're not the man I need. You can't help me." The last she said more to herself than to him and the pain in her words actually left him reeling. He should have said yes. *Yes, Rose, I'll help you bury the bodies. I'll help you murder and hide the crime.*

He took her arms and pulled her close, the wind whipping around them like a living being bent on forcing them to its will much like the trees around the house. "You won't give me a chance? I'm to be your husband. You can confide in me."

Her gaze took on a faraway look before she finally met his eyes. "No. You're not him. I don't need you. I need Richard Germaine and his son. You're not him."

His recent resolution to never claim kinship to his father again sprung in action but the words died on his lips. Voices carried from the terrace and Anthony was forced to release her. Forced to watch as she disappeared into the darkness. He couldn't follow her because he wasn't his father's son. He was a good man who believed in the law and upholding it. He believed criminals who stole, raped and murdered should hang. His father might not be a typical cut-throat man of the sea but he had murdered. He'd stolen. He may have even raped, who knew? Not Anthony. He didn't know anything more than that his father's occupation had ruined his son's life and had left his daughter on the same path. Straight to the hangman's noose. Only divine intervention and the love of a titled man had saved Daniella.

It was a good thing Anthony Germaine didn't need saving. He was a good man and he would do good deeds of which he could be proud. Rose Clairmont was only right about one fact. She didn't need him. No one did.

CHAPTER SIX

A PIECE OF the puzzle lay before Anthony's closed eyes. It had soft edges, wore unnecessary spectacles and bright shadows danced around it in a mixture of danger and allure. Pushing back the blankets, he fought his way through the bed's curtains and reached for another drink. His mind was slow to focus, his thoughts sluggish and consumed with several different possibilities, each more bizarre and ridiculous than the ones that came before.

Rose Clairmont was an enigma he should have washed his hands of. He should have fled to the Continent the second his broken ankle had healed. He could have started again somewhere new. Changed his name and grown a beard. Now it was too late for any of that. Too late to salvage his pride or prove to England she had been wrong about him. He may have the prince on his side but it had never done him much good so far. It's not like they were chums.

Forgetting the glass, he swigged straight from the bottle the housekeeper had delivered as Rose had run from the room earlier in the afternoon. She'd *run*, for heaven's sake. For not one second did the housekeeper appear surprised Rose was in his room to start with. She had simply given him the tray and then hurried off after her mistress. What the bloody hell had he gotten himself into?

Rose Clairmont was lighter on her feet than he was. Even before he'd broken his ankle, he'd run like an elephant with another on its back. No grace whatsoever. But Rose, Rose ran like a ghost and vanished like one. He'd gone after her in the garden but had very quickly lost her. He wondered if her feet touched the grass because she didn't make a sound or leave a trail. Not bad considering she had to be fourteen stone or more. Only, she wasn't fourteen stone at all. When she'd tripped and he'd caught her, he'd braced for a fall, thinking he couldn't possibly hold her up and not because she was so heavy, but because he wasn't particularly strong. He wasn't a huge man with muscles tearing his shirtsleeves. Only, now he knew some truth. Another piece to the puzzle. Rose Clairmont was not the heavy girl the unfeeling ton made fun of.

For the last few long hours he'd considered giving her his promise that he would help her without breathing a word of her problem to anyone. He just wanted to know what was going on. More than anything, he wanted to know how it involved his father. His retired pirate captain father.

Anthony's investigative mind was a whirl of activity and it needed an outlet. He needed a problem to solve. But he wouldn't just hand himself over to her. No. That wouldn't do. So he'd retired to his room but he couldn't sleep. The alcohol he'd come to rely on during his convalescence with a broken ankle didn't help either. How could anyone sleep when their brain just would not switch off? What was Rose so frightened of? Who in the hell was she really?

Eventually Anthony pulled on a pair of trousers and shrugged on a shirt before drifting over to the window above the desk. He really should drink from a glass. He wasn't an animal. A movement outside caught his eye. Was it a swaying tree? The howling wind was the only sound to penetrate the castle walls so he wasn't surprised everything moved about out there.

Only, the shadow kept on along the border of a garden bed, ducking beneath this branch and that. If the moon had been obscured, he would never have seen anything. Eyeing the brandy bottle and wondering if he'd had more than he thought, Anthony shook his head and turned the lantern right down to peer out the window again. There he was, a man, walking fast towards the garden's far end.

The wind changed direction and the man's cloak blew right out, the hood falling back while he scrambled to right it. Even across the shadowed garden and through a window three floors up, Anthony knew it wasn't a man. A man didn't wear a white ankle-length nightgown. Chestnut curls spilled from the cloak's hood and Anthony swore a blue streak.

She'd threatened him with violence when he'd accused her of having a lover. Was the rest just a ruse to throw him off the true path? He shouldn't have listened to her lies. Shoving his feet into a pair of boots, without time to put on hose or even do the laces, he was out the door and down a flight of stairs before he recalled he didn't know his way around the castle very well. He especially didn't know where he was going in the dark. Thankfully someone had left a few lanterns burning on each landing. He reached the bottom of the last stair and made his way to the front doors. He would be on the wrong side of the house but if he was quick enough, he might still catch her before she did anything silly.

One thought pulled him up short and nearly made him stumble as he rounded the damp stone corner of the castle emerging into the gardens. Was she running away? No, not in her nightgown, surely. He had refused her his help unless she told him what had happened. What if she wasn't on her way to a secret assignation? Had she seen no other way out and was on her way to throw herself off the deadly cliffs?

God, he'd been so stupid. He should have told her father at once that she was in danger. He wouldn't have cared for the information to start with but he could have intervened. He could have locked Rose in her room until she'd calmed down. The chit was cracked and hid it very well.

Damn it all to hell!

With each stride, his ankle throbbed. He hadn't run anywhere in months. Skirting the same hedge as Rose had the last he'd seen her, he hoped there was nothing deadly in the dark he could run into or fall down. Only by the light of the moon was he able to see anything at all but when he reached the corner of the garden, he didn't know where to go next. A narrow path disappeared into the tree line and he stopped, his hands on his thighs while he took heaving breaths of cold air into his burning lungs.

A sound carried on the wind and he straightened. Was it a gunshot? Or an explosion? This time he didn't hesitate as he took off down the path. Branches whipped at his face and grabbed at his shirt and trousers. A misstep nearly sent him tumbling head first into the undergrowth as he yelped, his ankle twisting. He righted himself the best he could and slowed down as complete darkness descended.

ROSE SHUTTERED HER lantern and dropped to a squat next to a wide-trunked tree. Though her heart thundered in her ears and the wind hissed and howled through the foliage, she'd known her follower was right behind her. She'd quickened her pace but so had they.

When the shriek came, followed by vulgar curses, she hoped whoever it was had come to grief and broken his bloody back. Only a short way ahead of where she hid was the end of one path and the beginning of the next. Rose knew Michael was bringing in a new shipment to the sheltered beach and hadn't wanted to miss out but the house party meant her actions were being watched. Or so she'd thought until she'd been completely ignored by her family for the entire night. They didn't give a fig about her or what she did. Judging by her brothers' vicious comments in the capital, they probably assumed she sat around and ate cake all day.

Yes, it had been a risk setting out but she was only going to watch from the safety of the cliff's edge. She'd even left her nightgown on just in case anyone from the house found her coming back in. She would pretend to be sleepwalking so long as they didn't see her boys' trousers beneath. It had worked a time or two in her younger years and she had become a much better actress since then.

Her lady's maid, Molly, would turn away anyone coming to her rooms in the night—not that there would be a reason for anyone to knock at her door—but if her mother or father suddenly worried for her wellbeing and came to check on her, Molly knew what to say and do. The servants in the castle were completely loyal to Rose. She paid them far more than the estate ever would, which is exactly why she was in the smuggling game to start with. They had become her friends and co-conspirators once she'd discovered how very little Hell's Gate provided for them to live, or rather, survive on. They had more to lose than she did if their antics were discovered.

If Mr Smith made good on his threats, they were all doomed anyway. Damn Anthony Germaine for being so soft. He clearly wasn't frightened to marry her yet he was a man of the law. A man who wouldn't abide Rose's smuggling activities or admire her adventurous spirit. She could never marry a man like that.

Which is why Rose had ventured out into the freezing cold, windy night to watch over the men's activities and make sure no harm came to Michael or their crew, not that she could do much to help them if something did go wrong. Staying away from smuggling while her family were in residence physically hurt her and they couldn't stop altogether because once the weather turned for the season, the goods would dry up and so would the money her tenants required to make their ends meet since her father didn't take proper care of them.

She herself needed a few good shipments so she could raise enough blunt to disappear into the night and never be found again. Right after the problem of Mr Smith was taken care of and she could rest easy knowing her friends could smuggle on once Rose was gone.

Confident whoever had followed had given up and gone back the way they'd come, Rose left the lantern and crept from the tree line to the edge of the cliffs. In the pocket of her cloak was a loaded pistol and she took it out before lying on her stomach and inching forward until she could see the beach. Waves crashed down on the shoreline leaving white foam behind when the sea retreated, only to crash back again and again.

It didn't take long for her eyes to adjust and she could make out a few men standing, waiting. She saw six but knew there would be more—staff from the house, tenants and some from the village between Hell's Gate and the Duke of Ashmoor's estate. The rowboats were missing, which meant some had gone out to meet the ship and bring the goods back. It was their only mode of transport since Mr Smith had ordered his pirates to intercept their sloop and burn it to the waterline.

Tea and lace were their trade for this evening. They'd already sent out their cargo of wool some weeks back and now it was the night to collect their swap. A whole seasons' worth of blood, sweat and even a few tears had departed the dock sheltered behind Hell's Gate—merely wool to the excise men's eyes if they were caught, but also gold beneath the sheep's clothing. And she wasn't a party to any of it this time, the risk of her discovery too great. Rose wasn't good at standing idly by.

Almost everything had now been shipped out to Calais. The brandy had come in on a successful midnight run already; now came the other half in tea and lace. The lace was to be sent straight to Michael's benefactor in London and the tea was to stay hidden for a few weeks and then be sold off in smaller amounts. They were to make double their money just from the brandy profits so it was well worth the risks. It wouldn't have been much of a risk at all if Mr Smith hadn't taken an interest in their comings and goings.

For at least five years the people of the estate and village had enjoyed reasonably hassle-free smuggling since her father and Ashmoor were veritable misers when it came to cottage repairs. Hell's Gate itself was mildly profitable but the inhospitable land made farming difficult and running cattle hard and dangerous work, which meant less money for her father and much less for tenants. From what Rose now knew, smuggling from this coastline had been going on for decades, if not a century or more even in legal times because the excise taxes were so high.

Now their French friends grew wary and had threatened to stop their trade altogether if the pirate wasn't taken care of. That's where Anthony Germaine was to have stepped in. His father was the most notorious pirate the seas around England had seen in many a decade. Now that word spread about Richard Germaine's retirement, Mr Smith all but owned the Channel. Anthony could have sent a message for her, calling on his father to help his bride-to-be since she'd failed to deliver the note in London, which was to beg aid.

Failing to deliver that missive after she'd been ruined,

Rose had needed a plan B. Or was it C or D now? It was the only idea any of them had come up with since that night. Just a tiny bit of blackmail. He would offer his assistance and she would offer him an escape from their impending nuptials. Only a tiny little bit of blackmail. But Anthony had shot it all to hell when he'd refused to help. She needed a pirate to fight a pirate. In her mind, it had made perfect sense. Of all the people in all the world to fall on her, it had been a stroke of luck.

Now she had no clue what to do. About any of it.

Activity just off the rocky beach drew her attention and she squinted a little to make out which of the men it was. Riordan, the blacksmith—he was the easiest to recognise as the rowboat crashed through the last of the breakers to slide ashore with a crunch. She let out her breath with a sigh of relief as Michael leaped down to help drag it further out of the waves. Behind him another two tiny boats were tossed about, one making it through, the other pushed back out by the retreating currents.

Half a dozen more men streamed from their hiding places to help carry the goods to a sheltered cave. They had the rhythm down to a fine art, each man with his own job to do.

Rose pressed her palms to the damp ground beneath her shoulders to push back to her feet and return to the castle but as the wind abated for just two heartbeats, there came a crashing behind her. Before she could turn or roll, she was pinned to the ground, sharp rocks biting into her thighs and knees, the breath squeezed from her lungs.

"Well, well, well," a voice crooned into her ear. "Just how many secrets do you have, Rose Clairmont?"

CHAPTER SEVEN

W HEN ANTHONY HAD lain in his bed earlier that night,
trying desperately to get to sleep but failing dismally,
not once had this scenario crossed his mind. He used his
body weight to press Rose into the ground and with each
buck of her hips to throw him off, he felt only pillowy
softness against his chest and stomach.

"A lady spy are you? Or your father's snitch perhaps?" he
wondered out loud.

"Get off me," she hissed beneath him with another buck.
She may have been lighter on her feet than he'd expected but
she wasn't strong enough to lift him.

Anthony raised one hand and tried to untie her cloak so
he could pull it back a little but she fought him every inch.
He didn't want to get rough with a lady, especially not this
lady, but he would know what she wore around her body to
make herself large and soft. Was it actual pillows? It certainly
felt like pillows as she kept trying to dislodge him. He knew
when he'd caught her at the dining table, when she'd
tripped, that there was more to Rose, or less as this case
might have been, but he'd been distracted and hadn't given
it enough thorough analysis.

"Be still for a moment," he commanded.

She ignored him but he was prepared for that. As quick as he could manage with his ankle still smarting like a horse had kicked it, he raised himself up and rolled Rose to her back, pressing into her right away with his body while he caught her hands in his own lest she punch him in the face.

She hissed and wheezed. "I can't breathe, you big oaf."

He'd never been called that before. He smiled and met her eyes. "You certainly don't need the spectacles," he said but more to himself than to her. By the light of the moon, her big eyes flashed a murderous gold but for a moment, he was entranced by the length of her lashes fanning across her cheeks as she blinked.

Anthony pulled away and swore. "Did you just try to butt me with your head?"

"Let me go," she said, still fighting him. "I told you I don't need your help now."

Careful of the weapons she made out of her body parts, Anthony pinned her two hands with one of his, noting a discarded pistol just above, and then began to undo the buttons marching down the front of her nightgown.

Rose went dead still. "What are you doing?" Was that genuine fear in her voice? He bloody hoped so.

"What are you wearing beneath your gown?" He straddled her now but he could feel laces or buttons or something digging into his backside right beneath where the softness ended. Ladies' drawers wouldn't have sharp edges at the front. He'd undressed enough women to know how their undergarments worked.

Rose resumed the fight, thrashing and attempting to knee him in the back. "You cannot do this. You're a gentleman."

He scoffed and paused for a moment, holding her wild gaze. "Who told you that?"

"I will kill you if you so much as lay a finger on me."

Anthony felt it pertinent to point out, "I could do more than lay a finger on you and then I could murder you and toss your body from the cliffs. This is why ladies do not wander about in the dark in their nightclothes. But then I'm beginning to think you are no lady."

With each button he undid—which was bloody hard considering how small they and their corresponding holes were—he revealed more and more. First was the fabric of her chemise, her breasts straining against the material, a little ribbon tied between. But then came the puzzling part. Just below her heaving chest was the pillowy softness. Clearly stitched well and showing a lot of use was a type of waistcoat. It pulled over her shoulders and down her sides beneath her armpits. He couldn't see how it was fastened and as he put three fingers between it and her body, he could feel the thickness. He gave a little tug but it held firm. "Ingenious," he muttered, staring at what seemed to be compartments of sorts. Individual pockets but to hold what?

She had gone so still, Anthony looked back to her face to make sure she was still alive. She watched him more intently than he had her. "What are you going to do now?" she asked right before biting down on the delicate flesh of her bottom lip to await his answer.

He was saved words, words he couldn't think up right then anyway, by a bright glow from the shoreline. From the roiling black ocean came flying lights. For a half second he marvelled at their beauty. Rose's neck craned back to see what he saw. But then a boat on the shoreline caught fire and the men scrambled back from the flames. He'd almost forgotten about the smugglers while he'd practically un-dressed his future wife in the scrub. The more seconds that passed, the more he was sure she had been giving him an act in the garden and at dinner. Clearly what Rose Clairmont really wanted was a man she could easily manipulate.

She gasped and turned her body. He let her up but then pushed her back down when she made to stand. Fumbling forward, she reached for the pistol and held it not at him but at the ocean.

"Put that down," he told her, grabbing the top of the presumably loaded weapon.

"I have to help them," she said, trying once again to stand.

More flying lights appeared, well-lit arrows hitting their mark over and over as fire consumed yet another rowboat. Within seconds the men on the beach had fled into the rocks without a shot fired or an answering arrow. Not that they could possibly see what they shot at. It was darker than dark across the horizon despite the moon and its light. The cliffs must have bordered a cove or inlet and deep shadows hid anything beyond the breaking waves.

Instead of cursing the darkness, Anthony was grateful for it. "We haven't been seen yet. Either we stay down or we go back into the trees."

"Michael will need my help. What if the pirates come ashore?"

"Michael? Is he your lover? Were you to meet with him after he stashed his ill-gotten goods?"

"For the absolute last time, I don't have a lover. Michael is my friend." She pulled away and made to stand again. "He might need me. Mr Smith will kill him if he is captured."

A deadly chill ran the length of his spine and Anthony leaped to his feet. He took Rose by the shoulders and propelled her back into the trees. Once he was sure they were hidden by huge branches and rustling leaves, he turned her so he could face her. He might have even shaken her a little as he said firmly, his tone low, his anxiety high, "I need you to repeat what you just said."

She eyed him warily, skittish now and aware something was wrong, more than her own situation called for, though that should have been bad enough. "Which part?" she asked.

"You said Mr Smith will kill him."

Rose nodded but didn't elaborate.

This time Anthony did shake her. "What do you know of Mr Smith?"

"He's the pirate I needed your help with."

"Have you seen him? Met him? Does he know you are involved in this?" He paused and then drew her closer so he could see her eyes better. Dread filled him. "What exactly *is* your involvement in this, Rose?"

"I'll need your word before I tell you anything."

His grip tightened on her arms. "You have no idea who

you are dealing with, do you? No idea of the danger you are in if Smith has marked you." Because of his broken ankle, Anthony hadn't been there the night Smith had kidnapped a duke's children and then attempted to kill them to prevent their witness to his awful deeds. Anthony's pregnant sister had also nearly died. His brother-in-law had been searching for the blackguard ever since but there'd been no trail left to follow. Perhaps Rose was wrong about the name or perhaps it was coincidence?

Only, Anthony believed in coincidence about as much as he believed in miracles. They were the stuff of faerie tales.

Rose's lips flattened to a thin line before she opened her mouth again. "I'll not tell you any more until I have your word you won't tell my father. I don't need his interference."

"You need a spanking is what you need. You need to be locked in your room or supervised around the clock. Damn it, Rose, tell me the truth."

She finally wrenched free of his grasp and bent to retrieve her lantern. "Unless you wish to make our fight yours, then you are better off not knowing."

He was left very little choice at that stage. It was either give her his word or be left in the proverbial dark, possibly even see her killed before the end of the week. Perhaps that was what she had meant by 'there won't be a wedding' the day before.

Rather than rushing back to the cliffs, Rose lifted a shutter on the lantern and began to walk back up the path to the castle, her cloak flapping around her ankles. The wind picked up, her hem floated and he swore again. Was the chit wearing trousers? Had that been the sharp edges he'd felt as he'd pinned her?

Swallowing back his pride, his questions, his honour, he spoke to her back. "You have my word."

Just as he'd hoped, she paused but didn't look back. "Be more specific."

He stepped closer, his front almost flush with her back. "You have my word that I won't tell your father about this mess you've gotten yourself into. But I want the whole truth, Rose. All of it."

Her chin drooped low but then she nodded. "After breakfast tomorrow, tell my father you would like to take a ride. Ask for a horse to be readied but no groom."

"There is no chance he'd agree to that. I don't know my way about. Tell me now."

She chuckled softly. "He'll agree. He'll probably hope you fall and break your neck. Be prepared for a feisty mount."

ROSE HAD SEEN dozens of men in their shirtsleeves, some even naked to the waist. So why did the sight of Anthony Germaine's forearms give her pause? She'd practically just lain there waiting for him to ravish her, her gaze transfixed on the patch of thick hair where he'd not fastened his shirt up to his throat.

Despite her antics with smuggling, her faux bravado and her best friend being on the wrong side of the law, Rose was still a good girl. And almost a spinster. She approached her twentieth birthday but felt about a hundred years old right then, on that path, in the wind and cold.

She lifted the cloak's hood to cover her hair and wrapped the wool tighter around her body as she hurried from the darkness of the trees, confident Michael and the men would be long gone to safety if Smith did decide to land a shore party. With every breath, she was aware of Anthony behind her. Aware of his thousands of questions and doubts. She had the same doubts, a thousand more questions than he did. Why did he have to follow her? Why couldn't he be on his way back to London? At the top of the list of what-ifs was how it was all going to end. Anyone who had ever done anything illegal must have had the same thoughts about their death or retirement.

Either she was going to die on the beach like so many had before her—generations of Clairmonts had given their lives for this land; Hell's Gate wasn't a name pulled from a Viking hat centuries before—or Rose was going to have to give up adventure and retire.

When she'd been all of thirteen, left at the estate rather than embarrass her family with her ungainly 'puppy fat', she'd been treated differently by the staff, taken under their wing and raised as their own children were. She and Michael, a stable lad, had become fast friends and easy-going comrades, helping with the smuggling trade to pass the dreary days. Her father never came to the estate for regular visits and always sent word of his arrival so the servants could be ready for him. Like he was a king or a god. It made it easy for Rose to suggest using his barns for the illegal goods and his horse and carts to transport it all. The Clairmont crest would never be questioned or denied passage. Her ideas had been welcome, as had she.

Hell's Gate had a long, sturdy jetty jutting out into a bay that led to the Channel. Appropriating a sloop had been a challenge but they'd prevailed. She'd only really ever known success, and a real life, for as long as she had called herself a bandit but it was beginning to get dangerous. She didn't want to give in to Mr Smith but she didn't want to give it all up either. The men *couldn't* give it up. They relied on the profits to keep their families fed and their houses standing. Her father was a very lazy landowner preferring to instead pour resources and money into the farming lands further north, bordering Scotland. If the tenants here had to wait for him to patch holes in rooves or fix roads, they would have to move away or risk perishing.

Rose kept the records in the ledgers of wool produced and lambs slaughtered. Well, she doctored the records in those ledgers exceptionally well. Her father didn't ask or acknowledge what she did for the estate. He cared that little about any of it. As long as funds were available to draw on for new dinner suits and gowns for her mother, he didn't care at all.

Coming to the edge of the gardens, Rose stopped to douse the lantern and hide it behind a dense shrub, the moon providing more light now that it was at a better angle over the castle. An involuntary shiver shook her but she firmed her chin and straightened her spine. Once the matter of Mr Smith had been taken care of, then she could worry for her own future. She'd half-lied when she'd said Anthony wouldn't have to marry her. For the life of her, she couldn't figure a way out unless she threatened to reveal her part in the smuggling to the ton. She would have to blackmail her father into giving Germaine a job. And then she would disappear. She could travel to France with one of the shipments and just fade into oblivion. At least her father and brothers would be rid of the family blight. Rose knew she would never be a treasured bride. She wasn't even suitable for the son of a pirate.

Anthony had been knighted by the king; he deserved a biddable minor daughter, not a hellion like her with a mind of her own.

Without so much as a glance over her shoulder, Rose started towards the house, sure that Anthony could make his way to his own room from there since he'd managed to follow her so far in the dark. She'd only made it a few yards when she felt his heavy grip on her elbow again. She was quite prepared when she was swung back towards him but the wind blew hard and she overbalanced, raising both hands to steady herself.

"What are you doing?" Rose hissed, unsure whether to slap his cheek or curl her fingers into his chest where her palms had landed. She'd known their conversation wasn't over, known he would have only more questions now after what had happened on the beach. He wasn't the type of man content with waiting until the morning.

"Someone is watching us," Anthony murmured. Right next to her ear.

Rose gulped. "Impossible. All were abed before I set out. I have done this before."

Strong arms wrapped around her as Anthony shuffled his feet, turning her so she now faced the house over his shoulder. "Second window up, fourth in from the left."

She cursed when her eyes landed on the window in question, a clear silhouette outlined behind the glass. "Damn it, I can't tell who it is."

Anthony shuffled her around again, his head tilted to try to catch her gaze. "They could have seen you leaving as well. We'll need a credible story, Rose."

"We need to keep moving. Perhaps they haven't actually seen us." It was a statement born of desperation and she knew it as well as he. If Anthony had seen her crossing the garden, then whoever it was watching now would have as well.

His grip around her waist relaxed but then Anthony's hands were on her face and he was looking at her with an odd expression.

"What are you doing?"

His eyes flashed beneath the moonlight as he whispered, "Buying us a credible story." And then he lowered his head and pressed his lips to hers.

Shock registered first but instead of pushing him away, Rose did curl her fingers into his shirt to pull him closer. Where her face and lips had been cold, warmth blossomed and wended its way along her nerves until she felt almost as though she could float away. When she sighed and leaned into him, he deepened the kiss, his tongue flitting across her

---

lips until she opened to him. He stole her very breath along with her sanity in that moment. Tentatively she explored him the way he was her and with a groan his hands dropped from her face to her back where he squeezed her closer still.

The spell was broken when Rose realised she couldn't actually feel Anthony touching her. God, how she wanted to feel his palms against her back and his stomach against hers. Despite his almost lanky appearance, he was like granite against her breasts and she wanted to feel more. But the blasted suit wouldn't allow it. She tore her mouth from his and tried to step away. This is not how she had imagined her first kiss with her maybe husband. There were too many lies. Too many barriers.

He wouldn't let her leave the circle of his arms. "Either slap me or stay where you are, Rose. If you intend to storm off, you need to make it believable."

How could he be unaffected by that kiss? How could he still form more than one thought in his head? She sure as hell couldn't. His breath came evenly, his face and eyes unreadable. She knew she was flushed, her insides felt like they were on the outside and she couldn't have stormed anywhere until she regained her normal breath.

He spoke again before she could decide on her next move. "The person watching will think us lovers having a secret rendezvous and if anyone asks, that is exactly what we were doing."

Finally, she raised her gaze to his. "But I'll be ruined and then you will definitely have to marry me."

"Better ruined than arrested for smuggling. You can say

anything you wish, like perhaps you wanted to test my mettle and kissed me."

"But you kissed me."

His lips curved into a full smile as he looked back down at her. "You very definitely kissed me back, Rose." He put his hand against her cheek again. "You should blush just like that when questioned about this."

How could she not? She was on fire. Gone was her worry over Michael and the men, although they knew how to take care of themselves. Gone was her worry over Anthony helping them or Mr Smith making his deadly move. Her only emotions were hot and bothered. How did he remain so calm? Unless he truly was unmoved? She was but an untried girl, and he was a man of London. Of course she hadn't affected him in any way. Even now she was openly displaying her virginity on her sleeve by playing the ninny over one little kiss.

Rose pushed him away and turned on her heel, back to the house, back to her room, away from him, away from his knowing smirk and his flashing eyes.

WHY HE'D TAUNTED her, Anthony didn't know. Why the bloody hell had he thought it a good idea to kiss her? Before that second in time, she had been a conundrum to his reasoning mind. A puzzle to solve or to save, whichever he decided after putting the pieces together. But standing there, with their discovery together in the middle of the night imminent, no other escape plan had come to mind. She'd

THE FALL INTO RUIN

bitten down on her bottom lip, her hands warm against his chest where he'd become a little breathless. He'd wanted to bite that lip for her, soothe the Cupid's bow with his tongue and more. So much more.

He was fairly sure she had been telling the truth when she'd said this Michael person wasn't her lover. The way she'd melted into his embrace and sighed and made little noises in the back of her throat told him she'd never been kissed quite like that before. As he followed her across the dewy grass, he wanted to do it again.

But he couldn't, or rather, shouldn't. Their goose was well and truly cooked now though. He only hoped their audience was a family member or a bed hopper themselves, unable to spread gossip without accounting for their own whereabouts. If it was Lord Clairmont, Anthony was probably as good as dead once he returned to his room.

"Rose?" he called after her fleeing form. "Please let me escort you to your room."

"No, thank you," she returned over her shoulder.

"What if that was your father watching us? I cannot let you face him alone."

"I have faced my father alone my entire life. Trust me when I say you would not be helping the matter by being outside my bedroom door if he did come to chastise me."

He certainly couldn't argue with that logic but as they approached the house, he didn't yet want to say goodnight to Rose Clairmont. Tomorrow was going to bring all sorts of new trouble for the both of them and he didn't want to rush headlong into it. He wanted to kiss her again. And then again. He caught her elbow once more, a little gentler this time when he tugged on her arm to turn her back. "Please, Rose. Let me walk you to your room."

She inhaled slowly, the action making her chest rise and her back straighten, but then she shook her head. "You have no reason to be in the family wing after midnight. My brothers would kill you and I would have a hard time explaining it all without my father truly thinking me a harlot of the worst kind. I'd be banished to the Americas or a Scottish convent."

"How will I know you have made it safely to your room?" He couldn't in good conscience just let the matter rest.

Rose huffed and pointed up the side of the castle above their heads. "My bedroom is just up there. If you wait here a few moments, I'll wave my candle so you know I have arrived. I always lock my door and won't be opening it to my father, my brothers or anyone else this night. Will that satisfy you?"

"Not nearly," he replied, still craning his neck to see where she had pointed. It was too dark in the shadow of the old stones and the ivy rustling back and forth made it almost impossible to train his eyes on anything in particular.

But it didn't matter because Rose darted through a door he hadn't even noticed and was gone. He probably could have chased her but what was the point? He stepped back until he could better see the castle wall and waited. Just as he was about to give up and go after her, a light flared and then brightened. True to her word, the candle flickered in a circular motion before the glass.

All Anthony could think was that she had come up with the solution very quickly for a girl thinking on her feet. Or was it how she communicated with her Michael? A series of lights and motions and they could signal each other from a short distance. He turned and surveyed the darkness behind the castle but the moon was now obscured by cloud and no answering flash of light was to be seen by him.

After several long breaths, he slipped through the door Rose had used and made his way towards the front of the house to try to find his way back to his room, but not sleep. How could he after discovering his intended bride was almost a pirate. He hated pirates. Hated everything they stood for. Hated everything they didn't stand for as well.

Her father was in charge of the men who investigated petty crimes all over London and here was his daughter up to her armpits in danger and illicit goods right under his very roof. Anthony knew he had promised Rose he wouldn't say anything to the earl about it but for a moment he wondered what blackmail might taste like. The Earl of Clairmont had already accused him of it once. He could threaten to leak the details of Rose's midnight dealings to the gossip rags of the ton if the man didn't give him a position.

Or he could go one better and take down 'Mr Smith' or Mrs Smith as Anthony knew her. Perhaps he could capture the notorious outlaw and drag her back to the city in chains? He would be seen as a hero and awarded a position with the Runners. It certainly couldn't hurt his credibility. If only he could prove that even though he was his father's son, he wasn't his father. He wasn't anything like Captain Richard Germaine.

For just one heart's beat in time, he thought about the kiss he'd shared with Rose. He thought about the help she needed to take down Smith. He almost wished he was the man she wanted him to be. If he was a pirate, he could have thrown her over his shoulder and carried her away from harm, from her family, from the ton, and no one would have dared to stop him.

Why couldn't Rose need a true hero rather than an outlaw? He shook his head, the walls around him beginning to look familiar as he made his way slowly. He would never be that man. He abided by the law and had to believe in a justice system for those who broke it. His every belief rested on the side of right and good.

So why did he suddenly feel as though good was never going to get him anywhere?

CHAPTER EIGHT

T HE FOLLOWING MORNING was the first in months where Anthony's head didn't thump like the devil's drums and his stomach wasn't full of stale liquor or empty because he'd retched it all up in the early hours. His butler back at home should have cut him off rather than let him drown his sorrows to avoid thinking about the woman he'd ruined, the enemy he'd made in her father, their situation, for three of the longest months of his life.

Last night he'd lain in the huge bed, sober—the curtains open to the drifting clouds and howling wind—and had thought of Rose. All right, he'd also thought about getting drunk but he'd finished the one bottle he'd been given already.

So instead, he'd passed the sleepless hours wondering what kind of figure she possessed beneath whatever it was she wore under her gown to make her appear ungainly. He wondered why she had been left to her own devices for so many years, getting away with only God knew what besides the smuggling. He also wondered when he would have the chance to kiss her again. Though those thoughts would not lead him anywhere safe, secure or sane.

He'd set out for the house party devising a way to get out of marrying Rose so Clairmont wouldn't see the need to stick a knife in his back so as not to have pirate spawn as a son-in-law. It followed him everywhere, his sire's reputation. But now his plans would have to change. He and Rose and their future would have to step back in line to the danger looming on the horizon. Literally. Smith was not someone who could go on as she had been. What was her game though? She couldn't return to London anytime soon and her clubs and brothels had been closed down, the thugs running them disbanded or arrested. Why hang about and cause more trouble rather than making a run for it and settling some-where new?

Never mind that as soon as Anthony had been old enough, he'd been sent to London for a 'proper education'. Unlike his half-sister Daniella. She had been kept aboard their father's ship until she was already well and truly damaged by piracy. Anthony had spent three quarters of his life in London but it didn't matter a bit.

As he eyed the earl over the breakfast table, smiling back when Clairmont only glared, he considered what kind of life Rose was going to have if she survived the month or even the week. It had to be freeing for her to be left alone without proper chaperone or family but it must also be lonely. Anthony knew all about lonely. He'd spent most of his life at school. He'd had nowhere to go in the holiday seasons so he'd stayed put even when all the other boys returned to their families and their gifts and their warmth. The few friends he had sometimes invited him home but when their fathers discovered who he was, where he'd come from, the invitations were rescinded immediately. He'd gotten used to it fairly quickly.

Mr Brayshaw, his history teacher, had taken pity on him and had let him spend time with the faculty, running tasks and doing chores. He'd eaten with his loner teachers, spent Sundays in church with them, walked alongside like he was one of their children rather than an almost orphan boy. It didn't matter that Anthony's father paid his tuition in full and donated hefty sums to the universities, he was still pirate spawn and always would be. He could have invented the wheel and he would still be the son of a pirate first, inventor of the wheel second.

He almost wished his mother had been alive the day it was decided he was to be sent away but the ague had taken her right after his fourth birthday. His father had rebelled and sworn vengeance on those who had rejected his wife and him, denying her the happiness of her family in those final days, denying her healthcare in London. Two years after her death, he began to torment the navy and any merchant leaving England. It became too dangerous to have a boy in tow. His father became the pirate captain and Anthony had been abandoned.

Josiah's voice broke through his melancholy and Anthony lifted his head to pay attention.

"What are your plans for the day, Germaine?"

"I was actually hoping Clairmont would allow me to ride the grounds for a few hours."

The earl scowled. "I didn't take you for a horseflesh sort

of man."

He wanted to tell the old bastard that he hadn't taken him for any sort of man at all but he bit his tongue on the retort. "I was polo champion at university. Three years in a row."

Samuel snorted and said, "Riding Hell's Gate and playing games of polo are a little different."

There were titters around the table but Clairmont seemed to ignore them all when he replied, "If the lad wants to ride, ride he will. I don't have any grooms to spare while they set up for the hunt later this afternoon but I'm sure we can find a mount to suit."

The evil smile Clairmont bestowed upon him gave him a chill. He had a feeling Rose had been spot on the money when she'd made her prediction the night before.

Where was his bride-to-be? "I wondered if Rose might like to accompany me, show me the pitfalls and cliff edges."

Three heads turned towards Anthony at the innocent enough statement but the eyes of the guests who'd risen early turned to Clairmont as he chewed his ham. Finally he said, "She won't rise before noon. If you want to ride, you'll have to do it on your own."

Anthony thought Josiah stared a little too long, which was interesting since Samuel had lost interest in the conversation and returned to his eggs. From the exchange, it was clear that Clairmont hadn't seen Rose in his arms the night before. Anthony had wondered from all the glares thrown his way if he had. Now he thought perhaps their audience had been her brother Josiah.

Throwing back the rest of his bitter coffee, Anthony wiped his mouth on a linen and then rose. "If you'll excuse me, I'll change my clothes and then present at the stables."

Clairmont grunted. "I'll send a footman to let the stable master know."

Before he'd cleared the room, conversations were returned to and Clairmont had dismissed him but he felt a gaze on his back all the way to the door. It prickled his nape and he wanted to look over his shoulder but didn't. Whoever it was would make themselves known soon enough, he was sure.

It took longer than he'd hoped for a mount to be readied but apparently just getting a bridle on the beast put men's lives in danger. Rose was definitely right. As three grooms fought to lead the animal from the stable, Anthony swallowed hard. He'd hoped the quiet grey munching hay in the corner had been meant for him.

"Are you sure you want to sit atop this beast?" one of them asked him after a great deal of hesitation. "He's a neck-breaker this one."

He was sure if he was any other guest, he would have received an ageing mare rather than a neck-breaker but he was who he was. Apart from being a champion polo player, Anthony had exercised Oxford's horses while the first and second sons had returned home for the special occasions. He was an excellent rider but this was new terrain and he didn't know the directions.

Anthony inhaled deeply of the familiar stable smells—manure, hay, horse—and then stepped forward to take the reins, holding them firm, gripping the bridle hard so he could look into one huge black eye filled with mischief but not terror. "We're going to be friends, you and I," he told the horse without a shadow of doubt.

The horse snickered and attempted to toss his head but Anthony held fast. "What's his name?" he asked the nearest groom.

"Malum."

Anthony tried to wrap his tongue around it. "Is that Latin?"

The groom didn't really answer his question, only replied, "We call him Mal for short, milord."

"Hmm." He was fairly sure *Malum* was Latin for *evil* but his languages had become rusty.

"The miss will think we're not coming if you don't get a hurry on," the outspoken groom said quietly by his side.

Anthony groaned. Were all the servants in on it then?

He nodded his thanks and swung into the saddle, squeezing with his knees and pulling back on the leather to get Malum back under control. "Easy there, boy," he murmured.

The groom mounted the grey. "He knows his way home so if you get lost, just loosen the lead and he'll find his way back."

"Eventually," one of the others said and they all laughed.

As Anthony and Malum thundered from the yard towards the towering cliffs, he sent up a prayer to the dark heavens. He was definitely not loosening anything, lost or not.

IMPATIENCE GNAWED AT Rose until her stomach threatened to tie itself into knots as she waited for Anthony. Why wasn't he there yet? She knew he would find a way to secure a mount if her father became difficult but what if something had happened to him? No. One of the grooms had instructions to ride out to her if anyone else took a horse from the stables or if Anthony didn't show.

Ned was to lead him to where she waited and then she'd take Anthony to meet Michael. Her friend had a note delivered to her that morning to let her know they hadn't lost any men or merchandise the night before although it had been close. Mr Smith was closing in and made it almost too dangerous to make runs but they now had only one more shipment expected before the movement on their end of the Channel became too treacherous with currents and winds and storms tossing ships all over. Mr Smith's interference had meant they hadn't collected all of their goods, their French counterparts deciding the danger was too high and returning home.

Rose shifted her weight in the saddle, her legs to the side, the smuggling suit threatening to unseat her with one restless toss of Belle's big head. When her family wasn't in residence and they didn't have a dozen extra houseguests, Rose rode astride in trousers, a shirt and a chimney sweep's cap. The freedom was exhilarating and the rides risky to her spine but she loved it. Now she just felt impeded and stiff. Much the way marriage would feel, she assumed.

The sound of hoof beats grabbed her attention and she

tightened her grip on the reins as Belle shifted impatiently. Her little mare had a not-so-secret longing for Malum even though he was the worst type of cad in the barn. She knew without even seeing the monstrous horse that he was nearby. No one else thundered in a way that made the earth vibrate just so.

Within seconds both Ned and Anthony came into view single file on a narrow track between centuries-old branches bent to withstand the vicious, unrelenting wind. Anthony peered around as though he was trying to see through the trees before his gaze came to rest on her.

A thrill of excitement stole away the cold as she returned his frank assessment. He looked every inch the gentleman this morning in his highly shined boots and pressed riding coat, which was almost disappointing in a way. She'd been picturing him in pirate garb, perhaps a bandana around his head and three-day growth on his cheeks, his shirt open to the wind. Belle clearly wasn't the only lady at Hell's Gate with a penchant for the wrong type of man.

"Good morning, Rose," he said, after tearing his gaze from her person and lifting it to her eyes.

"Anthony," she returned, unsure of what else to say. Suddenly she felt awkward and out of sorts and wondered if it was second thoughts that made her pulse gallop and cause her chest to feel heavy. Perhaps it was merely the use of his Christian name that caused her entire body to almost flutter.

Instead of more triviality, she turned to Ned. "Is anyone else up and about?" she asked him.

He grimaced but then nodded. "Everyone is awake but

no horses have been ordered yet. Your brothers came by in the night but they have their own men in the stable. There was whispering in the dark corner but nothing else untoward. No one went out."

What could her brothers possibly have wanted in the night, unless it was to do with the afternoon's hunt? She transferred her gaze. "Anthony, are you riding in the hunt later today?"

"I hadn't given it much thought," he said. "Though it probably would be wiser for me to stay away from your father if he's carrying a loaded weapon."

She smiled and answered, "Probably."

Ned took his leave and then it was just the two of them and their restless horses, only the wind and the creaking leathers making noise.

"What are we doing out here, Rose?" Anthony asked, seemingly no longer willing to make small talk. "We could have discussed this at the house."

"There is nowhere private in that place. Noise travels in directions you wouldn't even imagine." She hated Hell's Gate just as passionately as she loved it. It was a complicated relationship.

"Very well. I want to know how Smith found you and then I want to know how you found me."

"I will tell you everything, I promised you that much, but first you have to meet Michael. It's just as much his story as it is mine."

"Lead the way."

She hesitated, paused to reconsider the consequences if

he intended to betray her. "Remember you gave your word," she said, thinking the reminder was entirely necessary.

He gave her a nod. "I remember."

She hadn't expected the awkwardness though she should have. He might not have mentioned anything about their kiss from the night before but Rose was positively itching to discuss it. She knew why he had instigated it but more than anything else, she wanted to know if he would do it again. And then again.

"I didn't see my father this morning but was there any mention of...last night?"

She couldn't see his reaction as he rode behind but she thought his voice carried a smile. "One of your brothers behaved strangely but I don't know the man. Your father was his usual stoic self when it comes to my presence."

"Why does he hate you so much?"

"I don't think he actually hates me as such. I think he only hates the fact that my father is a pirate. Just the same as most of the men of the ton. He doesn't know me well enough to hate me for me."

"Are you close to your father?" She already knew he wasn't. It had disappointed her to know he couldn't simply reach out to the captain to help them with Mr Smith.

"I barely know him anymore but he is still my father and despite what the ton think, he is a good man."

"What happened to your mother?"

Silence descended until she thought he wouldn't tell her—perhaps it was painful—but then he spoke. His voice was so soft, she had to slow down to listen. "My mother died when I was four. The ague took hold and wouldn't let go."

"Where was your father?"

"At her side until her last breath. He wasn't a pirate then. He was a simple fisherman."

She had heard his mother had been disinherited upon her secret marriage to Richard Germaine. Despite their love story being an old one, there were still granddames who remembered. Her godmother had told her most of the story. Well, most of the public story. There was always a private side to the tales the ton retold as gossip.

"How did they meet each other? Wasn't your mother a baron's daughter?"

"That she was," he said, and then cleared his throat and went on. "It's all terribly romantic and clandestine; I'm not sure I should fill your head with that particular rehashing."

Rose leaned back and swung her right leg over Belle's head, turning in the saddle so she could see his face. He was laughing at her. What he found about their situation hilarious, she didn't know. "Are you making fun of me or light of their story?"

His grin fell away as he tilted his head to the side. "There is nothing light about their tragic tale, Rose. They met, were unsuitable, fell in love anyway and then it ended in her death. My father was cast out and turned to piracy to take out her passing on the aristocracy."

Cast out? She hadn't heard that. "There must be more to it than that."

"There is."

"But you aren't going to tell me? Are you?"

"No. Now where is it we are going?"

They were close so Rose let the matter rest for now but curiosity filled her. She was a lost cause for a romantic tragedy. How she used to long for a love so great that one would die for the other. She knew they existed in some form but not in their society. Usually the greatest romances were forbidden and quashed well before they could become a bastard child or an elopement to Gretna. That was the real tragedy in Rose's mind. But she'd thrown off the unrealities of a romantic age years before, taking up independence and adventure instead as her life's thrill. At least adventure couldn't break her heart or leave her cold. It's what she told herself day after day.

"Just over this ridge is an old hunter's cabin. It's where we meet."

"And your father doesn't know about it?"

"It's not on his land. My father doesn't care about anything really. Except his Runners and his public face. As long as he has good standing, he's happy enough."

"What about your brothers? How have you managed to keep this quiet for so long?"

She was about to answer but the sound of weapons being brought to the ready saved her words.

Behind her, Malum reared, his front hooves waving madly in the air, fear causing the whites of his eyes to shine beneath the tree's canopy. He smelled the danger but it was too late for Anthony. One moment he was in the saddle, the next he was on his back on the ground.

CHAPTER NINE

THERE WAS A rock digging into Anthony's hip and as he fought to regain his breath and his pride, he listened to Malum's hooves beating a rhythm as he fled what was about to come. Had it all been an elaborate set-up? The scene the night before at the cliffs? The smugglers on the beach? He'd been so caught up with Rose's puzzling babbling and actions that he hadn't prepared for any sort of reaction, especially not an ambush.

She'd led him far enough into the woods that she could put a ball between his eyes and let the scavengers finish him off, scattering his bones far and wide. He was an idiot. No wonder Clairmont doubted him and his investigative skills. Already his eye and his mind had been turned by a pretty girl.

"Are you all right?" Rose asked, her voice penetrating the fog of indignity. The last time a horse had thrown him, he'd been all of thirteen and showing off for his classmates.

"Not really," came his gruff reply. "If you're going to finish me off, you'd better do it now before I open my eyes."

Her tinkling laughter wasn't expected so he cracked an eyelid to the forest's gloom. There the vixen stood, a dozen men at her back with guns lowered but still in hand, all filled with the same level of mirth at his fall but not a one menacing or ready for the killing blow.

"*If* I wanted to kill you," she said dramatically, "I would have thrown you from the cliffs last night."

At the front of his mind he scoffed at the idea of her besting him in the dark, but in the back of his mind, he knew she was probably right. He had been stumbling then and he'd stumbled now.

Rose held out her hand to help him from his backside and he took it, once again surprised at how quietly strong she was.

He received several jolting claps to his shoulder and back as the strangers laughed and retold of the moment Malum had tossed him from the saddle. He took it all in, listening to the cadence of the conversations and camaraderie between the men. It was clear all were friends and as they fanned out alongside Rose, even clearer was that they were her friends too, protecting her from all angles as they approached a cabin. *This almost felt like a family.*

No smoke drifted from the chimney and overgrowth pushed the building to a lean. To the casual observer the entire place appeared abandoned. But he saw the scuffed boot prints, the trails leading to and away from the two steps to the rotting deck timbers to the door, which was the only thing not leaning.

"Whose land is this?" he asked Rose's back.

"The Duke of Ashmoor's."

He swore beneath his breath. Ashmoor was the most upstanding citizen London had likely ever seen. He was more devoted to England and patriotism than the prince himself. He swore again.

The cabin door opened from the inside and he followed Rose straight in. His gut told him to turn and run, to take cover, to go back to the castle and retrieve a sword or pistol. The dagger secreted beneath his coat wasn't going to do any real damage if he needed to use it. If he'd known this was her plan for the morning, he would have come better armed.

Anthony had to stand quite defunct and watch as Rose rushed forward to embrace a black-haired fellow with piercing dark eyes and a commanding air about him despite his not being very large or intimidating.

"Oh, Michael, I'm so glad you're all right. I saw every-thing and was so worried."

Anthony clenched his teeth when Rose placed her palm against Michael's cheek. When the fellow leaned forward and rubbed his nose against Rose's he had to restrain himself. Not lovers? The bloody little liar.

Michael smiled in return when he looked into her eyes. "Then why didn't you come to my rescue?"

Rose looked back at Anthony. Was that a blush on her cheeks? His masculine pride crowed. His face remained impassive.

"I was followed."

"Damn it, Rose, why would you take the risk? You agreed to stay away while your family are around."

Rose sighed and Anthony wondered why she would let this servant speak to her this way. She replied, "You know

I'm not good at sitting still while others put themselves at risk. Besides, no one else saw me. Our secrets are still safe."

Michael turned from Rose to look him up and down. There was no derision but Anthony had the feeling it wasn't far away. "I take it you're Germaine?" the fellow said.

"At your service, apparently," Anthony replied with a nod and a short, mocking bow.

Once again he was dismissed for the moment as Michael addressed Rose. "Are you sure you can trust him? We don't even know him."

Rose nodded but flicked a quick glance back in his direction. "He has given his word he won't tell Father or anyone else but I don't know how much help he can be to us now. He isn't in contact with Captain Germaine."

"Jesus, what have you told him?" Michael asked her.

"Not everything. Not yet. I have barely had time to think."

"I can help," Anthony offered, though he had no idea how since there were obviously pieces of the story missing still. From all sides.

Michael's lip curled as he came to stand before him. "Unless you have a ship with cannons and small arms then tell me how you're going to help us."

"First tell me why Smith is targeting you."

Rose leaped in. "It wasn't only us to start with. Smith has been a plague for months. We were the only crew to fight back rather than hand over a portion of our goods."

Michael gathered the threads of the story and with a wild grin, took over. "We're not sure why Smith is hanging about still. We can only gather that he's taken issue with the way we told him to stick his head up his arse and leave off."

The other men in the room guffawed but Rose watched Anthony. What was she waiting for? Outwardly he showed nothing more than calm as he crossed his arms over his chest to wait for the laughter to die down. When it did, he asked, "So you taunted Smith and now he's coming after you? Why don't you take action?"

That got the men serious. Michael's look of pain told a story of its own. "They crept in and burned our ship to the waterline."

"Your ship?"

Rose cleared her throat delicately. "Not our ship. One of Ashmoor's ships we had appropriated."

"Does Ashmoor know you are using his ship and his land to smuggle illegal goods from France?"

"Of course he doesn't," Michael said, growing impatient. "He spends almost all of his time in London with the other lords. And it's not the goods that are themselves illegal, just the way we're going about getting them."

They were children playing in a war they knew nothing about. "So let me get this straight. Smith just showed up one night and because you said something vulgar to the men on his ship, he's taken issue with you all and now is stealing your stolen goods?"

Michael nodded but Rose said, "There's slightly more to it than that, I think."

Anthony rounded on her, gripped her shoulders so she stood right in front of him. "What makes you say that,

Rose?"

Her gaze locked with his and for a moment she appeared as though she would shake him off and not respond but then she said something that sent chills all the way down his spine. "I think he has been trying to get someone's attention but I don't know whose."

He silently congratulated her. "Why?"

"He and his men taunt and cripple and issue threats but still they wait. If they were your run-of-the-mill pirates, they would have come to land, burned the castle and the village and taken what they wanted by now. Instead, they hang about on the Channel risking discovery and retaliation. But for what?"

Michael was quick to join the conversation with: "They're only pirates, Rose. Probably just waiting for a big enough haul of booty to make off with."

She pulled free of Anthony's grip and spoke to her friend around him. "If it was gold they were after, they wouldn't wait around in the one place. We clearly don't have what they want. So far they've got a few barrels of brandy, a small amount of lace and a tiny measure of tea."

A thought struck him. "Could they be intercepting notes? From France?"

Rose shook her head. "They don't get close enough for that and the war with France is practically over. We're really only dodging excise men and my father at this point. I cannot shake the feeling Smith is after something else. Something bigger. But it can't come from us; we have nothing bigger in hand."

"What exactly do you smuggle?" he asked the pair.

Michael looked to Rose, implored her, for what? Silence? To lie? She shook her head and went on. "We exchange a small amount of gold and a large amount of wool for tea, brandy, tobacco, lace and quality ribbons. Occasionally we also receive rare spices. We then sell it on and make a profit."

"Sell it on to whom?" A heavy feeling sank in his stomach when he thought about how many were involved in Rose and Michael's scheme.

"Michael has a contact in London for the lace and tea, the rest is distributed from the village by servants from the bigger houses. It's the way it's been done for years. Without a problem."

"Until now," Anthony murmured.

ROSE ALMOST FELT sorry for Anthony. He looked as though they had fed him too much information far too quickly and now had a stomach upset from it.

Only one thing was clear to her. "You've heard of Smith before, haven't you?" she asked, already knowing what he would say next.

He nodded. "I have, but I've never met him. Have either of you?"

Both Rose and Michael shook their heads. She wished she could arrange a meeting so they could figure out what he wanted once and for all.

Anthony spoke again. "I'm afraid you have all monumentally misread a few pertinent facts about Smith, which is why he has the upper hand right now."

Michael scoffed but Rose was all ears.

"The first is that Mr Smith isn't a mister at all."

Confusion set in. "You mean he's a lord?" Rose asked.

"I mean *he* is in fact a *she*."

The men drew breath around her and then laughed and laughed, Michael included. Rose didn't see anything humorous about the information. She shushed them and went on. "Are you positive? How can you be sure?"

Anthony nodded and crossed his arms over his chest to await quiet. "I haven't personally met the woman but I have it on very good authority. I'm guessing Smith's attacks have stepped up a notch in the last month or so?"

Her heart sank into her stomach. Rose nodded.

"She fled London two months ago after almost being captured by Trelissick—the Marquess of Lasterton—and his men. Since not many have seen her in person she has eluded authorities and has been on the run ever since."

His revelation changed the feeling in the room. Finally, one of the men spoke up. "How do you know she's Smith then?"

"I would give my life into the keeping of the men who were there that night." Trelissick was his brother-in-law after all and Darius, the ex-pirate, his unlikely friend now. He would not doubt their words. It had sounded fantastical to Anthony at the time as well, but his sister, Daniella, had confirmed everything. "She cannot return to London anytime soon." But why did she linger on the Channel? Rose had the right of it: there was something else, something keeping her there.

"I suggest you cease your activities at once until she grows bored and sails away." It went against his very moral fibre to school smugglers but these people had no clue as to what Smith was capable of. Anthony had heard the stories while his old school friend Harold had lain half dead. Stories about men being burned alive if they couldn't pay their debts. It didn't matter if you were first son or second, Smith's goons had a way with a bottle of oil and a spark from a flame that turned a grown man turn into a sobbing boy.

Michael was predictably the first to argue. "I say we go after her and take her down if that's true. She is only a woman who has been able to spread fear through the men around her by the sounds. If we can find her, we can put her back in her place."

From the corner of his eye, he saw Rose's full lips pull into a thin line as her spine straightened.

Anthony spoke before she could. "You and whose army?" He took a long moment to evaluate the other men in the room. Old men, young lads and tired farmers. "The best lords in London couldn't find her, how do you propose to?"

Puffing out his chest, Michael stepped towards him. "We already know she is on that ship. Smith has to have been giving the orders from the deck. We find the ship and we take her down."

"You are an idiot if you think it will be that easy."

Murder flashed in Michael's eyes but then Rose was between them, addressing her friend. Anthony's mouth loosened to a forced grin.

"I'm sure he didn't mean to call you an idiot, Michael,

but you have to admit if it were that easy, someone would have already beaten you to it." When she turned her glare on him, Anthony itched to tell them all they were all idiots, her included. Instead he let her talk. "What would you do? Other than turn tail and hide. If it is something she wants, I presume she won't stop until she has it?"

He inclined his head, resisted rising to her jibe. God, but she was a smart one. "Precisely."

Michael interrupted. "If she's dead, she won't be able to get whatever it is she wants."

"We can't just go about killing people, Michael. We are smugglers, not murderers."

"Even a good pirate doesn't gad about killing anything that moves," Anthony felt the need to add.

"We need a plan," Rose said, likely hoping to keep Michael from acting on the emotion still flashing across his dark eyes. Anthony was sure the other man wanted to hit him right then.

"Your plan should be to run and hide."

She glared at him again. "Would you? If everything you held dear was threatened, would you slink away?"

Everything he held dear had been threatened. First his sister the night Smith abducted the children of a duke and tried to burn them all alive, Daniella included. And then again when he'd fallen on Rose Clairmont and lost his future. After they said their vows, assuming Rose lived that long, he would be responsible for another person. A woman who was clearly used to getting her own way in everything. A woman who had been neglected to the hands of smugglers and left to her own devices for far too long. A woman who either couldn't or wouldn't see danger if it walked up and slit her throat while she kept on with that beguiling, beautiful smile. Her lips were impossibly full—

No. He shook his head. Cleared his thoughts. "I would never shirk my responsibilities, no."

"Then do not ask one man here to either. We need to find out what Smith wants and then figure out how to get it to her without further bloodshed."

"What if that isn't enough?" Michael asked, a challenge in his words.

Rose switched her gaze from Anthony's to look at Michael. "Then we can find her and bring her down."

Anthony groaned and rubbed a hand over his face. This meant he had to find Smith first, before these want-to-be pirates and would-be murderers got themselves killed. If he didn't bring her back to London in chains, he would never be respected. He would never be able to provide a future for Rose. No matter what happened, unless one of them was dead, they were still destined to be married. Nothing had changed there.

His little vixen had mettle but if she truly knew what it meant to kill a man, she wouldn't appear so bloody confident about it all. Anthony himself had never taken a life and didn't ever want to, but as a Runner, he might have to defend himself to the death against a foe. He prayed his first opponent wasn't going to be a woman. He definitely couldn't actually kill a woman. Although as he stared at the back of Rose's scheming head, he sincerely considered the notion.

CHAPTER TEN

I T SHOULD HAVE all been settled. For an hour they planned how to get word to Smith, Rose and Michael setting the details down for the men who would put their necks on the line for the rest. Anthony had sat in the corner of the room and silently taken it all in. She would be a fool to think he wasn't hanging on to every word. He'd said he could help but he was just as much in the dark as every other man there. The only assistance he'd given had been in the information that Smith was a she. Rose wasn't sure it was completely true but there *she* was, a female, the daughter of an earl and a smuggler.

Rose had led an entirely unconventional life to date. She had been born late to her mother and father, her siblings already much older than her. Terrible travel sickness as a toddler meant she was left behind when the rest of the family left for London. Her very lazy nanny controlled her by feeding her whenever she got restless and so the overweight toddler turned into an overweight child right about the time her sisters were being readied for their debuts. She remembered her family returning to Hell's Gate for a house party and hunt. It had felt like an age since Rose had seen any of them but time had held not much meaning to her then.

Her mother had swooned and her father had sworn upon seeing her that time. She was thirteen years old and should have left for the city when they returned to it. Instead, she was treated like the ogre from her childhood storybooks. It was the last straw for Rose who escaped the castle and headed for the woods, no sane plan in mind for a girl who had no idea about the world. She wasn't running away, she was simply running.

That's when she'd met Michael.

A few years older than her, he'd been very kind to a child whose family shunned her appearance. She'd cried to the stranger in the woods that day that she was good for nothing and may as well throw herself from the cliffs. He spent time with her and made her realise she had been sheltered. Why wasn't she running around the grounds of the estate? Did she like to dip her toes in the ocean on a warm day if the wind abated? Collect wild flowers from the fields bordering the forest? Why hadn't they met before?

The weather was always so harsh, her nanny had convinced her inside was where they should be always. She hadn't been a particularly inquisitive child. That all changed for Rose the day she met Michael. The day she accidentally learned the men of two estates and a village in between had to make their own way in the world in order to keep their families fed and their homes watertight.

Michael was the lookout that day and Rose had distracted him from his task, the men returning from the cove with a laden wagon of illicit goods. She'd sworn to never tell a soul but it seemed the only souls she could have told already knew. She was folded into the desperate arms of this family and became one of them, their secrets hers, their plight her new perspective on all the things she didn't know.

She came to truly hate her father in the years to follow. Everyone at Hell's Gate did. It wasn't hard to feed him lies when none were loyal to a fault.

Really, this Smith person could have been the daughter of the king and Rose might believe there to be truth in it with the kind of upbringing some children faced, with the kinds of fathers who were so selfish they didn't care about their duty or even common decency towards others. She learned very quickly it is far easier at Hell's Gate to stop asking the earl for help and to simply make happen what needed to be done. For that they needed funds.

As their scheming came to an end, Rose felt the glare of Germaine on her back. He would have words to say to her on their return to the estate, of that she was very sure.

Not able to put it off any longer, she bid farewell to Michael and the men, always the first to leave while the others dispersed slowly in different directions, back to the village, back to the castle, Ashmoor's estate and their normal lives.

It wasn't until she'd walked out of the little cottage, Anthony Germaine too close at her back, that she remembered they had only one horse. Malum had fled after throwing his rider.

Germaine seemed to read her mind as they approached Belle, happily munching bark from a tree. "Will she take the both of us?"

"She won't like it much, but I'm sure we'll fit." The side saddle meant Rose had to ride up front while Germaine clung to her back, his arms around her suit. Once again she damned her disguise but without it, she would have been married off on her sixteenth birthday had her father known she was no longer equipped with rolls of skin and pudginess like she had been as a child. That's how little attention they had paid her over the last decade. Mr and Mrs Foster had been the genius behind the garment she wore beneath her gowns. Molly, her maid, had once been assistant to a dress-maker before disgrace sent her fleeing London back to the village between the Duke of Ashmoor's estate and Hell's Gate.

Rose and Molly had taken an instant liking to each other and her maid knew the other servants and villagers well. She knew how to make Rose appear unattractive. Rose wished she'd never had to invent such a ruse but also thanked the Lord her father had too much pride, and no desperate need for the blunt, to foist her onto a man in need of a young wife.

Germaine's arms were tight around her middle as he rested on Belle's rump, the horse unsure as to how to go on until Rose assured the mare that they would take it slow back to the estate.

Only minutes passed before he was telling her exactly what he thought of their predicament. "It won't work, what you have in mind."

She bristled. "Then why didn't you speak up? Offer an-other alternative."

"Your hot-headed beau wouldn't have listened to a word out of my mouth."

Anger began to warm her from within. "He is not my beau. Michael is my friend, my best friend. Nothing more."

"I assume he is the one who got you involved? If they were discovered, they could blackmail your father to keep it all quiet?"

She hadn't ever considered that and she knew her friend wouldn't have either. "Michael would never do that."

"Where does he come from? Is he in your father's employ?"

Rose really shouldn't tell him anything more. He was not going to help them and if he broke his promise and went to her father, she didn't want him to know more than he already did. "I'll not betray my friend to you."

"You said you would tell me everything, Rose."

"That was before, when I thought you had something to offer me in return."

His grip tightened again. "I am the only man who is going to save your back from the dagger before you feel it. We'll rush our nuptials and I'll take you from this danger. Let Michael sort the mess out like the man he thinks he is."

Rose pulled back hard on Belle's reins, the horse disliking it and trying to nip Rose's foot with her huge teeth. She twisted in the saddle. "I'm not going anywhere. I'll not run from this and leave Michael to it. We are a team, all of us."

Anthony shook his head. "They are a ragtag crew of farmers with pistols and you are their safety net if they are caught."

She wished he'd stop saying that. "I am not leaving. I can't."

"Once you are my wife, you'll have little to say in the matter."

"My father will never allow it."

"He invited me to the castle to spend time with you before we stand before the vicar," he pointed out.

"He invited you so he could discredit you somehow before his friends so I can cry off with no ramifications." Damn, she shouldn't have said that out loud. Eavesdropping was her greatest misbegotten talent so she knew almost all of her father's plans. Sound really did travel in some parts of Hell's Gate. Not that her father or her brothers believed she would defy the earl and linger near enough to overhear. She was supposed to be spending her free time in her room, even with the guests in the house. Her father didn't want her appearance to upset anyone's delicate constitution. He was a buffoon.

"Don't you think I know that? But he has nothing on me, Rose. I have no mistress, I don't dally with unmarried ladies and I don't have anything to hide. The ton knows all of my dirty little secrets already."

"Perhaps he means to kill you after all?"

Anthony scoffed and Rose's cheeks heated as he looked down at her. She only just noticed how close his face was to hers as his warm breath washed over her.

His voice dropped low and her insides tumbled. "Do you share his feelings, Rose? I am the son of a pirate, a nobody. Why haven't you already plunged your knife into my chest?"

She licked her dry lips, drew a deep breath. His eyes were mesmerising up close, his heat distracting. "I…I need your help. With Smith."

"You said I was no help at all."

Her gaze dropped to his lips as he spoke the words, the memory of last night's kiss invading her mind and filtering through to her body. "I…I…" she stuttered, casting around for something to say. The truth was that he intrigued her. He was the first stranger to not grimace at her perceived size or openly laugh at her spectacles. Did he not guess that she'd never been kissed or why? Did he not know how she longed to learn about life aboard a pirate ship? He should have guessed how badly she wanted to be free of society, to fill her life with adventure.

"This is not going to end well for any of us," he murmured.

She knew that. Discovery or death breathed down the back of her neck all day and all night, vying to end her freedom. Anthony Germaine wouldn't be her death. He was very definitely going to be the one to reveal her part one way or another. But could she gain the upper hand before he did?

"Why did you come?" she asked, her voice only a breath above a whisper. "Why didn't you call my father out or flee the country?"

"Despite what anyone says about me, I am a man of honour."

"But it was an accident, a simple misunderstanding."

"I am beginning to believe it fate," he said with a small smile, one hand rising to tuck an errant curl behind her ear and then cup her cheek.

She shouldn't. She should be strong and push him away. Instead she melted into the warmth of his hand. He smelled of leather and soap.

"I don't believe in fate," she whispered, unable to get her voice or her body to obey, to find any strength whatsoever.

Now both of his hands cupped her face, his eyes glazed as he said, "Neither do I." And then he pressed his lips to hers.

Rose gasped when he pulled her closer, precariously perched on the back end of her mount. It was all he needed to deepen the kiss, one hand at her back, the other cradling her head as pins were loosened and curls fell from their anchors. His tongue invaded her mouth in a blatant sign of exploration. Never one to back down, Rose met him halfway, tasting his heat as she did a little exploring of her own.

Belle shifted beneath her and Rose came too with a start. How did he have the ability to make her forget where she was and who she was? What she had to lose? Hoof beats signalled the approach of another rider and within a breath, Anthony had her back facing forward and gave Belle a little kick to get her walking.

"You could try to act as though you weren't just caught with your hand in the sweetie jar," he said in her ear, his breath hot, his triumph clear.

Ned crested the rise ahead, worry etched into his young features.

"What is it?" she asked when he was close enough to answer.

"Malum came tearing back to the barn and your brothers' men were there to see it. We need a story and you'd better be quick about it. The house thinks you still abed."

That was the problem with so many lies. Uneasiness settled over her like fog as she wondered which unravelling thread she could afford to let go of now.

ANTHONY SHOULDN'T KEEP tempting whatever deity he'd upset into prolonging his torture. He was in enough trouble. But every time he thought about Rose's mouth, her lips, her taste and heat, it was as though he became possessed by spirits intent on seduction and mischief.

Even as she tensed in the circle of his arms—possibly the greatest excuse to hold her and not be called a cad—all he wanted was more kisses, more unschooled passion. In those moments when she wrapped her arms about his neck and made those little mewling kitten sounds, he forgot about every other woman he'd ever been with. His wife-to-be was quite possibly still a virgin despite her best friend being a man and surrounding herself with smuggler comrades. He smiled. God, how he'd love to add these details to the London clubs' betting books to raise the stakes. Or maybe to stake his claim.

He suddenly wanted to tell all of the naysayers they had it wrong about Rose Clairmont. Although no one would believe him. His first item of business after the marriage vows was to get her to burn whatever it was she wrapped about her body beneath her gowns. No longer would he let her hide her true self. No longer would he pull her close but have nothing to truly mould his hands to. He wanted to hold the curve of her hip, the line of her spine, the outline of her breast.

His smile dropped away. What if she wouldn't give up the wild streak embedded so deeply within her? He still had to keep in mind there were a myriad of pitfalls between now and the vows. Did she participate in smuggling adventures as a matter of rebellion, or boredom, or was it something else? He knew there were some people for whom the thrill of the game ran in their veins as surely as their blood. His sister Daniella was such a one. Despite the fact she was now married to a marquess and was about to birth their first child, she spent some of the year living aboard a ship anchored behind their estate. She was no longer able to behave as a pirate but given the first opportunity, she was in the fray, sometimes before one had even begun. It had nearly gotten her killed several times. Trelissick, her husband, could forbid her from adventuring until the end of time but she would never listen. It was a part of who she was.

Was it such a very big part of who Rose was? As she conferred with Ned over which tale to spin, he picked up on her nervous excitement, the way she revelled at being in charge and in control. Ned clearly would do whatever she told him no matter what. She could probably order he throw himself from the cliffs as a diversion and he would do so without question.

Anthony intervened when their story became more and more ludicrous. "Ned, tell the men Lady Rose had already taken her horse out but forbid you to tell anyone so she could surprise me with an unchaperoned meeting."

Rose's intake of breath actually made sound as she turned in her side-saddle to stare at him, the colour on her cheeks high, her beautiful eyes flashing her fury.

"And put your spectacles back on. If I noticed, then someone else will."

Ned looked between the two of them, waiting for orders from Rose, not from Anthony. He frowned and nudged Rose in the back.

"My father will kill you," she hissed.

"Your father will kill *you*. It was hardly my fault you were so desperate to see me alone."

She made such a noise of frustration that it brought the smile back to Anthony's face.

"Ooh, very well. Damn it. Ned will likely be in some trouble."

Anthony met the other man's eyes over Rose's head. "Ned is a big lad—he'll be just fine."

Ned nodded after a hesitation and then wheeled his mount back in the direction of the house.

Silence reigned for a few moments but then he found himself laughing and asking, "Do you often curse?"

Predictably, she bristled. "Damn is not a curse word. Not really."

"How is it that your father left you alone here for so long?"

"I was never really alone."

"You know what I mean. Has he really never had a clue

what you get up to?"

"The only thing my father ever notices about me is that I am very large, very dumb and very ugly. A nuisance and a blight on the family image."

Anthony's arms tightened of their own accord and his voice dropped low. "They only believe you hideous because that is the front you show them. If you styled your hair and wore a gown against your actual skin, what would you look like then? I don't believe you to be scarred or deformed. You are very definitely not dumb. Why do you do it?"

"My father considers women to be prize cattle. As soon as the calf is old enough to be of some use, old enough to be worth more than the name he gave it, he sells the calf to the highest bidder who will control her and..."

"And? And what, Rose?"

"You will think it silly."

He sighed. "And what?" he repeated.

"When my sisters were bargained into matrimony for political gain, they became...less. If they had light, it was dimmed by becoming a wife, a mother, a hostess."

"So this is your way of teaching your father a lesson?"

"I don't want to suffer the same fate. I won't. I'll not simper in the corner until I gain the attention of a dowry hunter and then be locked away for the rest of my life to birth babies and throw parties. I'm needed here. I like it here."

"It's what good English girls do, Rose. What makes you think you're any different from your sisters?" His very own sister had bucked the trend most viciously. But then again, she had spent the first significant parts of her life aboard a pirate ship. Rose had not.

Her head fell forward and the curve of her neck came into view between her tangled curls. "I feel so very different. I feel as though there is this thing…" She sighed. "You wouldn't understand."

"I might," he offered quietly. He had this *thing* too. Only he was filled with the right and just thing. He didn't want to break laws or kill or pillage. He wanted to stand on the side of peace and civil liberty. He wanted to help those who were helpless.

He didn't think Rose would answer but then she inhaled and said, "Each morning I wake up and I look out over the ocean and I want…I want…more. It's like a living, breathing beast inside of me and it needs to be freed. *I* need to be free."

"No one is truly free. There'll always be limitations, laws, rules and regulations. Part of being an adult means you have to toe those lines."

"Then I don't want to be an adult."

Anthony would have laughed had anyone else said the words. Rose murmured them with such conviction. Such childish conviction. She had only ever known this life. She hadn't seen the gaols full to the brim with thieves and murderers and cut-throats. She hadn't witnessed bodies being pulled from the Thames or cherub-faced children sold to workhouses. A man had only to get lost in the wrong part of London and he could witness all manner of things and more. A part of him hoped Rose never would see even half of those happenings but another part of him wondered if she might need to, to know the world wasn't what she thought it was.

Her men obviously sheltered her and kept her from any real danger but so far the most they had been doing was a little smuggling. Not even that really since they paid their French counterparts for the goods; they just didn't pay the taxes on it to the Crown. They'd never met the likes of a real pirate. Even Mrs Smith, or whoever the hell she was, wasn't a real pirate. She was a lawless criminal who got others to do her dirty work for her. If even one of those warning arrows the night before had hit its target, they'd be digging a hole in the cemetery rather than having a clandestine meeting in the middle of the woods. Anthony had been mulling over the events, trying to find a rhyme or reason to it all.

Rose's men had been mostly sitting ducks as they'd come into shore. If Smith wanted to kill to send a message, there'd be dead men—of that he was sure. She was very definitely sending a message but what was it? If he'd had to guess, he'd go along with what Rose had surmised: that she was trying to gain someone's attention and hadn't yet got it. Minor property damage to one sloop wasn't a slit throat or burned-down cottage with a family still inside. The message was tentative, subtle, almost not even there.

Rose tensed in his arms and the sound of more than one galloping horse reached them. As they crested the rise leading to the stables, a search party came into view led by one very angry Josiah.

"Your brother looks fit to burst," Anthony said in a

louder voice than necessary, before any other words or accusations could be spoken.

"He is not my keeper," Rose replied, her tone clear, her intent obvious.

Josiah clenched his teeth and looked as though he might ignore his sister's words but then he spoke, his gaze never leaving Rose's. "Would that I was; you'd be spanked for such forward behaviour."

Anthony tightened his arms about his future bride in warning. He prayed she kept her temper as he rushed to speak before she could. "You'll not lay one finger on her. Not this day or the next."

"You weren't supposed to either, Germaine, yet here we are. Here the two of you are, all alone, cosy and close."

"My horse threw me and it was a long walk back. That is all."

"Father might not believe it all innocence."

Anthony added, "We are already set to wed. Nothing short of death will change it."

Josiah's eyes lit to an almost unholy colour. "There's still time for my sister to cry off."

Rose finally entered the fray with: "If you two would stop discussing me like I'm not here, we might get out of the open and stop making a scene. Josiah, you do not own me. You are not my guardian or my keeper or indeed much of a brother at all so stop all of this protective business at once." She turned in the saddle and met Anthony's eyes. "And you are not yet my husband." With a small, apologetic grin, she gave him a shove until he slid from Belle's back to land heavily on his booted feet, almost overbalancing on the uneven ground.

Guffaws of laughter reached his ears but Rose ignored them all as she marched her horse through the assembled men and back to the stable, her back stiff and her chin held high. Anthony had to fight a grin of his own. If he'd thought for one moment Rose Clairmont couldn't handle herself or a tricky situation, he had been very, very wrong.

CHAPTER ELEVEN

THE THOUGHTS ROSE had mulled over for three long months came flooding in as she faced her father over the messy desk in his study. Why couldn't he have left her where she was? Forgotten and unwanted. Papers were strewn about, ledgers were open and ink lay in fat drops everywhere. Rose recognised several of the leather-bound books he waved at her as he shouted and a prickling began at her nape.

"How could you be so irresponsible? So reckless and na-ïve?"

In a practice as old as time, Rose let her mouth and shoulders droop and pretended to know what he scolded her over this time, pretended to be sorry, although it could have been anything and she wouldn't be sorry no matter what it was. A sudden fear that he had discovered her secrets had sent blood roaring in her ears so she hadn't actually heard his first words.

"How dare you dismiss my man of business! You have no right to meddle in the affairs of the estate!"

The words closest to her tongue were: *Why not? Because I am a woman?* She held them back. "He was stealing from you, Papa. I had to take action."

"Why was nothing reported to me? Collins should have come to me at once to discuss it."

"Likely he knew he would be arrested," she answered quite matter-of-factly. Maybe too much so.

Her father's eyes narrowed as he stared at her. "How did you know he was stealing from the estate?"

She couldn't very well admit that Collins caught her out first, playing with the numbers, skimming wool from the shearers before any totals had been tallied on paper. He'd threatened to go to her father and reveal what little he knew. So Rose had done what anyone else would have. She offered him a bribe she knew he couldn't resist and he left the next day. One of the many gambles she had taken but one that had paid off in spades.

"He tried to sell Mama's silverware two villages over. The Fosters were alerted and decisive action had to be taken. We only did what we had to."

"Who has been keeping the books since then? And why didn't Foster send word to me at once?"

Rose opened her eyes wide and took on an air of innocence. "He did write to you. Did you not get the missive?"

"Well I never bloody wrote back, did I?"

How her father's face could turn so purple and not explode from his shoulders, she would never know. "No, I don't suppose you did. Anyway, one of the footmen has a head for numbers and has been keeping the tally. I'm sure you'll find it's been a good few years."

If not for Rose's prompt actions, the estate would lie in ruins about her ankles, the tenants and farmers fled, the animals dead on the ground. Collins was a poor excuse for a man but it didn't surprise her really—her father was a terrible judge of character especially when he didn't have a care for the outcomes.

Another purple-faced glare was pointed in her direction. "You shouldn't comment on matters you know nothing about."

"Yes, Papa."

"Now, what's this I hear about you and the pirate's spawn spending time alone together?"

"His name is Anthony."

"And you should not call him that. You should not call him anything. I thought I made myself quite clear you were to stay away from him until I find a way out of this wedding."

That caught her full attention. "Have you found a way out?"

The purple faded and her father finally sat in his chair rather than attempt to tower over her. "I have indeed."

Rose waited for him to elaborate, a sickening dread filling her stomach. She pushed her spectacles up her nose and cleared her throat. "May I enquire as to the details?"

"What? Oh yes, I suppose you might have to be in on the plan. Do you remember Lord Harcourt?"

She thought about it for a moment. "No. Should I?"

"He has offered for your hand. Not really sure why, but gift horses and all that. He will arrive in three days to court you. On the fourth or fifth day, you'll leave with him in the early hours to Gretna to elope. Once you're married to

Harcourt, Germaine can't get his filthy talons into you."

"I've never even met the man; why would he agree to any of that?" Rose couldn't quite contain her shock or her disgust.

"Poor man has thrown out fourteen daughters and not one son. You'll be a marchioness if you play your hand right."

Play her hand right? "You're mad," she said. "Fourteen daughters? What happened to his other wife or is it wives?"

"Dead. Three of them so far."

"How old is he?"

"That makes no difference. If he can father a child, he can take a wife."

Rose got to her feet, wobbled a little, reached out for something to hold on to. "It matters to me. I won't do it."

"You have no choice, daughter mine. I'll not have you married to the son of a pirate."

"But you'd sell me to one of your cronies? Older than my own father? Do you not have a care for me at all?"

When the earl stood, Rose did not step back. She did not cower. He shouted again, "Did you not have a care for me when you met a pirate bastard in the gardens on your own in the dark? When you let him charm and ravish you?"

"Nothing happened! I had never met Anthony Germaine before that moment. If you'd listened to me, none of this would be happening. I won't marry Harcourt. I won't marry anyone."

"I am the lord and master here, daughter. You have no value to me now that you have been soiled by that filthy pirate. No one will have you save for the most desperate. Harcourt will arrive in three days and you will be here to greet him. You will not spend any more time alone with Germaine or I will confine you to the house."

"You cannot keep me under lock and key."

"Yes I can. Do not push me, daughter."

Rose bit her tongue against the railing her father deserved. It wouldn't help. It was highly unlikely her father checked the estate ledgers because they were interesting reading material. She wondered who had planted the idea in his head. He may lead the London Runners but for the most part, her father was a puppet and always would be. Like most of the lords of England, they danced to whatever tune was played for them on the day. She knew enough about society to understand at least that.

Now Rose only had three days to decide on a course of action. There was no way she would run off with an elderly stranger to a fate she loathed. She would be wiser and safer in the hands of pirate spawn.

THE MINUTE ANTHONY returned to his room to dress for a late luncheon, he sat down to pen a note to his sister's husband. Trelissick needed to know Smith was likely in the area. God, how he hoped Rose and Michael were wrong and it was a different Smith. There were a few in the world.

He sighed. It had to be her. There was no point operating under the assumption Smith was anyone but she.

Every move he made from that second on would be under the firm belief that it was indeed the same ruthless businesswoman from London, unafraid to exact lethal punishment when she deemed it necessary. He wished Darius was still in England. The ex-pirate would know exactly what to do and how to get it done.

Not that Anthony couldn't be the man for the job. He just wasn't one for underhanded tactics or outright murder. If he was going to bring Smith down, he would do it according to what was lawful. He'd like to see how Clairmont would refuse him a position then. Smith was wanted in so many circles in the capital. He'd likely get a parade when he brought her into the gaol in manacles.

A knock at the door had Anthony on his feet, the missive tucked safely into his pocket. He was sure someone in the house could discreetly get the message where he needed it to go.

"Ah, there you are, old boy," Zach said with more than an edge of impatience. "You've been missing all morning."

Anthony sighed and rubbed the bridge of his nose with forefinger and thumb. "I wasn't missing. I went for a ride and the damned horse threw me."

Zach raised both brows. "Threw *you*?"

"Yes, he threw me. Bloody brute of a horse. I think Clairmont wanted me to break my neck."

"Imagine his disappointment when you returned."

Anthony deliberately ignored the wry tone and finished tying his neckcloth before the mirror. "Don't tell me you've been pining for attention, cousin?"

"I'm probably going to die of boredom but never mind

me." As he pouted, Anthony watched as Zach walked around the room lifting a knick-knack here and an empty glass there.

The best idea would be to send Zach back to London. An even better idea came to mind. "I wouldn't mind if you wanted to go back to the capital. Today, even, if you wanted to."

"Sick of me already?" he said, stopping, both brows raised again. Halfway between anger and resentment.

"You've performed admirably as my human shield and as you've said, it's pure boredom. I really shouldn't have dragged you all the way here in the first place."

Zach came to stand right in front of Anthony and he wondered if he'd overplayed his hand. His cousin eyed him dubiously for several moments. "I saw the chit from across the room last night. You could come with me. Disappear to the Continent for a few months until it blows over."

Ignoring the curl of disgust to Zach's lip, Anthony stated, "Rose Clairmont is an interesting young lady. I could do worse for a wife."

"But you don't need a wife. Why would you want to weigh yourself down with the whale when you could very well continue to cavort with mermaids?"

Anthony curled his fingers into his palms. He wasn't a violent man, preferring to spar with words than fists, but right then, he wanted nothing more than to punch Zach in the nose. "She is not a whale."

"Neither is she a mermaid."

"How do you know? Have you spoken with her? Got to know her?"

"Why would I? Just those spectacles alone are enough to terrify. How would you even kiss her without the huge frames getting in the way?"

There were no problems at all there. The trouble was in *not* kissing her now he'd begun to know who she really was. "You should probably shut up now, cousin. That's my future wife you're disparaging."

"You're intent on marrying the wha—Her?"

"My honour is all I have right now and I will live by it."

"Even if that means tying yourself to Clairmont? You take the wife, you take the family."

He wasn't so sure. Clairmont and his sons clearly didn't care much for Rose. They hadn't taken an interest in the youngest of their family for years. Why would they start now?

He nearly slapped his head as the notion rushed at him. Why had they started now? Whose idea was it for Rose to have a come-out? There were families all over England with black-sheep spinsters, closeted away on estates forever, never to see society. Clairmont could have left Rose at Hell's Gate. London would have forgotten her existence altogether eventually.

"You've got that look," Zach said, his eyebrows finally lowered but his eyes narrowed.

"What look?"

"The one that tells me you've found a problem that needs solving. It also tells me you'll be a terrible bore, your thoughts on whatever it is that grips you."

"Nonsense, cousin. I'm merely puzzling over my bride-to-be and what the future holds for us."

"I just don't understand you, Anthony. You needn't marry a'tall. Why wouldn't you fight this? Why didn't you call Clairmont out and be done with it? He'll never give you a position. He doesn't even want to give you his hideous daughter. You could have even run away. It's what I would have done. Italy is nice this time of year."

Anthony sighed. He'd like just for once to be understood by another person. He'd like someone to see him for him. That he had honour and pride and all the traits a real man laid claim to. But. He also had his father's reputation and it had been heavy on his shoulders for too many years. What was wrong with wanting to show the world he was more than what they assumed him to be? What was wrong with wanting more for his lot in life? "Go back to London, Zach. I'll send word once it's all settled."

"So that's it? You'll marry her? Call Clairmont Papa?"

Anthony snorted and turned to the window. Once again the wind howled and dark storm clouds were moving in over the ocean. "I'll do what must be done."

"Well, you don't have to tell me thrice. I'll pack immediately and try to beat the rain. Good luck, cousin."

"And to you, cousin."

Luck wasn't what he needed. Anthony required a miracle. Divine intervention. Hell, he'd settle for a sign if it showed him what to do next. Of one thing he was sure: Clairmont hadn't got it into his own head to bring Rose out in society. He very much doubted his countess had brought it up either. Which left the brothers. Josiah and Samuel.

Anthony hadn't bothered investigating either of the brothers because it hadn't mattered much at the time.

He went back to his desk, penned another note and tucked it in his pocket with the one for Trelissick. He'd find Ned and have him send a boy to the capital since Zach was far too nosy to be trusted with the missives. Ned would likely show his mistress but Anthony didn't think Rose would hold them back. Not when it might mean help for them all.

Meanwhile, he would have to do some discreet digging of his own to pass the time.

THUNDER ROLLED AND lightning lit the afternoon sky, the smell of rain seeping into every crack of the castle at which Rose's father's guests did nothing but complain. The hunt was postponed until the next morning and lunch was taken in the dining room by grumbling men and nagging women. Cards were suggested and then the idea dismissed. Her father had wine sent up from the cellars for the men and tea for the ladies. Her mother floated in and out of the various rooms where boredom and complaints abounded. Not one of the guests had considered the library so that was where Rose currently hid. The fire was built up and crackled in the grate, the wood smoke soothing, the heat relaxing.

Mrs Foster was the first to destroy her serenity.

"Psst, miss, miss, come here."

Rose lifted an eyelid in the direction of the servants' stair. "What now?" she mumbled under her breath. After her morning with Anthony and then the argument with her father, Rose was out of energy and out of ideas. She wanted an afternoon where she didn't have to run about putting out fires. Smith wouldn't be on the Channel in the storm and they had no shipments scheduled for the night. All should have been quiet.

As Rose approached, Foster pulled her into the dark, narrow corridor. "Your Sir Anthony gave Ned two notes to send back to the city but we thought you might like to read them first."

Odd. "What do they say?"

"In one, he's telling a Trelissick fellow about Smith."

"And the other?" Rose tried to ignore the chill replacing the warmth she had been enjoying. She didn't want all of London knowing her business.

Foster looked as though she was about to enjoy what was to come next. "Germaine must think your brothers have something to do with this mess. He's having them investigated too."

"What would Samuel and Josiah know about Smith? They never come to Hell's Gate anymore either. Perhaps he is simply looking at it from every angle?"

"Or per'aps he suspects them to be in on it?"

In on what though? Neither Josiah nor Samuel could know she was part of a smuggling gang. They didn't care for estate business despite one day inheriting the lands and the castle and what little attention they did pay was on the northern property, not this one. Despite the lies they told to society about having good heads for agriculture, they'd shown zero interest for Hell's Gate or for her. She would have to tell Anthony to pour his resources in a better direction.

"Do we send the notes, miss?"

Rose nodded. "Send them both. It will be too late by the time they are received and acted upon anyway." She had three days to figure out how to set her plan into motion. She had decided to gain Smith's attention but still wasn't sure how to go about it. Despite what Anthony said about her notoriety, surely two women could sit down and sort their differences without further bloodshed? They had been keeping a watch along the coast but Smith only came near under the cover of dark, always leaving as quietly as she came, inflicting the most damage with flaming arrows to the items to make it to shore and then slinking off again.

Michael had begged their French friends to aid them but they were merely a village of fishermen themselves. They stole goods much like highwaymen and then swapped them for coin and fleece skimmed from both Hell's Gate and Ashmoor's takings. It was amazing how much could just disappear or rather, not appear to be counted in the first place, and not one of the lords noticed.

Their French counterparts' ship wasn't equipped for battle with pirates any more than Rose's had been before it was set on fire. It was a loss none of them had seen coming and it still hurt. Rose enjoyed sailing almost as much as smuggling.

Foster left to send the notes on to London and Rose went to her room to dress for dinner. There would be no reading, no relaxing and certainly no naps for her. Not that she could get comfortable in her suit anyway. The internal boning dug into her hips and would leave indentations on her stomach and ribs. The hall clock marked only six so there was time still before the guests would assemble for yet another awkward evening meal. It was good that her company wasn't sought after. She could disappear and no one would notice.

No one but Anthony.

He would mark her absence.

His eyes followed her about any room. He would be angry with her. Angry to be mixed up in their troubles. Michael was cross with her as well. She probably shouldn't have brought Anthony to their meeting place but they didn't have the luxury of sending him in the wrong direction. Rose was still sure there was a way for him to help them without his father's involvement. His information so far had shed so much light on Smith. Without that they would have remained in the chase for a random pirate rather than looking for motive for the pinpointed, deliberate attacks carried out by a woman.

For months Rose and Michael had attempted to reason why any pirate would linger on the Channel for long periods. The British Navy still patrolled the waters as well as French soldiers, some still on edge despite the relative peace but they were few and far between. It wasn't hard for their French friends to slip through and it was equally easy for Smith. But why? Why risk it all for a little gold, fleece, tea and lace? It was as if she taunted for the sake of taunting rather than for the goods. That's when Rose had decided the pirates were after something else.

Or *someone* else.

It hadn't occurred to her until their meeting in the woodsmen's hut that morning. Smith could very well be after *someone* at Hell's Gate. But for years it had only been Rose. The only member of the Clairmont family to settle in the inhospitable place. It was how she had remained so free to do as she pleased for so long. Smith couldn't want Rose for any reason. Or Michael. He was a stable lad at Ashmoor's estate. That left the villagers but they weren't anyone special either. Just farmers, boys and women. They had no riches or anything of particular value. Their port was about the export of goods. It wasn't a place for tourists or the gentility to take tea and cakes. The navy sometimes provisioned there but not always and not without fanfare signalling their arrival. Their ships were ostentatious and word travelled quickly along the coast when they were setting in for provisions.

Hell's Gate itself was entailed so it wasn't the castle or the lands. That only left the trade. The tea, lace, tobacco and liquor. But anyone with a ship and half a brain could illegally trade with France now that the Channel was open. There were just too many questions.

Molly met her at the door to her rooms and Rose asked for a bath to be drawn. She was beginning to get a very real headache and needed to relax properly, out of her suit, and think. Rain pelted the windows and the wind never ceased for a moment, causing the flames atop the candles to dance and sway, casting shadows upon the walls. Molly was a step ahead of Rose as usual with the tub already full of steaming, fragrant water, dried lavender heads bobbing on the surface.

"Molly, has Germaine been asking questions of the servants?"

Her maid shook her head as she untied the laces of the currently padded suit. When they had small goods to pass off, the padding was removed and the pockets filled. It had been necessary to wear it with her family in residence but there was nothing to be passed off now. The risk was too high. "He knows they are your friends so he probably also knows we won't help him."

"Nothing at all?" That was strange. If he was indeed an investigative sort, why hadn't he started investigating?

"I heard from Sally, the downstairs maid, who told the cook, who then told Mr Foster, that he was asking questions of Samuel over wine in your father's den."

"What kind of questions?"

"She only got snippets from their conversation but it sounded as if he was asking why you had been left alone here."

He wasn't supposed to be checking up on her or her past. He should have been thinking about Smith and how to get rid of her. Damn it, why couldn't the man follow a simple plan?

Molly left her to soak while she went to fetch her pale blue dinner gown. Rose's thoughts wouldn't calm or quiet. She let her head fall back against the tub and closed her eyes, brought forth a memory of the ocean on a calm day, the waves gently lapping the rocks and sand. A day when the wind was strangely absent, a true blessing. Families from the village came to enjoy the water, the little ones splashing in the shallows while their parents watched on from picnic blankets. A perfect day for the citizens of Hell's Gate. One where each and every man, woman and child was an equal to the next, even Rose. She wasn't the master's daughter or the mistress of the castle. She was just Rose. Their friend. She and Michael had set up a running race for the older children that had seen laughter and camaraderie filter through the generations as easily as the wind normally blew through the trees. She had been truly happy then. No regrets, no second thoughts, no worries.

Not anymore. Smith had ruined that. If not for the pirates, Rose would never have been in the garden that night. She would have still had her come-out ball—her father had been most adamant. But she would have passed the night without scandal, without offer, and been sent back to Hell's Gate to live as a spinster. Exactly the way she would have dreamed. Instead, she had spent months dodging a pirate, wearing her blasted suits and dreading marriage to a man her father despised with his every breath.

That last fact made Rose smile. She'd never been one to try to make her father happy. She smiled because it would make him miserable to lay eyes on his son-in-law at special events. He would be especially furious to know Rose wasn't the large girl he made light of.

When the door clicked and footsteps sounded, Rose called out from behind her ornamental bathing screen, "Leave the gown on the bed, Molly. I'll sit a while longer."

"Shall I wait on the bed too?" a deep voice called back with a hint of laughter. Not Molly. Not Molly at all.

Rose sat up, water sloshing over the edges of the tub, but then realised he would see more of her above the water than below, the soap making her bath milky. "What the hell are you doing in here? How did you get in?"

"I picked your lock," came that teasing tone again, closer this time.

"Well, get out. This is completely inappropriate."

Anthony popped his head around the edge of her screen and smiled, his eyes travelling the length of the bath as though he could indeed see through the water after all. "We need to talk, Rose."

WHAT PROPELLED HIM to seek Rose out in her rooms, Anthony wouldn't examine too closely. He only knew that they had to speak without her family or Michael or her friendly servants anywhere near.

"I didn't expect to find you in the tub," he said, the smile never leaving his lips.

"You cannot be in here," she shrieked, attempting to cover her nudity but only serving to bring his eyes to the movement below the water.

Anthony sat down on a low stool in the corner of the room, crossing his arms over his chest and getting comfortable. "We are going to talk, Rose. I'm sorry about the timing but I had no notion of where you might be later in the night."

She stared at him hard, her eyes a narrow golden glint between dark lashes, her cheeks taking on an almost unholy glow. "At least hand me a towel and turn your back. I will not have any discussions with you while I am undressed."

"I don't mind," he said with a grin. It was time he got a little more real with Rose Clairmont. He had to know what she knew. All of it. Then they could devise a plan that was better than hunting down and killing a villainess.

"You are lucky I am unarmed," she hissed through her teeth.

"Perhaps," he replied but stood anyway, picked up a towel and handed it to her. He turned his back after a long hesitation. Her skin was so creamy where the sun hadn't kissed it, not a freckle in sight. He'd had to tear his gaze away rather than follow the drops of water falling from her hairline, down her neck and further. He was too much of a gentleman to look but a part of him bayed to turn around, to see what she hid beneath her suits and gowns every day. His pulse jumped and his blood heated.

He had been hoping to find her without her suit on, not without a stitch on. The air moved at his back as she made to whirl past him and back into the main part of her bedroom. Perhaps to raise an alarm with the servants. He shot out his hand and caught her wrist. God but she was so soft and warm. She was also wet. "No you don't," he murmured, pulling her against his chest, his other arm snaking about her waist. He'd imagined her skin and bone there but was delighted to know she had substance. "We are going to talk. No one is going to come to your aid just yet."

"I wasn't going to raise the alarm, you ninny. I wanted to get my robe rather than stand here with only a linen. It's bloody cold."

Ninny? She could curse but she couldn't throw out a real insult? He was confused all over again. But first: "Why do you hide yourself, Rose?"

She stiffened in his embrace. "I beg your pardon?"

"I never imagined you would be so…so…this." Of their own volition, his fingers fanned out across her stomach, ridges of muscle beneath the softness under his palm.

She was exquisite.

He was lost.

"Too large? Too small? Is there nothing a man won't complain about?"

"I never said you were too large, not ever, but this? This is a welcome surprise."

"Kindly take your hands off me. Now."

He didn't want to. Ever. But he had to. He wasn't quick about it though, the pads of his fingers gliding over the thin linen, itching to explore further. But she wasn't his to touch like this. Every inch of his fibre should have been outraged that he'd broken into her room after dark while she was naked. He should have been fighting his conscience every step of the way. Should have. But his blood roared and his libido was very much awake in her presence and had been from the moment she'd walked out of his dressing room the day before.

He gave her his back but her reflection shone from the surface of the window, the rain making it appear as if she was fluidity incarnate. Her waist wasn't slim but neither was it large or even square. Instead, it tapered gently to a milky bottom and long, slender legs. He was admiring the curve of her nape as she pulled on a thick, maroon robe and snapped her attention to her intruder. Her cheeks flamed all the more when she realised he had been able to see her, colour staining her face and neck. Would it travel lower still? he wondered, his gaze lowering as he turned.

"Why are you here, Anthony?"

He had to give himself a giant mental shake to dislodge the picture he now had of Rose Clairmont in his brain. He sat on the edge of her bed so his desire wouldn't be as evident to her. "I need to know who instigated your come-out ball." Her gaze hadn't left his but it was only a matter of time when she stopped scowling and started pacing.

Only three seconds, in fact. "You broke into my rooms to ask me that? It could not have waited until dinner?"

"I need to know who made the suggestion to your father, Rose."

She paused but only for a breath. "What are you talking about? Father came up with it on his own. Didn't he?"

Anthony shook his head. "I don't think so. Why now? Why at all?"

She had spent months wondering 'why at all'. "He wanted to be rid of me once and for all before I could get any bigger, older or more embarrassing to him."

"I doubt it. From what I've seen and heard, you practically run Hell's Gate. Who would be custodian if you left with your new husband?"

"Father wouldn't have thought that far ahead, I assure you."

"He didn't come up with this on his own, Rose. Has he given you more than a passing thought these last years?"

"No."

"Then why now? Why launch you on the ton knowing full well you might not take?" She openly cringed and Anthony regretted the frank way in which he'd stated the facts. He wasn't always the most diplomatic when he was making lists of the whys, the whens and the wheres. "I'm sorry, I didn't mean it to sound like it did."

"You can be honest with me," she began, her voice small, her arms hugging her middle. "You were horrified when you first saw me, weren't you? They all are. I only keep it up to annoy him further."

"If I'm being honest, I don't remember much of our first meeting. I couldn't even remember your name or being in your father's office. I suspect he drugged me to get me out of the house because I didn't walk out on my own broken ankle and I woke with the devil's own headache the next day."

Her chin dropped to her chest and he wondered what it was that he'd said. Where was fierce Rose? Where was the woman who was strong and independent and uncaring of what others thought of her?

He stood and walked towards her though he knew he should have stayed seated. "If it is real honesty you want, I'll tell you that our first meeting here, at Hell's Gate, when I thought you a wh—"

Her chin lifted and her spine straightened, her eyes once again flashing. "When you thought I was a whore? A trap set by my father?"

Here was his fierce, thorny Rose. "When I thought you a trap, I considered giving in to it." He reached out both hands and gently pulled the hair from beneath the robe's collar. It was still damp against his fingertips. "Your curls were tumbled about your shoulders like a doxy and your cheeks were flushed, your breasts rising and falling with your uncontrolled, anxious breaths." He moved his hands to her shoulders, her arms, his thumbs skirting the edges of her ribs as far as he could reach without scaring her as he drifted ever lower, his touch moving to her waist, her hips. "If you were a doxy, I could have had you, right then. I could have bedded you, broken the engagement and fled once my lust was satisfied."

The edge of her lip curled. "Now you sound like a pirate."

Anthony chuckled softly. "Never that. I was a man facing a woman just as I am now. You might not believe it, Rose, but you tempt a man to sin."

"Liar," she breathed, but she lacked conviction.

With two fingers beneath her chin, he pressed until she met his gaze. "Never underestimate your feminine charms. They can and will bring any man to his knees with only a promise of what your body offers. A man—be he pirate, gentleman or chimney sweep—will do anything a woman asks of him so long as she gives him a hint or taste of what comes next." He touched his lips to hers intending to immediately break away, to go back to the bed and continue their discussion in a platonic way. He only wanted to make her realise how desirable she truly was. To raise her spirits.

But it didn't happen that way.

When Rose sighed against him and licked her tongue along the seam of his mouth, Anthony's blood finally surged to a full gallop and he lifted her in his arms, walking her until her back hit the wall and her legs wrapped around him, her fingers speared through his hair as the kiss deepened to infinite depths. She tasted sweet yet with a hint of danger, truly a rose. Beautiful to look at but could slice you open if you weren't careful of her sharp edges.

Right at that moment, Anthony fully believed his own words. As he ground his hard pelvis into her softness, he would have done anything she asked of him. Anything at all. He created just the right amount of space between their bodies so he could untie her robe, spreading one half to the side so he could fill his palm with her bare breast, flick her nipple with his thumbnail. She cried out, her back arching, but he swallowed the sound and kissed her even more senseless, kneading the soft mound with one hand while he ground into her, pressing her against the cool stone and trying to remember why he couldn't open the fall on his trousers and enter her in one swift movement.

Her heat was everywhere. She was soft, warm, wet, mindless. Little mewls of delight emerged between frustrated sighs as she tried to get closer to his body, seeking something, anything to satisfy.

Virgin, his mind whispered.

Caveman, came next.

He tried to quiet the voices but they held a hint of reason, of reality. He would not ruin Rose against the wall in her bedroom on a stormy night right before her own reckoning came. As tempting as it was. At least if they perished this week at the hands of Smith, they would both have known bliss. But he couldn't. He wouldn't.

He slowed his movements, softened his kisses, lowered her to her feet carefully then finally stepped away after he was sure she could stand. The wall held her up, her robe loose, her body bare beneath it, one pinkened nipple on display for his eyes to feast on, fabric clinging to the rest of the bounties he'd not yet laid claim to.

"I'm sorry," he said, forcing his errant body to turn, to sit back on the bed and take stock. A gentleman would never do what he had just done. *But a pirate would.*

ROSE CAME TO but was slow to act, slow to close her robe and retie it, slow to step away from the wall that had surely held her up for a little while.

It was as though a storm had captured her and lifted her high above the land, a maelstrom so wild and turbulent she had all but forgotten her own name. Had he not been whispering it while he'd touched her, kissed her, really made her come alive, she might have forgotten who and where she was altogether. For long moments she hadn't known where her body ended and his began. They were almost one being, mad for the dizzying heights she knew now to be just outside of her reach.

She'd thought she'd been living her life, revelling in her freedom. So what the hell was that? And how did she get him to do it again?

"What did you say?" She realised a little too late that he spoke to her. Her own body was so loud. Blood rushed in her veins to pool right down low in her body where a dull thud had taken up residence.

"I said, I didn't mean for it to go that far. I guess I got carried away."

"You and me both," she said, but more to herself than to him. Was it possible? What he'd said about a woman completely controlling a man with just one taste and an unspoken promise? And what came next? She knew the mechanics of how a man and a woman would lie together but she wondered if the act itself would bring more of the out-of-control feelings she had just experienced. How did one know what to say or do if there was no control?

Rose smiled and licked her lips. She'd liked it. Really liked it.

"Don't do that, Rose." His voice came as a soft warning but she ignored it, finding splendour in the way her body almost seemed to hum in expectation. She felt so heavy in some places and so light in others. Had she captured a flock of tiny birds inside of her stomach?

"Do what?" she replied, her mind absent from the room still.

"Don't look so dreamy. It should never have happened."

Eventually her brain caught up to his words. "Why ever not? We are either going to be married or dead in the coming weeks."

"If I asked you right now which one you would prefer,

what would your answer be?"

He knew full well she didn't want to marry. She'd told him as much that morning on their ride. But now she wasn't so sure. "Is it always like that?"

"What?"

She hadn't really looked him in the eye yet, afraid of what she would see, afraid of what he would see reflected in her eyes. When she did, it didn't do much to quiet her pulse or her thoughts. He was as scared of this as she was. "Between a man and a woman. Is it always so...so...intense?"

He shook his head and the fear of the noose fell away. "Not always. It does help when lust comes into the equation. When two people are attracted to each other."

Her mind absorbed the latter but immediately went back to what he'd said about her feminine charms. "Do you think that is how Smith does it? Uses her charms to get men to do her bidding?"

"Probably, although her lover was killed some months ago."

"Wouldn't she want vengeance for his death?" If the man Rose loved was killed, would she not want to spill the killer's blood in return? She'd played at being quite bloodthirsty since Anthony had arrived but the truth was, she'd never sunk her dagger into the skin of another. She wasn't actually sure she could. Yet, she'd never been in love or close to it. She loved her friends and might be able to avenge them, but none had ever made her want to remove her own skin so she could climb into his.

"If it was an eye for an eye she was after, she would have

stayed close to England, struck like a silent assassin rather than in the open attracting attention."

"Could she be trying to gain your attention? Or your friend's—Trelissick's?"

"Not from here."

He seemed very sure but they were running out of answers and the list of questions grew and grew. "We need to set up a meeting," Rose stated, beginning to pace once more, back to business, now that her body had cooled and her conscience was a little more awake.

She had behaved so wantonly. Just like the doxy he'd thought her. Closer to the pirate she'd wanted him to be. If she still had her ship, she could eliminate Smith and then sail away. She wondered if a female pirate could be as successful as the male ones. Smith obviously knew what she was doing and was very good at it.

"Dear God, are you mad?" A minute passed and then another. "What are you thinking about now?" he asked, with sincere dread attached.

She wouldn't tell him she was wondering how to manipulate a man with her body so she could truly get away from Hell's Gate. From her father. From the life England had in store for her. Perhaps if she helped Smith get what she wanted, she might give something in return to Rose. She might even take her with her when she left the Channel?

Excitement buzzed through her, exhilarating her to higher heights than Anthony just had. Their plan had been to take Smith down but Rose would have to readjust now. She would have to do it with neither Anthony nor Michael in on it. Both men would tell her it was insane. Completely cracked to even consider it. That's why she needed a woman on her side…

CHAPTER TWELVE

"WE'VE FOUND HER!" Molly exclaimed as she came rushing into the room, skidding to a halt and taking half the rug with her.

Rose closed her eyes again and groaned. It had been a late night full of nightmares and feverish dreams after a dinner that had gone on too long and a supply of wine that had seemed likely to never, ever end. Rose only wanted to be alone so she could sort her thoughts into actions for the next day but she couldn't plead a headache every evening as she had been. Her mother would want to summon the physician.

Each time she closed her eyes to try to think an action through, Anthony would appear in her mind, his eyes hardening as his head shook and he forbid her from making a sound, from moving a muscle. Despite it all being in her head, she'd not been able to banish him completely. Not surprising that his image would invade her nightmares and turn them into the stuff of heaven-sent dreams though. Never had anyone touched her so intimately. She almost believed him when he'd said he would desire her no matter what size she was. He had kissed her in the garden in the dark but it was because they were watched. She was mad to think his conduct anything other than lust in the face of a naked body. Or perhaps a distraction method? That would work in his favour also. But he'd touched her so reverently. Hadn't he?

"Didn't you hear me? I said we found her. Get out of bed and dress before the whole house wakes."

"Found who?" Rose asked, shaking her head free of beguiling eyes, urgent fingers and hot kisses.

"Smith. Damn it, woman, get out of that bed." Molly ripped the blankets back and dragged her the first few steps but then Rose was up and ready, pulling her nightgown straight over her head and holding her arms out for stays and then the suit. Rose had learned long before to wear both layers in case she had to remove the suit to ride or swim.

"Where? How?"

"Michael sent some of the lads out into the storm to perch on bar stools and street corners. He knew she'd have to come to ground what with last night's wind and hail and all."

Excitement rippled through her followed by a keen sense of doom. Doom for her newest plan to become ashes to the wind. "Does Michael know?"

"He's waiting for you at the cottage. Ned has your horse ready with more clothes but you need to hurry before your brothers' men or Germaine are alerted."

Both gave her pause. "Why do my brothers have men watching? Watching for what?"

Molly gave the laces one last good tug and then pulled

out a riding habit to go on over the padding. "Josiah has men in the stable until all hours. They don't take horses out or bring any in. They huddle in corners talking amongst themselves. Samuel has three also. Strange, quiet lot."

"Perhaps they are in the stables because there is little room in the house? Or perhaps they are horseflesh men?"

Molly met Rose's eyes in the mirror. "Or maybe they are waiting for something or someone? Josiah even had a watch set last night on the ground floors. The Fosters both were unhappy with the lack of answers about why it was necessary."

Peculiar indeed. "Do you think you could dig up some clues, Molly?"

"I've been trying, miss, but they're a tight-lipped lot. I can't be too obvious."

"No. No I don't suppose so. And do be careful. Perhaps Anthony was right and there is more to this whole situation than we are aware of?" It had to be a wild coincidence but even as she had the thought, she knew it wasn't. Josiah and Samuel were sure someone was coming but surely it wasn't linked to Smith? Perhaps one or the other had left an angry husband behind in London and feared he would come for revenge? They were both known profligate rakes. Reasonably rich, titled, unattached. A London lady's favourite kind of cad.

But Rose had enough to think about and do without worrying for her brothers. Either of them. They were big lads and could look after themselves. If they couldn't, they could ask Father to take care of the mess like they had in the past.

News always filtered back to Hell's Gate of the escapades of the males in her family. Never the women though. Her two sisters and her mother were the epitome of style, grace and boredom. No mention of scandal would ever carry their names. It was the reason Elizabeth and Emma hadn't attended the house party. Rose's current scandal would not touch them if their respective husbands had anything to say in the matter.

Rose on the other hand… She hurried to finish dressing, jammed her feet into her boots while Molly tied a ribbon in her hair, and then she was running down the servants' staircase and out to the stable.

Ned held her mount steady just behind the main building. Rose spoke to another groom nearby. "If anyone follows us, Kendle, I'll box your ears."

He grinned but gave her a quick salute and then they were off, galloping as fast as they could beneath the cover of trees for as far as they could, Rose in her ridiculous side-saddle with Ned right behind.

She breathed a half sigh of relief when the little hunter's cottage came into view, some of the men milling about, readying horses, checking weapons. It looked as if their little band of smugglers were professionals heading for war.

Rose quickly greeted each man but continued into the cabin to find Michael talking with the blacksmith.

"What news?" she asked before even a hullo.

Michael's gaze flitted over her shoulder before returning to her face. "Where is your hound?"

"My what?" Confusion held her for a moment.

"Germaine. Did he come with you? Follow you?"

Anger replaced confusion. "He is not my watchdog and you shouldn't treat him as such. He is probably still abed for all I know or care." Anthony Germaine wasn't her anything as far as she was concerned but her cheeks warmed thinking of him abed. But he'd never actually asked her to marry him and she had never accepted the forced betrothal. As of that moment, he was simply an intriguing man she liked to kiss. End of story.

Michael hesitated but then said, "Smith and her men are holed up just this side of Ramsgate."

"Why would she risk being anywhere near a navy port?"

"Simon heard a tale that her ship ran aground in the storm and is wedged fast in the sands just past Deal. There's a tavern known as the Cock's Wobble. That's where we'll find 'em."

"How can we be sure it's her?" How could they be sure Anthony was telling all of the truth about Smith's identity, that he knew all of the facts?

Michael drew a deep breath and pulled her aside from the other men. He lowered his voice and said, "There's more. It seems the lady is heavy with child."

"A ruse?" Rose asked immediately. She was no mother but how could this woman stay on a ship harassing others, knowing it might come down to a fight to the death?

Michael shook his head. "Simon didn't seem to think so. She is parading herself as Lady LePedle, on her way back to France as soon as the weather clears."

"They don't really like the French around these parts,"

Rose pointed out although Michael already knew that.

"She paid her tab in full in coin for her and her men. Thirteen in total. We think. There's a lot who are light in the pocket who don't mind hiding a few frogs for a bit."

"I have to change out of this godawful suit and think. We need a very good plan because we can't just ride into town, run down the door of the Cock's Wobble and storm the place. Anthony says her men are ruthless, that she herself is ruthless. We have to proceed with caution."

"I'm not going to go on everything your Anthony says about her but we'll be careful nonetheless. Leave your suit on and we can enter the tap as weary travellers, a husband and wife, caught in the rain?"

"She wouldn't have reason to suspect, would she? But I can't ride that far in the rain. I would be waterlogged and fall from my horse." Rose's mind was a whirl of activity, of excitement and the thrill of catching their predator before they became the prey. But she only wanted to talk to the woman. She didn't want all-out war. She also didn't want Michael to know she had a bargain to strike with the pirate. "I'll change into my buckskins but carry the brown woollen gown in a saddle bag. I can put it on right before we arrive." Rose especially liked how Michael didn't try to talk her out of going along. Any other man would tell her it was far too dangerous. As she secreted sheathed daggers inside each boot, she wondered if he should have at least tried.

"We could take one of Ashmoor's carriages?" he suggested. "Hide some of the men inside?"

"This is not a hostile mission. Think of it more as reconnaissance. If it is at all possible, I would like to simply talk to the woman. If she wanted us dead, we'd be dead. There's something else she is waiting for and if we can find out what it is, we can find out if it is feasible to give it to her and send her on her way."

"It's very risky," Michael supplied, finally giving voice to what Rose had known was coming eventually. "If not many know her true identity, what's to stop her from killing us both right there?"

"We'll tell her Anthony Germaine knows where we are and is under instruction to release her whereabouts and description if we don't return."

A tsking followed her words and then Michael rolled his eyes. "That will never work."

"It might." But they couldn't rush off on a maybe. "Perhaps we'll think of a better plan on the way but we can't dilly-dally here and let her disappear again. This might be our only chance."

In the end Michael capitulated. They took six of their biggest, strongest men with them and left a few to stay at the cottage in case Rose and Ned were followed. Ned was to head back to the stable and tell anyone who asked that she had gone to town to see the vicar's wife for advice about her impending nuptials.

Simple. Too simple. A shiver of dread worked its way down her spine as she fought to pull her boys' pants on while the men changed her saddle for another. When things were too simple, they were often fraught with flaws yet unseen. If Rose thought she had any other choice, she wouldn't do it.

Wouldn't risk her neck or Michael's. But her time was limited. Her father's crony would arrive in two days so she had to decide on her future before then. It was either marry an octogenarian stranger chosen by her father, marry Anthony Germaine, or put her life in the hands of a ruthless lawbreaker to escape it all.

Only one of those options could lead her to happiness. She just hoped she chose the right one.

ANTHONY COULDN'T THINK of anything worse than spending the morning making small talk with the other houseguests. He was attempting to get closer to Josiah and Samuel Clairmont but so far had been passed off to a distant cousin who laughed like a barking seal and another man who had a strange propensity for bawdy jokes before noon.

"If you gentlemen would excuse me," he said, rising from his chair to quit the room altogether. If one could describe in graphic detail what lay between the legs of a fishwife, then Anthony should sure as hell be able to drink this early in the morning. He had plenty of sorrows to drown that day.

He assumed Rose was hiding from him since she hadn't come down for breakfast. Had he frightened her? He almost snorted. Rose Clairmont may have been frightened about her shaky future but there was no way a few harmless kisses could terrify her into hiding for long.

Perhaps she was dredging up the nerve to face him and pretend she was unaffected? He bloody well couldn't stop thinking about her silky skin on his hands, her nipple pebbling beneath the pad of his thumb, the little groans of delight she made as he kissed her. Or rather ravished her. That word was probably more than apt for what happened between them the previous night.

After returning to his room frustrated and as randy as a lad outside a brothel, he'd attempted to alleviate the problem with vigorous exercise. He'd crunched until his stomach hurt and he couldn't breathe as the wind howled, almost screaming for vengeance against him. If he was the fanciful sort. And he wasn't.

The storm lasted well into the night reassuring him that Rose wouldn't be leaving the castle after everyone else retired for the evening.

Anthony was just about to turn the corridor into Clairmont's library, where his liquor cabinet was always stocked, when he heard hushed voices. He crossed his arms and leaned against the wall, expecting Rose to be passing something along to the servants. Probably instructions to poison his luncheon or drug him over dinner so she could make her escape.

It was neither. It wasn't even Rose. Two male voices, hissing at each other so he almost couldn't make out the words.

"You can't station men outside of the house without someone noticing," the first said.

"Let them notice," the second replied. "I'll say there was word about a robbery two shires over and that we can never be too careful. Mother will be happy. Father will dance a jig that Mother isn't nagging him about an extra watch."

"And if she is seen? If she comes for us or sends her men? What then?"

"If she comes, then we'll kill her. We'll kill them all."

Anthony's blood ran cold but he stayed hidden.

"You can't kill a lady."

Derisive laughter accompanied: "You and I both know she's no lady."

"We cannot kill her."

The laughter stopped. "We took everything from her. Every last guinea. She won't be so forgiving this time, Samuel."

"Perhaps if you let me marry her like we promised, then she would forgive it all. She would be on her way to having the protection of a title."

Oh dear God.

"You were being ridiculous offering her marriage like that. I merely offered to make her my mistress. She never wanted our protection before all this business with Trelissick. She merely wanted the two of us to take a fall if she was caught. Now that she is one thread from the hangman's noose, she can't come crawling back to see what bones she can be offered."

"You should have never gotten us mixed up with the likes of her, Josiah. Not ever."

"You weren't complaining when your prick was buried deep within her body, drinking her alcohol, playing at her tables and with her girls. Where were your objections then, brother?"

Anthony was so deeply focused on the words the two

Clairmont men were exchanging, the chilling foreboding that every new syllable spelled for all of them, that he didn't hear the footsteps behind him until it was too late.

"Skulking about in the corridors eavesdropping, pirate spawn? Can't say I'm much surprised." The earl's voice carried from the corridor and beyond. He'd bet even parties behind closed doors would have heard him proclaim Anthony worse than the lowest of the low.

Josiah and Samuel rounded the corner and closed in, one scowling, the other worried. Samuel should be worried. They had no idea of the mess either. Why did everyone underestimate Smith? Was it because she was a woman? Women committed atrocities too. They were just cleaner and quieter about it. The men investigating were never in a hurry to admit they'd been bested by a female so the tales didn't spread as far or as wide.

Smith was calculating as well as ruthless. She was patient and sure of herself and her crew. She was bloody dangerous and it boiled his blood to know that smarts obviously didn't run in this family. They were all out of their bloody minds. He wanted to tell them so but bit down on a reply. Instead he waited for one of the brothers to say something. Anything.

Josiah broke the oppressive silence first. "We'll deal with this, Father. You go and entertain your guests."

"Don't kill him, mind," came the only reply before the earl sauntered off in search of a gossiping ear to listen to his tall tales.

Once Clairmont was out of earshot, both of Anthony's

arms were taken in crushing grips, an angry brother on each side. Anthony didn't even care about the beating they probably wanted to give him. As they propelled him into the earl's study and slammed the door, turning the key in the lock, he very nearly would have welcomed a good old-fashioned fist fight. He had frustrations to vent.

"How much did you hear?" Samuel asked, his tone whiny and worried.

"Enough to know that you two are in it up to your eye-balls right now."

Josiah scoffed. "I have the situation well in hand."

Anthony raised a brow and sank into a chair by the coals in the hearth. His feet wanted to move, his body wanted to lash out. He tried for an outward calm instead. "Do you now? In what way do you have it *well in hand*?"

"The business of gentlemen does not concern you."

"I don't give a fig for what you and your brother do but you've put your sister's life in real danger."

Laughter sounded from both brothers. "She also shouldn't concern herself with matters she knows absolutely nothing about."

If he got up from his seat and punched Josiah in the face, would he have time to tackle Samuel as well? His fists clenched and he counted the steps between the two while they stood there with stupid looks on their stupid faces. "You really have no idea what Smith is capable of, do you? Or are you in denial because of her fairer sex?"

Josiah's upper lip curled with disdain. "Another woman who thought to play in a man's world and emerge the victor.

Look at her now. She's got nothing and she knows it."

Anthony used one hand to the crack the knuckles on the other. "And what are the spoils of this game? How much money did you fleece from Smith?"

Samuel stood taller, his chest puffed out, his hands on his hips. "Now, see here, it wasn't her money to begin with. Her tables were rigged and her liquor watered. She no more deserved that money than the next blighter. When she disappeared without a trace, we merely helped ourselves before someone else could."

"I'm afraid that's not how Smith obviously views it. You two are the reason she risks all to hang about, aren't you? She can't go anywhere because you have her only means to support herself in a new city."

"We don't have it," Samuel said.

"Not anymore," Josiah muttered.

"Well, you had better get it back and hope she doesn't take your balls with her when she leaves."

Josiah's temper finally snapped; Anthony had been waiting for it. All three men surged but Anthony's fury was more urgent, driven by the knowledge of what they had been putting their sister through. He swung his fist and connected with a cheek but not hard enough to break any bones. He was never a great fighter.

Out of nowhere, pain exploded in his own face, his jaw, cheek, chin. Both he and Josiah dropped to the carpets, Samuel the only one left standing but cradling his knuckles with a curse even Rose could have uttered with more conviction.

THE FALL INTO RUIN

"Did you just hit me in the face while my back was turned?" Anthony asked the one brother still on his feet.

"You think I won't defend my brother from the likes of you?" Samuel spat.

Anthony sat up, out of reach of Josiah, who held is face in his palm while he got his scowl back in place perfectly. "The likes of me?" he repeated, almost dumbly, unable to really understand where the brothers' brains were at. "You told me to marry your sister and take her away." And then it clicked in his mind. "You've known all along she was in danger, haven't you? You must have already upset Smith before her lover, Frederick, was killed; otherwise she wouldn't have come here so quickly once her identity was discovered."

He knew he spoke more to himself than to the so-called gentlemen in the room. Never in his wildest dreams would he throw Daniella to the wolves just to save his own hide. Who were these people? "I take it your father doesn't know?"

"Of course he doesn't," they snapped in unison.

"Which one of you is going to apprise him of the situation?"

Both brothers looked at him then, murder written all over their faces. Josiah said, "Remember the part where this has nothing to do with you?"

"It concerns me because Rose is involved *and* you are breaking the law."

Josiah got to his feet. Anthony did the same, taking several steps away from them both.

Samuel taunted with: "You are not yet a Runner, Germaine. You don't uphold any laws."

Anthony wanted to bang their heads together. "Your father does though. What do you think will happen to him *if*, no, *when*, you are found out?"

"We have been hiding it from him long enough now. If it's just us and you who know anything, then there's only you to blame if word of this is leaked."

Anthony reached for the bridge of his nose to massage a growing headache away. He couldn't tell the earl anything without revealing Rose's place in it all and he'd made a promise not to do it. Not to tell her father anything. He'd known none of it would end well then and he knew it now too. "How do you propose to 'handle' Smith? I can assure you, it won't be easy."

Josiah smiled and Anthony realised he was the cunning one. The one who thought he knew it all. When Josiah said, "We're going to have to kill her."

Anthony tipped his head back and roared with laughter.

He needed a drink. Or three. He ignored the words for a minute and poured himself a scotch from a decanter on a sideboard beneath the old estate ledgers and papers. He sniffed it first but found it unlikely there would be drugs in it. Unlike last time when he couldn't remember much more than the threats and the shouting after falling on Rose in the dark. "Did you two drug me that night I fell on Rose?"

Samuel lifted a hand in the air. "That was me."

"With what?"

"Belladonna."

"I didn't taste it."

"Few ever do in small doses." He didn't have to look so proud about it.

"Could you do it again?" Anthony asked as an idea formed. If they could get close enough to Smith, and the brothers could, they could render the pirates unconscious and then have them taken in. The problem hadn't been in capturing Smith so much as discovering her whereabouts. Thin air had seemed to swallow her up.

"It would mean a trip to London but yes. Providing my contact has enough in stock, it might work."

He tried to ignore the fact that an idiot like Samuel Clairmont could just walk into a storefront, probably on Mayfair no less, and order copious amounts of a killer substance. This was why he had wanted to be a Runner in the first place. After Smith was in custody, he would work on undoing Samuel and Josiah. Clairmont didn't deserve his position if his own sons could help a notorious criminal run her businesses undetected and take part in it. "Does Smith have any leverage against either of you other than the fact you were helping her?"

One brother looked to the other. Something he wasn't privy to passed between them, but then they shook their heads. "No. Nothing."

That meant there was definitely something.

Damn. When were the complications going to come to an end?

ROSE HAD NEVER ridden so far on horseback in the rain and

she was miserably cold, a little bit wet and shivering like a robin in the snow. The storm worked up to a level of intensity she'd always had the smarts to stay away from and indoors. Perhaps it had been foolhardy to set off the way they had but what choice had she been left with? She had to meet with Smith, take measure of her character, see if there was anything at all to be done.

Two days.

That's all the time Rose could take to set her own path. Her father would not be stalled. Once he had his mind set on a way forward, he wouldn't back down from it. Rose knew also that any husband of her father's choosing would be better in his mind than the pirate spawn who'd accidentally 'compromised' her.

So Rose was going to forget the almost tempting option number one in Anthony Germaine as her husband. Waking up next to him in the morning, his hands on her body, his lips kissing hers. It could be a grand adventure. For a time. But marriage was permanent. Very permanent. It's not like she could one day say to him, "Let's go our separate ways."

Option two—her father's crony—was not even on her list of maybes, perhaps or I might consider its. Not for one second would she entertain the notion of running away with a man at least forty years older than her to be married till death do us part. The death part she had a feeling would come sooner rather than later, especially if their first child happened to be a girl.

Anthony likely wouldn't mind a girl, she pondered. He talked about his sister with such affection. But did he even want children? They hadn't talked about it yet. There were a million subjects they'd not discussed in the few short days they'd been given to get to know one another. Did he like the weather hot or cold? Did he abhor pigeon pie like she did or did he enjoy the foul taste? What was his favourite colour, food, drink, poet, king and country?

Rose wasn't stupid enough to think they could talk about it all in a few days; it's why a husband and wife had a lifetime. But. Only if they loved each other. A marriage of convenience is what her father had in mind. Quick. Dirty. Impersonal. If she did have to marry one day, there would at least have to be a measure of feelings. There had to at least be the likelihood that they wouldn't murder each other over breakfast.

Anthony made her laugh, which happened to be an excellent start. He also didn't speak down to her unless it was about Smith. He'd so far touched her and kissed her like he really enjoyed her company but was it all lust? And was lust really a problem if it was a precursor to love?

She shook her head and her entire body gave another shudder, causing her mount a mild shock of alarm. No. Her future lay with Smith and passage anywhere with safe harbour. Perhaps their comrades in France would house her for a short time? Her future didn't lie with Anthony Germaine, her father, his crony, or her brothers. She was still in charge of her destiny.

"We're nearly there," Michael said quietly as farmland gave way to houses, which became closer and closer together as they approached the town. "The Cock's Wobble is by the wharves and warehouses so keep your hood up and don't draw attention."

Rose didn't point out that her hood was keeping the pelting rain off her head or that she had no desire to attract any attention at all. If one whisper got back to Hell's Gate that she had made the trip to a sordid establishment surrounded only by males of common birth, her father wouldn't worry about a suitor. He would probably shoot her and then toss her off her beloved cliffs.

Michael seemed to know well where he was going as the small group made their way down filth-slicked streets, past doors missing paint and even panels. She tried not to stare as women leaned from upper windows calling suggestively, one with her bosom entirely on display. Rose pulled her hood down further over her eyes as her cheeks burned and the churning in her stomach made her want to retch. *Hold it together*, she kept telling herself. She knew bawdy houses existed; she just hadn't expected to ever be right out the front of one.

At the end of the warren of streets, brothels and leaning buildings, they came to a large yard with a structure made of iron, mismatched tin and timbers, relatively new, relatively inviting. A few men milled about under a portico at the front, smoke drifting skyward in puffs from pipes and cigars but there weren't too many. Not enough to deter Rose from her goal this day. Of having a conversation that could well save time and lives.

A brief thought floated into her mind that she hadn't donned the brown dress in her saddlebag but she never got the time to dwell on it. Michael pulled on his reins and then jumped to the muddy ground, coming around to Rose's mount but not helping her down. He took the bridal in his hands and leaned in as close as he could. "Pretend you are a boy, Rose, but do not speak. For the moment, you are mute."

Her lips thinned to a narrow line but she did as he said with a nod, careful that her hood didn't slip, careful not to raise her face to the drizzle or the audience they'd attracted. She trusted Michael and he would take care of her.

A few mud-stained urchins came and took their horses and the men's, Michael dropping coins into their hands with whispered instructions on the feeding and care he expected for such a sum. Rose thought it more likely the horses would be sold before they could even order an ale at the bar.

Two men were left outside by Michael's orders and the other four placed her between them as they entered the tap. Her hood was still pulled so low, she could really only see the ground in front of her now. Warmth stung her freezing cheeks after only three steps into the room, the stale scent of yesterday's food and unwashed bodies coming with it. Here the silence was almost unnatural. Where was the din of voices? Of afternoon drinkers?

"We're closed," came from one side of the room, the loud, rough voice cracking the unusual quiet.

"You don't appear so," Michael replied. His boots turned and Rose had to lift her head a little to follow his movements. He approached the scarred timber bench where the man who'd spoken stood, a scowl on his broad face, a beard half grown on his cheeks and chin.

"Don't much matter how it appears, lad. I said, we're closed."

"How about just one ale? For me and the lads. Then we'll go on and find another establishment? We only want to dry off and satisfy the thirst."

The barman raised a brow and ran his gaze over Rose and then the men. "Where are you off to then?"

"Ramsgate."

"Navy lads?"

Michael shook his head. "Just brothers heading to town for a little mischief."

"And the girl?" he asked, pointing a meaty finger in Rose's direction.

"Our sister. But she won't drink your ale."

"If she won't drink the ale, then out she goes. It's all I got."

Rose stepped forward, mentally prepared herself for the changing of her speech. This was something she was very good at. "I'll drink the ale. Please, sir, just one ale and a few moments out o' the bleeding rain."

The other brow rose but then the man nodded and rounded the bar to begin filling cups with what would probably taste like poison and would hurt her gut just as much.

"Why's your sister wearing breeches?" he called across the tavern.

Michael laughed and gestured for them all to sit. Damn, she hadn't held her cloak closed at the front. She was so cold and scared that she'd forgotten. "She's no good in skirts, this one. Our mam says she should have been another lad, trippin' and cursing all over."

"Askin' for trouble," the barkeep commented.

"Not today," Michael said with meaning.

Rose followed the conversation, inane and without purpose, but she wondered when Michael was going to ask about Smith. How would he broach the subject over only one short ale?

As the barman placed a drink in front of everyone including her, Michael dropped his purse on the table with a clink of coins, some spilling out onto the surface, glinting in the lantern light, far more than a few ales demanded.

"Sumfink else then?" he asked in a low tone, not moving away now he'd seen their blunt. Rose rather thought her friend had overplayed it a little. That was a lot of money for a tavern owner to lay his greedy eyes upon.

"Would you mind telling Lady LePedle we are here to see Smith?"

The man's huge hand had already begun to lift a few coins but then he dropped them back down with a clatter. "No one here by either of those names."

Michael took a few of the fallen coins and handed them over. "We're not here for trouble. Just a quiet conversation between weary travellers."

Rose held her breath. Everyone held their breath. It felt like a whole week passed before the man nodded and stomped off towards a rickety staircase, muttering to himself.

When she opened her mouth to speak, Michael shook

his head and said, "Drink the ale."

Tension coiled inside her until every movement or small sound made her want to jump to her feet and reach for a weapon. Anthony had asked her if she'd ever killed a man. If it did come down to a fight, how would they escape the tavern and flee the city without being caught or at least chased? Rose could use the daggers she carried, had been taught by the men to defend herself, even hunt a little, but they hadn't discussed this part at all. Damn, they really weren't ready to be fighting pirates or the likes of Smith and her men. Anthony was right about that.

"I think we should leave. We shouldn't have come," she whispered from her place next to her friend.

"Patience, Rose. We're only here to talk. I'm sure she won't shoot us dead where we sit."

A voice—sharp, clear, feminine, amused—sounded from the stair. "How can you be so sure of that I wonder?"

The six of them jumped to their feet, the men immediately sheltering Rose and retreating to the closest corner. A few curses were thrown about. More when the woman appeared at last, moving into the room as though she hadn't a care in the world. They'd been prepared for her, for Smith to be a woman. Perhaps a little rough, closer to the brothel creatures they'd passed. Anthony hadn't actually seen her so he hadn't a description to give.

Rose hadn't expected to face a lady. Her dark gown was fashionable and expensive even despite its simplicity, her black hair perfectly coifed, and was that a little rouge on her cheeks? Perhaps she too was warm or nervous or even anxious, though she gave nothing away. Her movements were hindered as she sat, letting out her breath like it was painful, her stomach so distended before the rest of her, Rose thought she might have her baby right then and there on the dirty floorboards.

How could she just sit and face the six of them? She had no idea of the weapons they carried or the harm they might intend. Where was the woman who was supposed to invoke fear just by the mention of her name? In front of her was someone who wouldn't be able to defend herself or run from a room or even rise from her chair in a hurry. Rose was shocked, so shocked she didn't make a move or utter a sound.

"What is it you want?" Smith asked, impatience clipping her words.

"We want to meet with Smith," Michael finally said.

"How do you know I'm not him? State your business and then we'll see, shall we?" she replied, her shrewd gaze travelling over their party.

And then Michael began to laugh and the men relaxed a fraction. Rose wished he'd shut up. Insulting someone before you'd taken measure of their character, or their men hidden close by, could be fatal to them all. Smith wouldn't appear so nonchalant unless she was well protected. Rose was well protected and she was still in fear of losing what little she'd eaten that day.

Rose pushed through from her shelter of strong bodies. "I wish to speak to Smith so if that isn't you, perhaps you could point us in the right direction?" Of course this was

Smith. There was no way their information could be so wrong.

"And who would you be?"

"Introductions will be made only to Smith."

"And how do you know I'm not him?"

Rose returned to the table with a courage she didn't know she had inside of her and drank the last of the ale from her cup. She then said to Michael, "We're wasting our time here. Let's go."

"Is time of the essence?" the lady enquired.

"Time is always in short supply. Sorry to have bothered you." Rose made her way to the door, the men following, Michael hesitating.

They'd only made it halfway across the tavern room when the woman spoke again, amusement still ringing in her words as she stood unsteadily and said, "Come back, Lady Rose. I was merely toying with you."

Rose stopped but didn't resume her seat. Her stomach was in knots and she was fairly sure her character was being assessed by her actions. Best she make them count. "I am not a plaything."

"No, no you are not."

"Shall we have a conversation as women of business or shall I take my leave?"

"Is it all so serious as that?" Smith asked, one brow raised.

"It is when lives and livelihoods are at stake."

"I suppose you are correct. Please, have a seat. I cannot stand overly long these days." Smith punctuated the words by running her hands over her abdomen, her belly huge beneath the fabric.

"When is your baby due to be born?"

"Not for weeks yet I wouldn't think."

"Will you stop pestering us then? I've heard you are headed to France?"

Smith sat back down. "Who did you hear that from?"

Rose approached slowly, Michael giving her a small nod and holding the chair opposite their foe for her to sit. Being at the same table as a notorious criminal mastermind was a little bit exciting. The fact that she wasn't hostile in the least was puzzling but Rose would take it. They needed to talk and talk they would, so it seemed.

"Why have you marked us?" Rose asked, without answering the previous question.

"Marked *you*? I haven't."

"You've been annoying us for quite some time. There must be a reason for it." And then something else occurred to her. "You knew who I was the moment you saw me. How?"

"You have the same features as your brothers. Same eyes. Same nose. Same stubborn tilt to your chin. But I do believe you might be smarter than both of them together."

"I should hope so," came her first words, but then: "Is this about them, then? Josiah and Samuel?" *Had Anthony been right about everything?*

"Your family took something from me and I mean to get it back."

"What did they take?" Rose leaned forward on her seat,

the end in sight. If she could get it back, then Smith would leave them be.

"Did you know I was to be a countess?" Smith told her, her attention completely on Rose in that moment, watching for a reaction.

She wouldn't get one. "Oh?" The knots in her stomach began to unravel, almost causing a shudder. "Were you engaged to an earl?"

She half nodded. "He spoke of marriage, yes."

She couldn't be talking about her father. He was already married. Rose was beginning to get the very awful feeling that Smith wasn't after something that could be found under a bed or in the corner of a room and placed in her hand. "What did my family take from you?"

Just two words. Two very frightening words.

"My life."

CHAPTER THIRTEEN

B Y THE TIME four o'clock sounded on the huge, irritating clock in the entry hall of Hell's Gate, Anthony knew something was very, very wrong. The Fosters, both Mr and Mrs, were extremely, transparently, nervous. Rose was nowhere to be found about the grounds and when he'd been informed by Ned at the stables after lunch that Lady Rose had made a trip to visit the vicar's wife, Anthony had nearly called bollocks on the whole charade.

The vicar's wife was an insipid thing with barely an intelligent bone in her little finger. At dinner on their first night, the vicar had looked at Rose with disgust and had been less than happy to hear about their nuptials despite offering to marry them out of obligation. If Rose had gone to the vicar, she would be back by now. Unless she had been injured? Thrown from her horse? Or just not there?

As he entered the front salon to peer out through the thick glass, he ground his teeth and smothered an incredibly bad word. Rain drifted down in sheets causing the landscape to appear foggy. The incessant wind had finally died down to a breeze that only just moved the trees, unless they were so wet and heavy, they had nowhere to go. All outside activities had been cancelled for at least the day, and not a soul had ventured out. Most of the men were getting thoroughly drunk in the library since the hunt was cancelled for a second day. Clairmont and his sons thought everything to be hilarious, their cackling grating on his already stretched patience as they waited out the weather.

Josiah's men sat outside, hunched into their rain slickers, murder in their eyes for a master who would expose them to such elements. No one would be fool enough to venture out on a day like today. Except for Rose. *Damn it.*

Perhaps she and Michael were plotting? Double damn. It took only minutes to gather his wet weather gear and head back out to the stables.

"Ned, saddle Malum," he ordered on his first step into the musky warmth of the barn. On an ordinary day, he would want an ordinary horse but the thunder was close and the ground wet. He needed the devil steed.

"You can't go out in this, milord."

"I can and I will." Anthony walked straight up to Rose's loyal servant and grabbed his shirtfront, pushing him up against a stall door. "Do you think you're protecting her by lying? She could be in very real danger out there."

Only a little fear flashed in Ned's eyes but then his stubborn obedience reappeared. "Michael will look after her just like he always has."

"And if he doesn't? If he can't? What then? Where did she go, Ned?"

"She went to see the vicar's wife."

Anthony gave him another shove, which saw Ned's head

slamming back into the timbers. "If anything happens to her, I'll be back for you. Saddle. The. Horse."

Another lad showed up then, Malum's bridle in his hands. "Let him go, Ned. If he breaks his neck, the lord will shake yer hand."

Ned mumbled as he set to work opening the barn door. Something that sounded like: "It's not the lord I'm worried about."

Once Anthony was finally seated atop the devil horse, the rain coming down so hard now the sound was deafening, like the roar of a waterfall, he looked to both men one more time. "Tell me where she went."

Both heads gave a shake. "We can't. We'll not betray her."

A curse filled the space. "No, but you may very well have killed her."

If she'd gone off to find Smith, what would be left? Her particular brand of torture was fuel and flame. He still didn't think Smith wanted Rose for anything and now that he'd spoken to Samuel and Josiah, he believed more and more that the brothers were her true targets. But why? Surely not just for the money they'd stolen from her? If she was captured now, she'd be put to death. Still the biggest question remained. Why linger? Why hang about for gold? She had a ship she could sell once she'd crossed the Channel. He had to presume she had other riches to pawn to start over. A resourceful woman like Smith could start over with next to nothing. So why linger?

Many times over the last few years that he'd been putting

on a civilised front, he'd had to put himself in other men's shoes. He couldn't put himself in a woman's shoes though. They were complex creatures, most vexing and most irritating. They often acted without thought. Rose was no exception. She hadn't given an ounce of thought to what might happen if she'd been caught in the garden alone at her own come-out ball. She hadn't thought about the consequences of smuggling or having friends who were her father's servants and villagers. She certainly didn't think a man as a best friend was anything out of the ordinary for the daughter of an earl.

Why did he have to like that so much about her? That she bucked convention? If he had to take a wife, he wanted one who would bend to society's dictates. A proper woman of good family. Someone who would make him happy, not drive him to distraction. But he'd never wanted a wife in the first place. She was already making him think about dinner parties, long cold nights and more importantly, intimate blushes over breakfast.

If he was to be a Runner, it would be dangerous work. There would be days or even weeks when he wouldn't return home. He would be running with the worst of the worst to catch the criminals at the heart of London's underworld. Well, actually, he wouldn't be doing anything of the sort since Clairmont would never give him the position. He had to be the one to take Smith down. It had to be Anthony. Clairmont might then be leaned on by those in higher places to give him the position he so coveted.

But what about Rose?

If Michael had led her into a mess that would get her kidnapped or killed or anything else detrimental to her remaining in a breathing state, he would have the boy arrested and hanged. Anthony might not have any power himself but his brother-in-law did. Trelissick could bring forward a charge to pin on his liveried shirtfront.

Rain blinded him but Malum knew where he was going. He would start with the meeting place because it was better than doing nothing. Darkness began to shroud the countryside earlier because of the heavy cloud and Anthony hunched over the big horse's neck, urging him to hurry though he slipped and slid in the mud. Trees flashed by and thunder boomed.

They were upon the dilapidated cottage before he knew it and he leaped from Malum's back before the monster could attempt to throw him into the mud. Tying his reins tight to a nearby tree, he stomped up the steps and threw the door open wide, blistering words in his tongue for his intended and her feckless friend. But there was no one there.

Tucked in the corner was a screen of sorts and when he looked closer, Rose's padded undergarments were folded into a chest beneath a ratty length of old canvas. Other than that, the cabin was empty. Cold. Clueless.

Just as he was.

OF ALL THE necessities in life, being Mr Smith had been the one to keep her alive the longest to date. It was her most used alias and had been her best kept secret until a few months before. Bloody Wickham had started a chain reaction of events she couldn't hope to ever control. Smith's savage reign in London was at an end but she wouldn't go quietly. She wouldn't slink away never to be heard from again. She was going to take down the men who had promised her the world only to leave her high and dry when she needed them the most.

How could Josiah and Samuel sit back on their laurels, perfectly disillusioned thinking themselves safe, thinking themselves smarter than her. Lucinda knew differently. Lucinda knew their deepest, darkest secrets. She knew things about the men of London that they barely knew about themselves. She wanted them all to pay but none more dearly than the Clairmont brothers. Josiah and Samuel had offered her a partnership, a way out of the slums and into a life of grandeur and luxury. Bloody liars.

As she met the gaze of Clairmont's daughter over the stained surface of a tap room table, she couldn't help but admire the girl who'd had to grow up under the thumb of an uncaring earl. She was there, almost unprotected, completely out of her depth and faking courage better than any man. She already admired the chit and that was not good for business.

Rose Clairmont had been silent for all of three seconds before she drew breath and said, "Explain to me how my family robbed you of your life. You sound like you've led one adventure after another for quite some time, free of rules or indeed, laws."

Adventure? Only a romantic at heart would see Lucinda's

life as an adventure. Or a naïve girl who'd been sheltered from the likes of her lot for too many years. "How old are you, Rose?"

"Old enough to know I haven't given you leave to address me informally. Unless I may know your name also?"

Touché. Point one to her. "My Christian name was Lucinda."

"Was?"

Intelligent too. Damn. "No one gets close enough anymore to use it."

"Well, since we are getting chummy, you can call me Rose and I will call you Lucinda. Smith is rather ambiguous don't you think?"

Lucinda inclined her head. What was she going to do with Rose Clairmont? This girl was an enigma. When she'd discovered Rose was behind the smuggling activities at Hell's Gate, she'd almost regretted interfering with what was obviously a well-run operation to fight the boredom of the country. But she'd needed to gain the attention of Rose's brothers. It would have worked too if either of those halfwits had known what their sister was up to with the stable lad of their very own neighbour.

Smith had relied on the idiocy of the ton for too long. She'd grown complacent in her power, put some of her waning faith in love and hope, and now Lucinda was paying the price. She was almost right back to where she'd started all those years ago, useless to anyone but a man. And men only wanted her for one thing. Luckily enough she'd learned how to manipulate anything with a cock at the early age of seven.

Rose Clairmont would be hard to manipulate. She already knew that. Then again, leverage had a strange way of becoming the perfect weapon.

"Tales of you abound, Rose. The stories have it that you're quite hideous. Fat. Bespectacled. Sometimes smelling like the inside of a chicken shed."

Rose chuckled. That chicken thing worked quite well once and then fable had stuck. "Stories have a habit of being wrong occasionally."

"Except that I saw you at your come-out ball. You were huge. And very yellow."

That got her attention. She sat up straighter, dropping her faux cloak of nonchalance. "You were there? Where? How?"

"The details aren't important. Why do you fool your family into thinking you so large and uninviting?"

"The details *are* important and that is none of your business."

"I'm making it my business." Lucinda looked at the men at Rose's back, each one of them on alert for danger to their mistress but would any of them die to protect her? If Lucinda decided to take her for ransom, what could they do? Smith's men were everywhere inside and outside of the building and would lay down their lives for the promise she gave each and every one of them. She wondered if the other girl knew she didn't stand a chance?

"We should be discussing what it is you actually want. What can I give you to make you go away?" Rose said.

Lucinda ignored the rudeness to the question, putting it

down to frustration, and replied, "Before I tell you what I have planned for you and your family, how about you tell me a few things. Like why you think smuggling is an acceptable pursuit for a young lady?"

"Acceptable pursuit?" Rose actually laughed. "You're practically a pirate. You are a wanted criminal all over London and beyond."

"How exactly did you find out about me?"

"The details are unimportant."

Lucinda lifted her gaze to meet the eyes of the men around her. "While you're sitting at my table enjoying my hospitality, they are most important."

"How did you come to be at my ball?" was her counter.

Lucinda shrugged, hiding the hurt away like she always did. The truth was all she could come up with. "I wanted to see how your family lived. I wanted to witness the extravagance thrown away on a daughter born on the right side of the blanket. You are perfectly legitimate yet your father still doesn't seem to care for you. Why not?"

"Do you know my father well?"

She shook her head. "How did you find out about me?"

"Anthony Germaine."

Lucinda had heard of him. Several times recently. Bad boy turned want-to-be gentleman. She'd come to the Clairmont garden too late, after Germaine had already disgraced himself further and Rose's fate had been sealed to his. It had been entertaining to watch though, from the cover of trees and darkness. She couldn't have planned the moment better herself. Well, most of it had been her idea anyway. Rose's come-out ball so she would no longer reside in Dover was a master stroke on her behalf. It had done exactly what it was supposed to. Turn her family against one another. A minor distraction but a helpful one that added the happy bonus of bringing both brothers to Hell's Gate. She couldn't exactly play with their lives in the city any longer.

Samuel had been a player at her tables for years before she took him as a lover. Her initial plan had been to seduce the brother so that if Clairmont ever managed to catch her out with his Runners, she would have the necessary leverage to be set free. She hadn't counted on Josiah or his passion, or his need to take the things his brother had. In her mind, two brothers had to be better than one, so she allowed them to share her. It wasn't the first time she'd taken more than one man to her bed and it wouldn't be the last. Her mistake had been in the falling. She wouldn't say she *loved* either man but they had wriggled their way beneath her armour and she'd thought the feelings were mutual. She even let them into her private world, showed them her clubs, shared with them some of her profits to keep them malleable while Frederick tricked London into thinking he was Smith at her behest.

When Lucinda had discovered she was pregnant, Samuel offered to marry her. Josiah offered to whisk her away to Hell's Gate and let her live there with servants and money and everything her heart desired. They only had to have their sister married off first. Simple enough to two men who thought more with their cocks than they did with their brains.

Then that wicked business with Wickham had cost her Smith's cover face, Frederick. After she'd been forced to flee, both Samuel and Josiah had taken her earnings from the clubs not yet connected with Smith and left her to the wolves. Never mind that she very well may have been carrying Clairmont blood or that Samuel had professed to love her more than life itself. She was on her own again and Hell's Gate was her destination.

She would not let them get away with fleecing and humiliating her.

Lucinda was used to lengthy revenge schemes. It was one of the ways she had yet to be caught red-handed. When would she meet a foe worthy of her rather than these inbred halfwits? Was Anthony Germaine her adversary or would he prove as useless as the rest had? Either way, she now had to work to a timeline.

The bottom line for Lucinda was that she couldn't leave the country until she had the funds the Clairmont sons stole from her. Destroying a few unworthy gentlemen along the way would put the smile back on her face. She would watch them burn and then she would take her child to a place where beauty didn't equal a tool of men. Where love was honest and so were the citizens. Her child would have a happy life and be cherished, bastard or not.

Lucinda should have been one of those children herself but she had been wrenched from the arms of her dying mother and forced into a workhouse until she was old enough and strong enough that her little body wouldn't be ripped apart by the depravities of the sick and twisted. She'd learned very early in life that her beauty would make her an even bigger target in London's underground society and that her bastardry was a stain that would never wash away despite who had sired her. Had England's elite forgotten that one could not choose one's father? Why was the child always blamed for the parent's shortcomings? She had that in common with Anthony Germaine. Both she and he were persecuted for their origins. She had used it to her advantage while he still thought some good could be salvaged.

"Where is Germaine?" Lucinda asked Rose, interested in the fact that he wasn't there—her fiancé.

"He has nothing to do with this," Rose assured her, but there was a strange flash in her eyes and it wasn't anger or stubbornness.

Lucinda had also learned about a man's expressions. His telling signs. "He does if he's telling the world about me."

"Not the world," Rose was quick to add. "Just me, Michael and the lads. No one else knows."

"And his brother-in-law, Trelissick, his sister Daniella?"

"I don't know anything about any of that. It's none of my concern. You are though. You must give me something attainable otherwise I'm afraid you're going to wind up disappointed and never be able to leave here."

"Something attainable?" Lucinda tapped her finger to her chin as though deep in thought. She already knew what she wanted. "Bring me Germaine and the money Josiah and Samuel stole from me and I might consider the matter settled. With you at least."

"I didn't ever harm you in any way. Why have you been

coming after me and my men instead of going directly for my brothers?"

"Your men?" Lucinda scoffed. "They are your brother's men through and through. They are Ashmoor's men and your father's villagers. They do not belong to you nor will they be loyal to you when they are offered more or the truth of their treachery is revealed."

A murmur went through Rose's comrades and a few denials sprang forth. Lucinda didn't want to hear any of them. Rose Clairmont was useful to them because it was her land, her money, her jetty, her goods. If they were discovered, chances were they would throw Rose over just to escape with their own hides intact in the same way her brothers had done to Smith. It was the way of men: pass the buck, find the scapegoat. Why hadn't Rose yet realised she was their scapegoat? Any fool could see it.

"These men are my friends. They would give their life for mine as I would for them," Rose declared.

Lucinda stood, taking her time, ensuring all who saw her noticed her delicate condition, considered her slower and less of a danger. "Would you?" she asked the men at Rose's back. "Would any of you die for your mistress?"

"I would," came from a dark-haired fellow, a few years older than Rose by the looks. "We all would."

"Excellent." Lucinda put two fingers into her mouth and gave one long piercing whistle. Her own men, those who feared and admired her rather than liked her or felt obligated to protect her, swarmed the tavern, weapons in hand, ready to do what she commanded of them. Good men were really not good at all as Rose would soon find out. They relied on the coin you paid them. They were only as loyal as the depths of their fear and the amount you paid them to be.

Rose's friends went for their weapons but their mistress jumped to her feet and called, "Hold steady. We didn't come for a fight."

"And you're not getting one," Lucinda assured the now frightened girl and her panicked men. "I need you to return to your home and gather up what I need."

"I will do as you have asked but upon two conditions of my own."

"I hardly think you're in a good place to bargain."

"Neither of us have the time nor the leisure to do this any other way," Rose pointed out.

Lucinda held her palm up and curled her fingers back and forth. "What are your conditions?"

"Germaine is not to be harmed. At all. And you have to take me with you."

Lucinda almost swallowed her tongue. "Take you where?"

CHAPTER FOURTEEN

ROSE'S NERVES WERE absolutely shot. She had not much energy left both from the harrowing journey and from the day's events. There was one more feat to be accomplished for her though. Two if you counted just surviving the room. She felt hemmed in with nowhere to turn now that there were so many large men in the small space.

"You must take me with you to France or the Americas, wherever you are headed next."

"Why would you want to leave England? Why would you want to go anywhere with me?"

"You burned my ship already and I can hardly waltz into the next port and book passage. I need to flee my father and it's you or it's marriage. I am out of time and out of options."

"That's the most ridiculous thing I've ever heard," the villain said but Rose was buoyed by the fact that the other woman hadn't said no immediately. "What if your father comes after us?"

"He won't. I'll get the servants to cover my tracks well enough. My family will think me dead in the ocean. Suicide. No one will question it."

Michael grabbed her arm in a fierce grip and hissed in her ear, "Have you lost your mind?"

Rose turned to face her friend, her hand over his where it almost bruised her arm. "I am a grown woman, Michael. Why should I stay here and marry? Smuggling has been fun, helping the villagers worthwhile, but we have danced with the danger for too long. It's time for my next adventure far from here."

"But with her? She's a criminal. A pirate. A thief and a murderer."

Lucinda sighed and said, "I can hear you."

Michael dismissed her with a quick glare but then came back to Rose. "I won't allow it," he said.

Wriggling from his hand, Rose put her hands on her hips and stepped back. "You won't? How are you going to stop me, Michael?"

"I'll tell your father."

Rose rolled her eyes. "He's not going to believe a word you say unless you confess it all and then you'll be off to the gallows while I am either locked in my room or married off to Germaine or Harcourt. No one wins then."

"This is not a game where there are winners or losers, Rose. Only dead or alive. You're a woman and you'll be all alone."

Just the way she bloody well wanted it. She turned back to face Lucinda or Smith or whoever she said she was. "Do we have a bargain?"

"You want to go to France and Germaine is not to be killed?"

"Not to be harmed. At all."

"What am I supposed to do with him if he's not dead?"

She couldn't believe she was about to say her next words but she couldn't let him die because of her. Because she had asked him to come, to help. "Bring him along but leave him where you leave me. By the time he makes his way back to England to reveal your part, you will be long gone, living under a new name with your baby, somewhere safe."

Smith was thinking about it. Rose waited. Smith held her hand out and Rose shook it. "Looks like we have a bargain."

A thrill danced through her veins and Rose couldn't prevent the smile on her face. She had almost done it. She was nearly free of it all. Her father, her family, society, her suits and her suitors. She could make up her own rules and be free to do as she pleased. She wasn't daft enough to think France didn't have restrictions but she would be an unknown there. She could gather enough funds to make a comfortable life for herself as no one in particular. Just a woman with the means to take care of herself. She could claim to be a widow and even take a lover. Or not. She could look for a husband of her own choosing. Or not. She wouldn't even have to eat pigeon pie ever again. Her day was looking up and up.

"Rose," Michael began again. "I won't let you do this."

Smith stepped in with a gesture to a few of her men. "If you're not with her, then you're against her and I can't risk that." Two of her men took Michael by the arms, another wrapped an arm about his throat as soon as he began to fight back.

Rose reached for the dagger in her boot and approached, ready to defend her friend as he would her. Until an arm snaked about her middle and she was pulled roughly against the chest of a beast of a man who smelled as though he had rolled in piss. She kicked out, called out, writhed against the man-prison. "Let him go," she shrieked. The others in their party were similarly subdued until not a one of them could help themselves let alone Michael. They were hopelessly outnumbered after all.

"We have a bargain—you can't do this," Rose yelled and attempted another kick, her head jolting backwards viciously trying to find a point where she could do some damage.

Smith tut-tutted and shook her head. "You didn't say anything about your men not being harmed."

"He must return with me. We won't leave without him."

Smith gave another signal and the men began dragging Michael out towards the back of the tavern.

"You can't take him," Rose screamed, terror rising inside of her until she was almost unable to breathe. He was more a brother to her than her own ever had been. She wouldn't risk his life to fulfil her own.

Smith stepped before Rose, twisted the dagger from her grip and then slapped her hard on the cheek. Rose flinched, swore, met the cold eyes of a woman she realised she had underestimated.

"You have given your conditions, Rose Clairmont. You will return here before seventy-two hours have passed with Germaine and my blunt. For every hour you are late, your man will lose parts of himself he may value. A finger, a toe, an ear. If you fail to return at all, I'll kill him and then come to collect what is mine from your father's home and I won't be using the servants' entrance."

Moisture collected on her eyelids but Rose didn't cry. Defeat filled the places she had previously been happy, in control, hopeful.

The vice around her eased and then disappeared. She stumbled but then caught herself, straightening her shoulders and stiffening her stance. Smith offered her the dagger back, ivory handle first, and for one moment, Rose wondered if she could press the heel of her hand against the knife and drive it home, straight into the heart of London's worst.

Not only could she not stab an unarmed opponent, she could not kill a pregnant woman either. No. All she had to do was convince her brothers to hand over the money and get Anthony to follow her back to Smith. Smith's men would capture him but he wouldn't be hurt. Smith had given her word. Hadn't she? Was her word worth anything to Rose?

Probably not but Michael was. It had been him and her against the world for too long. He was like the brother she'd always wanted. She would do anything to save him. Even if it meant betraying everyone else around her…

LUCINDA STEEPLED HER hands before her chest and gave a chuckle. Rose Clairmont was on her way back to Hell's Gate to get her money and the man who would be her one-way ticket out of the Channel. She wasn't stupid enough to think

Trelissick wasn't close to tracking Smith down but he would never fire upon the ship his brother-in-law was held captive on. Neither would Clairmont send a fleet after a ship carrying his youngest daughter. The threat of scandal alone would leave the earl dawdling to even put on his boots.

"There's no need to look quite that happy, sister."

Lucinda looked to her 'hostage' and her smile grew broader. "You were fabulous, brother. So very convincing."

"What if she returns to Hell's Gate and calls the authorities down upon you?"

Opening her eyes wide and putting her hands beneath her chin, she mockingly put on the airs of a naïve chit in love. "But she loves you, Michael. Didn't you know?"

Michael, Lucinda's brother and fellow bastard, beamed. "In her own way, yes she does. Silly girl."

"All girls are silly," she remarked. "Rose is no different from the rest."

"I've spent a long time grooming her, sister. Don't completely disregard her ingenuity."

"And don't you disregard her worth to us. The only way to draw the Clairmonts out will be with their sister. The fact that she will willingly come along with us is a great boon but in the end, she too will have to die."

"She hates her father just as much as you do. She would probably kiss you for ending her misery," Michael pointed out. This was why he was better served on Ashmoor's estate than at her side. He was softer around the edges. He'd been raised as a bastard but as a useful bastard in his father's house. He'd never known real hunger. He'd never known real danger or pain or terror. He had a hatred for his sire much the way Lucinda did only hers burned so much brighter, hotter, deadlier.

He hadn't spent a decade exacting vengeance the way she had. The blood of the men who had hurt her was on her hands, in her memories, a part of her soul. There were plenty more left but she was running out of time. Her baby would not be born into hatred. Her baby would not endure even one second of London's prejudices. Her baby would never be taken from her, never know defeat or loss, never be broken inside until all the pieces felt like they would fall out.

Her vengeance would be final. It would be swift. It was going to be deadly.

CHAPTER FIFTEEN

TOO ANGRY TO doze. Too angry to ride. Too angry to do much more than sit and brood and grind his teeth together. Anthony thumped his clenched fists against his thighs and stood, resuming the pacing that was the only action stopping him from roaring to the ceiling like a depraved animal. He couldn't go after the fool girl because he had no idea where the hell she went. It wasn't to see the vicar's wife.

Bloody hell.

If Rose's padded undergarments were here, then she would have to return, assuming she didn't have several sets hidden away in her rooms. She could have anything hidden anywhere. She was out of control. Reckless. Immature. Naïve. Stubborn. She was just like Daniella only worse. At least his sister had the wits about her to keep herself alive and reasonably safe. Rose had no idea the consequences that could befall her and if she did, she clearly didn't care at all. She had no idea the mess she was making of her life or that of her men.

Would it stop once Smith was out of the equation? Would she see the light and give up the smuggling and 'adventure' as she put it? He rather doubted it. She would have to be sent to an abbey or an asylum just to preserve her own heartbeat. He'd like to take her by the arms and shake all the nonsense out.

But she wasn't his.

Not yet.

Not likely, ever.

A very, very small, no, infinitesimal, part of him admired her tenacity. But she was going to get herself and those around her killed. He liked the way she had avoided marriage like it was a deadly pox. He liked the way she commanded her men and the way they respected her in return. But. She wasn't the right woman for him. She had too much passion. Too much fire. Too much yearning for the thrill.

Anthony had worked so hard to bury those traits in himself.

He wanted to help protect the city and her citizens. He wanted to work on the side of good and just. There was a thrill in that too. A sense of pride. Of logic. Of fairness for all those who stayed on the side of honour and respect. Criminals belonged in prison or hanging for their crimes. Newgate wouldn't be necessary if there were more men like Anthony and fewer like Smith and her cohorts.

"Fuck," he roared into the growing darkness. If Smith had taken Rose or hurt her in any way, Anthony wouldn't bother handing her over to the authorities. He'd kill her himself. Honour, principle, righteousness be damned.

He thought the thought and a small voice in his head

told him he wouldn't. He wasn't a murderer.

A commotion beyond the door had Anthony backing down behind the screen and calming his nerves, schooling his breath. He didn't have to wait long. The door opened and in filed Rose, flanked by her men, all looking defeated, bedraggled, soaked to the weary bone. Rose sniffled and wiped her face on the back of her hand. She looked like something the cat might have dragged out of a pond.

All thoughts of being gentle, of catching her off guard or going easy on his future bride, went out the proverbial window as he stood and made his presence known. "Where the hell have you been, Rose?"

She jumped and the men around her drew weapons, closed ranks, immediately alert.

"What are you doing here?" she asked, her hand at her throat, her eyes red-rimmed and wide.

"Where did you go today, Rose? And think carefully before you answer because if you tell me you went to see Smith, I'll lay you over my knee and spank some sense into you."

The last thing he expected was for her face to fall and then crumple, tears running tracks over the dirt on her cheeks, her hair in complete disarray as huge sobs racked her body. He reached for her, just made it to her side before she let go and fell to the floor, half collapsing, completely giving up the pretence that she was strong and in control.

Anthony looked up at the men from his new position on the floor, cradling the distraught woman in his arms. "What did Smith do to her?"

No one answered or spoke. They all looked to be in shock and didn't know what to do with their lady's tears.

"Did she hurt her?"

The men shook their heads. One added, "She took Michael hostage."

"In exchange for what?"

"Not what," the man said, his huge barrel chest sucking in and then puffing out, his eyes never leaving Rose. "Who."

Another scraped his hand over his full beard, hesitated for a moment, but then met Anthony's furious gaze and said, "You."

"Why would she want me?" he said out loud, not really expecting much of an answer from any of them.

Rose's sobs had subsided a little but she gripped his coat front in her shivering hands like she'd never let go. Or couldn't.

Anthony pointed to two of the men. "Build up a fire so we can get her warm."

"It'll give away our position," one argued. The other went to work and quickly had flame licking timbers.

When he scooped Rose up to carry her closer to the heat, she whimpered but didn't protest. She was like a little girl in his arms. A frightened, defeated child. He couldn't rail at her now. Not when she had lost someone close to her. Perhaps this was the consequence she needed? But at what cost?

Anthony thought the likelihood of her friend being alive by morning to be very slim. Then again, Rose would do anything to save him. Michael. Damn it.

Once her body started to relax and her limbs didn't shiver and shake, Anthony told the men to return to their homes, the servants back to the house.

"I'll look after her," he assured them when they looked as though they would fight him. A few glares were exchanged but in this meeting of wills, he was the only one with the strength to hold out. Then it was just him and Rose. His fury was banked but only just. What if it had been Michael who'd walked through the door with tears in his eyes for Rose? Would he have stayed long enough to tell them where Rose was being held and then run for his miserable, rotten life? This was why their relationship was strange. The daughter of one house and the stable lad of another. It was an imbalance that infuriated him. Michael had taken advantage of Rose's position, her naïveté.

"Rose, are you going to tell me what happened?" he coaxed gently.

He thought she wouldn't answer but then she shook her head, a hiccup and sniffle following.

"I need to know. Where was she? Where did you meet her?"

Muffled words met his silence. "I…I can't tell you. She'll ki-ill him."

She was shaking so much. Anthony pulled away and took her hands in his, held them before his mouth and blew gently against her fingers.

"Wh-what are you do-ing?"

"You need to get warm before you catch a chill. Although it would serve you right, you little idiot." His temper bubbled and he fought to gain hold. Fought the urge to hurt this woman who couldn't defend herself. Hurt her until she saw what she was doing was beyond foolish.

"I-I am n-not an i-idiot." But her tone held no conviction and he couldn't warm her like this.

His fingers went to her muffler. It fell to the floor. Her sodden cloak followed.

"Jesus, fucking Christ. Are they trousers?" *Put the lid back on. Put the lid back on.*

She was soaked through every layer by the looks and he wasn't surprised. The rain fell in wild sheets, whipped by the wind and driven down by the heaven's response to her actions that day. Clenching his fingers into fists, he went to the chest where her dresses and padded underthings hid and pulled them out one by one until he found a blanket beneath. It was dusty but it was dry.

"Take your clothes off."

Her golden eyes went big and wild and Anthony had to wonder if she didn't get hurt, why was she so dazed? Was it shock? If that was the case, he was going to need more than a blanket to warm her. "Do you have any strong liquor here, Rose? Brandy? Scotch? Even port will do."

She shook her head. Stood there like a simpleton and stared at him while her teeth chattered.

"Take. Your. Clothes. Off. Now." He was no longer in the mood to mollycoddle, not that he had ever been.

She shook her head again. That special, shiny, Rose-like glint returned to her eye and buoyed him despite her refusals and shivers. Whatever had played out hadn't broken her after all. He let out a breath he hadn't been aware he'd held.

He didn't waste time on more commands she wouldn't follow. He marched back to her, dropped the blanket next to the puddle she was making on the floor with her tears and wet clothes, and started on the buttons of her shirt and then the laces of her boys' trousers.

"You are quite possibly the most reckless, most stubborn, most pig-headed girl I've ever met and that's saying something since my sister used to have that honour before I met you. I'll put money on you catching your death this day from the bloody wind and rain and if that doesn't happen, I'll throttle you until you see the sense of your stupidity!"

He knew only a few ways to warm a person up from the inside. They had no alcohol so that left anger or passion. He'd try the easiest one first and leave the most tempting one for last. If he made it that long. If *she* made it that long.

ROSE TRIED TO slap his hands away but she was beyond exhausted. Her tears were dry for the moment and her face felt odd, tight, scratchy. She couldn't remember the last time something had upset her to the point she had found herself in only moments before. If that wasn't bad enough, now she had to endure name-calling from him? If he'd been the pirate's son she'd needed, she would never have been alone out there. His father's reputation might have been enough to end Smith and keep Michael safe. They should only have to mention Richard Germaine's name and Smith should have run a long mile.

Who the hell did Anthony Germaine think he was anyway? Taking the high road while he relegated her to the shit-stained ditch? A renewed sense of self-preservation sparked to life inside of her and she tried again to slap his hands away from her clothing. She didn't need to get warm. She only needed to get back to the house and confront her brothers, get them to give her all of their blunt and then she would go back for Michael. She'd cried her tears, now it was time to get on with it.

"You could have been killed," he ranted.

"I know that."

"You're an idiot. A child. So naïve."

"Are you finished?" she said to the top of his head as he reached the last button on her shirt. She knew she had to get dry but she could do it without his help.

"No, I'm not finished. Rose, do you have any idea… Of course you don't otherwise you wouldn't have done it."

The fire at her back had stopped her teeth from chattering at least. "It was my only chance. *Our* only chance. I had to go. I had to do it."

That made him pause for a moment. "Do what? Only chance for what?"

She wondered, did his nape prickle? Did his sense of whatever held him forewarn she'd practically thrown him in with her lot without much thought? Smith had promised he'd be safe but then she'd been brutal and fast in taking Michael. Would she keep her word? Rose had to hope so.

An errant shiver rocked her body and she almost fell, had to reach out a hand to Anthony's arm to steady herself. She had lost the feeling in her feet nearly an hour ago on the return trip and didn't know how much longer she could stay upright. It was as though ice water ran in her veins where her blood used to be. Why couldn't he save his arguments for later? For when she was warmer and could think in straight lines?

Anthony lowered her to a stool and then bent to take off her boots. The only part of her, except for her back, that felt any heat at all was her cheeks and she had the feeling they flamed. One boot came free, her dagger falling to the timber boards with a thump. He didn't look at her again until the second dagger shook loose to join the first.

"At least you were armed," he noted, his tone tight, his lips pulled, his grip rough. "Stand up."

She couldn't do it on her own and had to place her hands against his shoulders where he kneeled at her feet. In only one more moment, he had her buckskins peeled down to her knees, the wet leather clinging like it never wanted to let go. When he put his hand behind her bare knee to pull her foot out of one leg hole, she yelped and nearly toppled.

"Not the time for maidenly protests, Rose."

She didn't answer. Just prepared herself for his touch on her other leg. She was essentially bared to him now, her short chemise wasn't long enough to hide the fact that she had no smalls on beneath the soft leather of her pants. She needed to be able to move freely when riding. She needed to be able to hide herself from him now.

"I can do the rest," she insisted.

But he wasn't paying the least bit of attention. His hand hadn't left the back of her knee nor had his eyes left her legs.

When his fingers tightened, the anxiety that had been balled up inside of her all day was released. It fell as heavy as a stone in her middle yet it was almost liquid, warm but with edges.

When he finally did release her it was only to raise both hands to her rough shirt to push the edges aside and pull it off completely. Only he hadn't undone the button at her cuff and the fabric caught there, pulled, restrained until her breasts jutted out when her shoulders pulled back.

A second thrill shot through Rose and where she had been cold before, she now began to burn. The way his eyes ate her up, the way his hands skated down the outside of her thighs, his calloused palms scratching, all did things to her. Delicious things. Another shiver rocked her and she watched as Anthony physically shook his head and removed his hands. It took great effort, she could see. She almost begged him to keep going.

"Sit." His voice was gruff, husky, clipped.

Rose realised she had him then. Could make him do just about anything she wanted him to. He was the one who had given her the key to unlock this unusual weapon she hadn't realised she'd held. Dare she use him to see how dangerous it could be? She didn't even know how far she was willing to go. She didn't know how far she *could* go. Frustrations had built inside of her until she could almost explode. Frustration that she had been bested by Smith. Frustration that she'd had to leave her friends behind. Frustration that Anthony Germaine wouldn't cross the ultimate line for her in any way that she needed or wanted him to.

She was likely to be on her own soon enough and what if

someone took her innocence from her? She'd never before thought of giving it up but then she'd never considered it an important possession either. Could she brush it aside in order to achieve her ends?

She sat.

He swallowed. The bump on his throat rose and dipped. Sweat beaded his forehead as he bent over the buttons at her wrists.

Of all Rose knew about Anthony, the first was that he held himself to the same standards as a gentleman of the ton. The loftiest and the most noble. Yet, last night he'd picked the locks to her rooms like a thief and kissed her as rake would. Who was he and where did he fit? Was he like her after all? Tempted by all things illicit, his honour only holding on by a jagged thread?

Once the wet shirt lay on the ground in a puddle of her outrageous clothing, Rose was left in a thick chemise. They had come to a stalemate. Anthony reached for the hem. It had to go. It was wet. Lord, she was wet. The air she tried to suck into her lungs felt as though it wouldn't stay long enough to give her life-sustaining oxygen, rushing right back out again. She bit her lip. What was she supposed to do next?

The only thing she could do was raise her arms as he stripped her of her very last piece of modesty, leaving her bare, raw, flushed and wanting. When he dropped to his knees again to reach for the blanket, Rose steeled her spine. She lined up her resolutions. She came up with a plan that could have only two outcomes.

Keep Anthony on her side and at her side.

Or...

Know pleasure at his hands before she passed him over to Smith to possibly doom them both. He would no longer see her as a potential wife after that.

CHAPTER SIXTEEN

G ONE WAS THE mess of tears and sobs. Gone was the padded suit, frizzed hair and thick spectacles. In place of the Roses he'd so far met, sat a new one. A seductress with powers she didn't even know she had.

She played a dangerous game.

He let her.

Anthony had come to recognise when Rose was thinking hard, she bit her lip. When she'd come to a point in her mind, she soothed the bite with her tongue. Now she sat before him, naked, thinking, scheming. Whatever it was, it wouldn't work. He was too angry. Too angry to let her get to him. He may also have been slightly distracted by the thatch of curls he'd uncovered when removing the soft deerskin from her long, shapely legs. What a crime it was for her to cover her body with her padded suit. With any type of clothing at all.

All the yearning he'd spent the last few years pushing down into a box threatened to tumble forth. His cock hardened and his mouth went bone dry. Back in the days of carousing, he would have bent Rose over and entered her in one smooth movement, holding on to her ample hips as he drove into her. Had she been a doxy, a tavern wench, or an indiscreet widow out on the town. But this was Rose. His intended wife. His future boss's daughter.

All of that should have been important. It should have beat a warning with the sound of his heart in his ears. But it didn't. He couldn't look away. He could only think of how big her breasts were. How heavy they would sit cupped in his hands. How wide he would have to stretch his lips to suck her nipples and more into his mouth. Then his gaze dropped lower still.

How he wished he could hold on to the anger, to the rage, to the knowledge she'd deliberately set out in a howling storm to meet London's most dangerous criminal this decade, hell, perhaps this century.

But he couldn't. Hold on to it that was. He could barely function as anything but a man in those moments. He was harder than the stone of the castle and she looked softer and more delicate than a spring raindrop clinging to a flower petal.

He was close enough to reach out and touch if only she was his. If only she gave him a sign, an invitation that she was tempted to sin as much as he was right then and there. No one need know. Instead, he kneeled before her and retrieved the blanket, his fingers closing around the scratchy wool.

The remaining moisture left his mouth when Rose blatantly opened her legs, her bare little toes crawling along the floor until she'd found her balance and was leaning towards him, her arm outstretched.

"Thank you," she murmured, the tips of her fingers brushing his as she took it from his hand.

He let her take it but then stilled her with a grip on her wrist, gentle, undemanding, completely at opposites with how he was feeling inside. With his other hand, he smoothed the silky satin of her thigh, his thumb so close to her core he almost dared to close the distance.

He'd become someone else overnight, over the last few days, and he wasn't sure how he felt about it. This wasn't the boy who'd run wild in the night drinking, gambling, fucking anyone who looked his way with a smile. It wasn't the man who'd broken his ankle and spent two months drinking alone in the dark. It definitely wasn't the man he longed to become, one of honour and integrity. "Do you know how much I'd give to taste you right now?" he said as he was held spellbound by his own movements, by her lack of virginal outcry, by how achingly close he was to curls that glistened with moisture and promise.

"How much?" she responded, breathy, feminine, alluring.

"Everything." But then reason finally clashed with wanting. "But it's wrong. So, so wrong."

"No one would ever know."

His heart gave an almighty thump. "You don't know what you're saying." He went to lift himself back to his feet and give her some privacy, some distance, but then she was tilting forward from the stool and straight into his arms again, her chest pressed to his, her hands on his face, the blanket discarded much the same as all the common sense in the room.

"I'm so cold." She gave an almighty shiver as if to shore her story with some substance but all it did was rub her breasts against his shirtfront.

Flashbacks of the night before invaded his mind and supplied him with the memory of her pink nipple, the weight of one tear-dropped mound in his hands as she'd mewled like a baby kitten before a saucer of cream.

He nipped her jaw and then pressed an open-mouthed kiss to her neck. He should step away. "Not a good enough reason to do this, Rose," he said, between tastes of her salty, rain-washed skin.

A smile curved her lips just before she tilted his face back to hers, pressed her mouth to his, her tongue sweeping right in as all coherent thought fled.

Thinking with a mind of their own, his palms floated over her back until he reached her derriere where he found purchase and both squeezed and directed until her sex came to rest against his, the fabric of his trousers the only barrier left now. In minutes she would be so frightened, or daunted, she would call a halt to the sensual onslaught. He had to let her find her own boundaries and then call a stop.

On and on their tongues duelled and his hands mapped her curves. His body ached for satisfaction but his mind knew no matter how far this went today, he would find no relief within her body or at her hands. Rose was an innocent no matter how much she wanted to play the harlot, to distract him from her madness.

When next they came up for air, Rose was earnest when

she murmured, "I hate this feeling."

Anthony's hands and lips came to a complete stop, as did his heart. "What feeling?"

She closed her eyes and tipped her head back, her sigh long, loud, frustrated and obviously unaware how close to his mouth the movement lifted her breasts. Still he didn't let her go as he should have. "This intensity inside of me like I could explode if only I could find the trigger. You make me want to crawl out of my own skin."

Her honesty did him in. It wasn't his place in the bigger scheme of things but he wanted to show her pleasure in a world where she'd so far only known rejection.

Anthony did finally let her go then. He picked up the blanket and spread it before the flames in the hearth. "Lie down," he said, unable to utter more than two words at a time when she had him on fire. She did as he said, the movement of her breasts hypnotic to him. He removed his jacket and then loosened his shirt cuffs.

"What are you doing?" Her voice was so small. Was she finally thinking about what she asked for?

He lowered himself down on his arms, nudged her legs apart and settled over her. He didn't say anything at first, only undulated his pelvis over hers, ground his hardness into her softness until she gasped and writhed.

"Do you want to know pleasure, Rose?"

She nodded, her head thrashing, her curls everywhere, fanned out on either side of her head as she bit her bottom lip. Her eyes closed then and her hands fisted in the blanket beneath her.

"You have to make a promise to me first."

"I won't tell anyone, I swear it."

He chuckled and leaned down to glide his tongue over her neck, stopping only to nibble on her sweet, soft earlobe. "That's not what I meant."

"What then?"

He met her gaze, the firelight reflected there, her skin flushed and her lips wet. "Promise me you won't see Smith again. Ever."

He knew his condition would end her willingness. He spoke hastily before she cooled altogether. They'd come this far and he didn't want to turn back. He wanted to touch her, to make her wild, to give her release. "I'll go to her, get Michael back for you. But you need to promise me you won't ever see her again."

"I cannot do that and you know it."

He didn't think so. He placed his lips against hers and kissed her until she was arching her hips against his, desperation making her reckless. This was a lesson he'd never be able to teach her. Patience. But he knew he could distract her until she agreed to just about anything. On a groan, he said, "Promise me then that you will not see her again without me there. You have to tell me what moves you are making so I can protect you properly."

Breathlessly she responded, "You don't own me. Not yet, Anthony Germaine."

To own Rose Clairmont would be paramount to taming her and they both knew that would never happen. She would never belong to anyone. "This part of you that feels as though it will explode when you're in my arms?" He pressed into her again, kissed her senseless again. "I have a feeling also. I have this need to protect you. To keep you safe. It's just as frustrating as yours because you are still working against me, Rose. Say you'll work with me and I'll show you sweet release." Another drugging kiss. Another gentle roll of torture as he drifted a hand down to squeeze the curve of her backside, his fingertips so close to her wetness. "Together we'll bring Michael home and take Smith down, but only together, or not at all."

WHAT WAS SHE supposed to say to that? To him? She couldn't make promises knowing she would wind up breaking every single one before the end of the next week. He had to stop making her feel so alive and frantic and anxious so she could think. She had to be the most selfish creature on the planet because she wanted it all. Freedom. Pleasure. Him. He'd evoked in her this strangeness that was all bliss mixed with just a little bit of pain. Rose hovered on the edge of something amazing, and the excruciating knowledge that she needed the very thing only he could give her taunted all of her senses at once. She wanted it all. She *needed* it all.

"I promise not to go to Smith again without you."

He pushed himself up to watch her. Did he try to catch a glimpse of her soul through her eyes? Did he suspect anything? She wasn't lying so there was nothing to hide there. Her words were completely honest. She needed him to go with her to Smith. She wanted to tell him her plan but she knew he wouldn't trust her or Smith and he would do anything he could to ruin her groundwork. It didn't matter that he wasn't to be harmed; he wouldn't like it one little bit. She didn't like it much either but her options were limited. She could control the situation. She was sure of it. Smith would not dupe her twice.

She couldn't, however, control this one. Each swipe of his tongue over her skin or sweep of his hands over her body drove her crazy. She should have felt fear or shame or embarrassment but there was only that intensity again, the feeling as though her very insides would come tearing out through her skin. Rose raked her nails down Anthony's back and kept going until she got to his bottom. She squeezed just as he had done to her. His groan and the answering pressure when he rolled his hardness against her again had her moaning in reply. When her legs opened fully to wrap around his waist causing the delicious friction to hit another spot entirely, she cried out. He captured the sound with his mouth but still he didn't stop. On and on and on he kissed her, rubbed against her, left her reeling until she didn't know which way was up.

She took his full weight as he ran both hands down the side of her body, lifting his chest just so and then torturing her nipples with the pads of his thumbs only to replace them with his warm, wet mouth sucking on first one nipple, and then the other. When he reached her hips he kept exploring with hands and mouth, shifting his body down hers until finally he left her completely, unlocking her legs from his waist so he sat between her knees.

Rose heard a whimper and realised too late it came from her. Did that tiny sound amount to begging? If it didn't then she was prepared to say the words to him. *Don't stop. Keep going. Give me all that you can.*

She watched with fascination as he reached for her with his finger, sliding it between her curls.

"I won't take your innocence, Rose."

She made a strangled sound as the edge of pleasure became a never-ending curse and said, "Take it, I don't want it. It's yours."

Another slide, almost dipping his nail into the place she'd only ever touched herself. The flock of birds returned to her stomach and rose and fell with each barely there touch.

"You say that now but later, when you've thought on it, you will hate me."

"I hate you now. You're killing me."

He smiled and withdrew his hand. "Do you want me to stop?"

She reached around on the floor until she found the hilt of one of her dropped daggers. "I might have to stab you if you do."

"Threatening a man to make love to you, Rose?" In one deft movement, he reached for her again and slid that knowing finger right into her, up to the knuckle, hard and fast and rough. "Or is it a fuck you're after?"

She gasped both from the intrusion and from the vulgarity. She cursed often and the words were never pretty but from him, like this, she'd never expected it. His eyes had

THE FALL INTO RUIN

become black pools reflecting only the flames from the hearth and the knowledge that if he wanted to break her, he probably could. Was this the pirate she had been looking for? The flutter of thousands of tiny wings moved lower inside of her abdomen and the dagger fell from her fingers to clatter at her side.

"Whatever it takes to make you give me what I need," she ground out.

"Are you afraid of nothing?" he asked but his attention had drifted from her face to what he did with his finger and thumb.

"I'm afraid if you don't do something, I'll combust. I need…I need more."

His gaze was still on that place between her legs. Had she known this was the kind of explosive feeling she could experience, she might have explored her own body more in those long lonely nights at Hell's Gate. When he added a second finger, they both groaned. Rose's eyes shut and she had to fight the impulse to squeeze her legs together to make it all go away. Was there an ending to this or had he awakened in her a storm that would never pass?

HE HAD DIED and gone to heaven. Though the wind howled and thunder boomed all around them, Anthony no longer saw it as the Lord's displeasure—he could only think of *her* pleasure. Of *her* undoing. God, how he wanted to witness her orgasm, feel it around his shaft as her insides clenched. He wanted to be the one who brought her to it and then to hold her as she came back down to earth. He wanted to taste her and fuck her and love her all at the same time.

He'd never in his life been so hard. He'd never in his life used the word fuck in the presence of a lady and now he'd said it at least twice in one night. His erection pressed so hard against his trousers, he wondered if the fabric would hold. As he readjusted himself, she lifted her head and stared at him there. His cock jumped as though she touched it. When she licked her lips all sorts of carnal thought took over.

"Can I see it?" she asked.

He nearly died. "No you can't see it."

"You're looking at me," she pointed out with impatience mingled with desire.

"I cannot completely ruin you, Rose."

"Is it because you don't want to? Because you don't want me?" The fire in her eyes cooled a degree and he wanted to tell her to shut up so he could think for a moment. He was supposed to be distracting her but the moisture on his fingers and the smell of her sex in the air turned him from a want-to-be gentleman into a sex-starved cad.

His fingers tangled in her curls again and he fought and fought. Truly he did. Here she was, begging, ready, willing, and he was going to add to the rejection that had become her life. The gentlemanly way to proceed would be to give her what she wanted, he reasoned. Clearly his rationale had taken a hit if that was all he could come up with.

"Anthony, please."

Two of his fingers slid into her heat again and when her

hips bucked this time, she cursed and groaned and thrashed her head. *Fuck it*, his mind roared. *Fuck her*, his body insisted. He kissed and licked her stomach, gently rounded, soft, perfect, dipping his tongue into her belly button.

"Are you sure?" he asked against her skin, his own voice strangled, his own need rising to dangerous levels. It had been more than a year since he'd touched the heart of a woman. He was trying to be respectful, respectable, a gentleman. Where had it gotten him so far? *Nowhere*. He should remove his fingers from her and run into the night but he didn't. He continued to feel her, to dip into her heat and find her places of pleasure.

She nodded, no fear, no second guesses, just desire and need.

"In for a penny, might as well be in for a pound." He hadn't intended it as a pun but as the words left his lips, the weight lifted from his shoulders and he was light as a breeze and free as a bird. A smile curved his lips and he met her gaze as he continued to move his fingers in and out of her. "But first, a taste."

CHAPTER SEVENTEEN

R OSE COULD ABSOLUTELY not take any more. Her body tried again and again to find what it was she needed to be satisfied, to be normal again, but it was out of her reach. Anthony had even kissed her, *down there*, his tongue mimicking the way his fingers had slid over her earlier. He didn't stop and she begged him for more, for everything, her pleas falling on deaf ears as he continued to torture her slowly while he drank of her body. She reached for his head and pulled his hair while she thrashed and moaned. Higher and higher she flew until she could no longer feel the hard timbers at her back, only the teeth that grazed and the hands that wound her up and up.

All at once, her vision fractured and her body clenched like it would not explode but rather collapse back in on itself. Over the edge she fell, finally, fully, all of her being splintering beneath his ministrations. She thought she might have screamed but didn't much care, such was the oblivion in which she found herself and her insides pulsed and her skin turned molten.

At the edge of it all, was Anthony. He moved up her body, licking, laving, sucking and nipping, his fingers still at play within her. "Do you still want more, Rose?"

She met his gaze over the rise and fall of her bared breasts but then her eyes dropped to the fall on his trousers, his other hand running over the hardness there as though just another taunt in a long line of promises. When her brows rose, he did it again. Touched himself. When she licked her suddenly dry lips and nodded, he straightened, looped the buttons through the holes and freed his member.

"Oh my," she breathed. She'd never before seen one. Her men had bared their chests at laborious work but never had she witnessed this. "Can I touch it?"

He choked, coughed, shut his eyes on a nod.

Coming to a sitting position, she was tentative at first, only daring to poke it, but then it sprang back and her instinct was to take a hold. When she did, it jumped in her hand. She marvelled at the softness of his skin but the hardness beneath. "What word should I use?" she asked. She knew a few but was not ready to test them all.

"It depends on the context," he ground through clenched teeth, stripping his shirt from his arms in manic, sharp movements, although she hadn't seen him undo the buttons.

"Is it very strong?" she asked, ignoring the ridges of his stomach and the hair dusting his narrow chest, instead running her hand up and down the length of him. "It feels as though it would be very strong."

She let out a little shriek when he grabbed her shoulders and pushed her onto her back, her body once again trapped by his. "That's enough," he growled. "One last chance, Rose. If you're going to say no, now's the time to do it."

His hardness pressed into her folds and the heat of him almost burned. "I won't say no. I want this. I need you."

I need you.

He stilled.

No one had ever said those words to him before. They fired along his veins and a crack appeared in the wall he'd built around his mischievous nature and the part of him that was probably, most definitely, the son of a pirate. He'd conjured a box for the side of him that got him into trouble and shot his credibility as a genuinely good man. Had he known Rose was the key to unlocking it all, he would never have come anywhere near her.

Stars appeared before his eyes as he nudged at her entrance, making sure she was ready, that she could take his width and length without harming her or causing her pain. "This might hurt a little, but I'll try to be gentle."

He'd never lain with a virgin before, even in his days of debauchery. When he'd become so sick of trying to change society's opinions of him and acted the way they'd always assumed he would, he'd never taken an innocent into his bed, or anywhere else. He started slowly, inch by precious inch, sinking into her, waiting for an obstruction, a tearing, something to slow him and remind him she was new to this.

It never came. Once he was fully seated to the hilt, their eyes clashed. Hers filled with first discomfort and then with wonder. His, he had a feeling, filled with the devil's need to let it all go and just take her, just be himself here with her.

Her inner muscles clenched and it was all the invitation he needed, sliding nearly all the way out and then back in until they were pelvis to pelvis once more. She was so gloriously tight, like a glove that was a size too small. With each stroke and glide, she adjusted, her breath coming in moans and pants, her nails surely breaking the skin of his biceps and back as she seemed to try to find purchase, a handhold that would see her secure in the hurricane between them.

His movements quickened and she met each one with a lifting or a tilting of her hips, her moans turning to begs and pleas to keep going, harder, *harder*, don't stop now. He captured her encouragement with his mouth and kissed her like he was starved of her oxygen, all the while slamming into her welcoming body over and over and over. Until finally, he just let it all go and the ground beneath him shifted.

Thrust.

Fuck being a gentleman.

Thrust.

Fuck being a Runner.

Thrust.

Fuck being Anthony Germaine, son of a pirate first and the daughter of a baron second.

All he wanted in those helpless moments of release was to be one with her, with Rose. He wanted only to be her all, to give her the world, the moon, the stars. When she screamed his name and her body clenched around him, he tossed away the notions of who he'd wanted to be and gave over completely to what she needed of him. His body clenched and his climax washed over him in waves until he was spent.

He smiled and collapsed atop her quivering body.

Perhaps this was where he was meant to be all along.

CHAPTER EIGHTEEN

I T WAS A funny thing, Rose thought, lying next to Anthony, his body a shield against the cold at her front while the fire warmed her back. She'd never known. She had read books and eavesdropped on cheek-burning conversations amongst the servants but never could anything have prepared her for what they'd just done.

He stirred, kissed her head and wrapped her tighter to his side. "When we are married, I should like to do that every day. Perhaps twice."

Confusion chased away the lingering bliss and she lifted her head to meet his glazed eyes. "We aren't getting married."

Instead of the stubborn tightening of his lips she'd expected, he simply smiled and shifted his focus to the darkened ceiling above. "We're definitely getting married."

"I am practically a spinster and a hoyden to boot. Just because we...we...did...that, doesn't mean you owe me anything. Your honour is getting in the way of common sense."

"How so?" he asked, his voice rumbling from his chest where she rested her hand.

"No one ever has to know. I won't tell anyone."

His chest swelled and he laughed. "I should like to shout it from the treetops right now."

"Oh." A dawning realisation made her chuckle along. "You're teasing me. Very funny."

He rolled his body until she was pinned once again to the floor, his expression serious, his touch gentle where he held her wrist down to the blanket. "We are getting married. As soon as possible. Tomorrow if I can make it happen. Of course, I'll have to ride back to London for a special licence so perhaps the day after."

A new horror dawned. "You can't leave." She had to present him to Smith. There was no other way around it.

"I suppose you're right. Trelissick should arrive in a day or two depending on when he received my note about Smith. Fine," he declared. "As soon as this business is done though, we're getting married."

She cast about for an argument. What they had shared had been beyond this world but that didn't mean she would tie herself down for it. Her plan was still to flee England, her father and her familial 'duty'. If Smith kept to her word, then Anthony would be released with her somewhere along the coast of France and then Rose would send him back to London without her. He couldn't very well drape her over his shoulder and carry her back. Could he? Would he?

"Rose, I am coming to know that look of yours." He put a fingertip to her lip where she had bitten down on the flesh. "There is no way around it now. We have prematurely shared our wedding night." He looked around the room. "In a leaning shack." Lightning flashed and the room brightened for a moment, revealing dust in the corners, cracks in the timbers and several leaks where water pooled, making mud.

"What about Michael?"

His expression darkened as thunder boomed outside. "You're thinking about bloody Michael while you still lie naked in my arms?"

"Not in those terms." Her cheeks burned. "We must act tomorrow to get him back. We cannot wait for Trelissick or Smith will punish him for every hour that I do not show. How could I think about marriage when his life hangs in the balance?"

His tone was dry when he answered, "How indeed."

"We need to go after Michael tomorrow, give Smith what she wants, and then we can sort this business of nuptials."

"There is no getting out of it, Rose. I agree that we have to take Smith down first but then we will be exchanging vows before the vicar." His warm touch drifted up her arm, over her shoulder, and then down, to rest on her stomach. "What if you were with child after tonight? We cannot have a six- or seven-month pregnancy to set the tongues to further wagging and I'll not leave a bastard for you to raise."

Blast, she hadn't thought of that. She refused to dwell on it now either. Smith was pregnant and on her own and she seemed to be handling it quite remarkably. Rose only needed to buy herself some time. "After we take care of Smith?"

"After."

She breathed a sigh of relief when Anthony looked to

take her question as acquiescence. He rolled back to stare at the ceiling and pulled her with him to tuck her once more into his side.

Rose had almost fallen asleep when Anthony tensed and said, "We should head back. They'll be looking for you."

She shook her head and nuzzled his chest. "They all think me abed. Molly will cover for me."

A longer silence passed but then he spoke again. "What kind of husband do you want, Rose?"

He'd come to Hell's Gate without fully knowing what he was going to do about their impending nuptials. Not much had changed really. He still had very little clue about marriage. He was certainly warming up to Rose though. His body swelled knowing her bare leg was draped over his and her breasts rested against his ribs.

The woman in question lifted her gaze and speared him with a glare. "I didn't want a husband, remember?"

"Never?"

"Not ever."

"What about children? Had you never thought about a baby of your own? A legacy? Love?"

Her silence spoke volumes but he'd give just about anything to know what went through her mind. Why hadn't she argued with him more? Usually her protests were far more insistent. Anthony prodded a little deeper, this newfound sense of self, the person he actually rather thought he wanted to be instead of the kind he thought society would accept. It really never occurred to him that there could be a middle ground. He'd had a goal, a path for his life; he hadn't wavered from that until now. "What kind of man would I have to be to capture your heart?"

"Capture my heart?" she scoffed, her breath huffing over the muscles of his stomach. "I didn't take you for a romantic."

No one ever really took him for anything but he didn't point that out to her. "Humour me. Please?"

Rose's sigh was audible and her chin lowered from the permanent stubborn angle she kept it at as she toyed with the dark hair on his chest. "I suppose I would want a husband who is my equal."

"Equal how? Give me an example. I promise I won't breathe a word of it to anyone."

"You'll laugh."

"I won't. I'm merely trying to understand you. What kind of woman you are. What you really want out of life."

"I already told you this. I want to be free to have adventures and fill my time as I please. I don't want to be told what to do and when to do it. I don't want a husband who will put demands on my time, my body, my *self*, whenever the fancy strikes."

"The only demands I will put on you will be like this, when it's just the two of us—naked, wanting, needing."

"Tell me something," she said. "What do you want in a wife? Someone biddable? A quiet, meek thing who will launder your clothes and take care of your guests? That won't be me."

How little she knew. He had hoped that she'd started to understand him like he was coming to understand her.

Rose's insecurities were born of fear. Anthony's came from persecution and humiliation. "I rarely have guests so you may be easy on that score and I do have a servant or two to launder my clothing."

"Please don't patronise me. If you want the truth then I deserve the same in return."

"The truth? The truth is that my wife will face a world of ridicule and cold shoulders. I am neither a gentleman of the ton nor am I in trade or rich enough to do as I please and tell society to go to hell. It has never mattered that my mother was the daughter of a baron or that my father wasn't always a notorious pirate. It doesn't even matter that I saved the prince's life all those years ago and was knighted for it. All people are going to see when they look at my wife is that her husband will never amount to much." If she thought she was judged now, wait until she was a Germaine. Only then would she know true ridicule.

"And you wonder why I wouldn't want to marry into a society like that? When will men stop placing so much value on a person based on their lineage or their sex? Since when did my total worth equal my birth and appearance and nature? Since when did yours equal the total sum of your parents' mistakes?"

Anthony wondered if she knew she was championing him? Her total sum could have come from her spirit alone and be worth more than all of England's treasures combined. "My parents never once considered their actions mistakes. They truly found in each other what made them whole." Had he also found that elusive *thing*—feeling, emotion, whatever—to make him whole? He'd thought a career helping those who couldn't help themselves would fill the missing pieces he knew lay within him. They howled sometimes, for peace, for justice, for a fair chance. But lying there next to Rose, those pieces finally felt full, quiet, right. And it had nothing to do with a job.

"I am not a bucket in need of filling. I don't have missing places in my heart or in my head that I can only make whole by marrying. And how do I know you won't become a tyrant? How do I know you won't want to…to…to nail me to a bedpost?" She finished the sentence with finality but her cheeks flushed and Anthony wondered if she truly believed her own words.

"You sound exactly like Daniella."

"Your sister?" There was no disgust in the two words, only interest. He instantly regretted bringing her into the conversation.

Rose smiled and tilted onto her back, her breasts high, her nudity on display though she didn't seem to mind. "I should like to meet her. A real pirate. Oh, the sights she would have seen, the countries and the people and the customs."

"Yes," Anthony replied in a wry tone, ignoring the siren call of her body. "All of the above. But then she married."

"Because she was compromised."

He heard the whisper of *just like me* but didn't call her out on it. "You don't know Daniella. She wouldn't have married Trelissick in a thousand years if she didn't feel something for him. I suspect he wasn't the first man Daniella took to her bed. She was like you in so many ways, craving adventure and terrified of being curtailed."

She met his gaze again. "I am not terrified. It's just not going to happen to me."

Anthony let her think that for a long moment.

She spoke again. "Did he curtail her?"

"Not in the least. He even bought her, her very own ship. They were to live on it when she became restless on land."

"He did not."

"He did. But since she is with child, she cannot sail away even if she wanted to. Which she doesn't. My sister looked forward to marriage with as sour a taste as you do but she loves him. They will still have adventures, of that I am sure."

"Well, then, they are the exception and definitely not the rule."

"How do you find the energy to be so cynical of everything all of the time?"

Rose smirked as though she had won an argument. "I eat a lot."

Anthony couldn't help but laugh at that but deep down Rose was exactly like Daniella. Neither woman could believe in something they had never experienced. Anthony wasn't an expert on love by any stretch but he wasn't stupid enough not to know it made people do crazy things. Love had made a titled ex-assassin marry the outrageously scandalous, common daughter of a pirate. Love had turned his mother from her own family to marry a fisherman.

Love was a dangerous emotion.

If it could make a man consider giving up his own hopes and dreams in order to make another person happy, to give it all up so they could truly live the life they wanted, then he hoped Cupid's arrow wasn't embedded too deep into his shoulder...

ROSE COULDN'T BELIEVE Anthony Germaine would have such romantic notions. How could someone who had lived the life he had still believe love to be a great and wondrous thing? It had torn apart the lives of his parents and had repercussions on the next generation and probably the one still to come. She resisted the urge to turn in the saddle and face him again. The last time she'd done that on this short ride home, he'd kissed her and Belle had nearly stumbled.

Daniella Germaine had raced horses through the park against the very gentleman who thought to mock her. There was even rumour that she had swum naked in the moonlight on a mere dare. She was raised on the decks of a pirate ship surrounded by cut-throats and thieves. Even if only half of her exploits were to be believed, she had more than tasted adventure; she had dined on it at every meal. And now she was happily married and expecting a child.

Rose didn't need to be quite that outrageous. She was reasonably satisfied living with very few constraints, coming and going as she pleased, having friends and comrades she could trust. The notion of babies had been relegated to the same place marriage had been. It was a box with a large label that read *'Unlikely to ever happen'*. But now that it was likely, she didn't know how to feel at all.

The threat of rain was still heavy in the air and the storm continued to rage with lightning flashing in the distance and thunder rumbling but they'd had to make a break for home and the weather would hopefully work for them rather than against. Malum had worked his way free from the knot Anthony had tied, or rather more likely chewed his way free, so once again they both sat pressed against each other atop Belle. If that devil horse, Malum, would do as he was told, Rose would have known Anthony waited for her at the cabin. Would she have still gone in knowing now what she did?

Her body felt thoroughly well used, aching in a few places, satisfied in others. Of course she'd have gone to him knowing this would be the result. It could just as easily have gone the other way for her though. She knew there was a time he would rather have throttled her today than kissed her. That too had passed. She hoped.

He hadn't spoken of marriage again and she was glad. Once he discovered her willingness to hand him over to Smith to gain her own selfish ends, he would no doubt be back to the throttling stage of their tumultuous relationship. She could handle that better than this foreign easiness descending on them. He had his arm around her waist like it belonged. And damn her if it didn't make her want to melt back into him and return his optimism about a combined future.

But. She didn't. It wouldn't be long until he was asking her where his dinner was, his spare sock, shine my boots this and scrub the floors that. She knew he had a townhouse and a couple of servants but if he didn't get his position with her father's Runners, what else would he, or could he, do? If he stayed with her in France, would he find a position there? Would he bend to working harder for their supper or would he always resent her for changing the course of his life so dramatically? Money would be scarce, friends even more so. They would have no family to lean on, not that they had much of that anyway. They would be alone but for each other for a long time. She would probably kill him if he ate with his mouth open or snored or left his muddy boots on the washroom floor.

"You're doing it again," he said, his chin resting on her shoulder.

She resisted the urge to swat him away. "Doing what?"

"Thinking too much. Worrying. We'll get Michael back. Your brothers and I have come up with a half-reasonable plan."

Dread hit her so hard in the stomach, she nearly vomited. "My brothers? What did you tell them?" And why hadn't he informed her of this development earlier?

"I overheard those two idiots talking in the corridor and your father caught me listening in. It was sort of hard after that to hide my knowledge of anything."

Rose twisted in the saddle and shot him an accusing glare. "You told my father as well? You promised not to."

Anthony shook his head. "I didn't tell him anything. Only your brothers. I told them they were irresponsible to draw you into their mess."

"Their mess?" Rose asked, playing dumb so she could know what he knew. She turned back to face forward in the saddle. He had an uncanny ability to sense when she wasn't being very honest.

"It seems they both made promises to Smith. When she fled her clubs in London, your brothers fleeced her."

Rose sighed. He already knew just about all there was to know. "That's not all," she said. "Smith is heavily pregnant and the baby could belong to one of them."

He tensed at her back. "Damn it. Could this whole mess get any more complicated?"

It could. Rose should tell him about Smith's demands, that Anthony come along and be taken hostage. Perhaps there was another way though? Perhaps Rose could simply turn up with the money and that would be enough? Except that she'd given her word. They both had. If one broke the rules of this particular game, then the other could too and probably would.

Rose was pulled from her musings by lights heading their way. A party on foot by the looks. She squinted, tried to make out how many and who. Of course her absence couldn't be ignored for this long. She guessed the best way to respond would be to fall further, tell her father that she and Anthony had spent a passionate afternoon alone and nail the lid shut for good on her marriage coffin. But if she was too cocky about it, her father might just shoot him where he stood.

"We have company," she said in a low voice over her shoulder.

"Your father?" he guessed.

"One would assume. Let me handle it, please. The less you say, the longer you stay alive."

Rose breathed deep and called out, "You have found me. No sense in having it out in the dark. Let us ride back to the castle and settle everything in comfort."

But as the party got closer, Rose could make out black hoods and cloaks but not a familiar face. These were not her father's men.

CHAPTER NINETEEN

ANTHONY KNEW THE moment Rose froze in his arms that something was very wrong. What it was though, he couldn't make out. He also couldn't ask her since the men in cloaks were now within earshot.

He did the only safe thing he could think of with his brain cold and his body sapped of energy both from the earlier fury and the lovemaking. He had to protect Rose, no matter what.

Sliding from the horse's rump, he said, "Go straight to your rooms and lock the door. I'll make my way."

She twisted to look at him, to voice a protest, but he gave Belle an almighty slap, which set the horse straight into a gallop. Hopefully they didn't break both of their beautiful necks in the dark. Luckily he didn't get kicked in the head for his trouble. Although it would be quicker than what these men had planned, he was sure. Would they simply shoot him or would they beat him to death first and then toss him from those damned cliffs?

"Surely we can work this out like men? Tomorrow? The girl has come to no harm—we're to be married anyway. Let's go back to the house and have a drink."

One of the men stepped forward, his lantern high, his hood tipping back to reveal his face. "You're not going back to the house."

Josiah. Of course. "Is this your father's idea then? Get me out of the way?"

Rose's brother laughed. "We're not here to kill you, Germaine. Smith wants you. She needs you for some reason and it might just save my own neck to give you to her."

"What would she want with me?" Anthony was genuinely puzzled about this turn of events. He had nothing of value, no line of communication with his father who was officially retired anyway. He had no riches and barely a name.

"Rose didn't tell you?" Samuel asked as he moved in from the shadows.

"Tell me what?" Dread descended to the pit of his stomach where before a measure of joy and determination had settled. He had forgotten the moment her men had brought her back to the cabin and said a very similar thing. His mind had been on Rose, her tears, the way she'd collapsed against him.

"Rose was to bring you to her to use as a hostage for safe passage across the Channel and perhaps beyond."

A strange sense of unreality rose from his chest in the form of laughter. It cracked the silence that stood before him and a few very obviously mad men. "What value would I have as a hostage? This is ludicrous. Are you sure someone isn't playing some sort of prank on you?" Anthony had been with Rose from the moment she came back from this, her first meeting with Smith. Where had the brothers got this information? "Have you spoken to Smith, made contact?"

Samuel shook his head. "No, but we know about the little meeting this afternoon in the village."

"Shut up," Josiah hissed.

"How?" Anthony asked but even as the word crossed his lips, he knew someone had sold Rose out. "Never mind. Did this man give the information willingly?"

Josiah's mouth took on an evil slant and his eyes flashed in the lantern light. "Not willingly."

So they'd beaten one of Rose's men, maybe even killed him for the information? Anthony would do well not to underestimate Josiah but was Samuel as dumb as he came across or was that also a ruse?

Anthony spread his feet on the dirt and raised his fists, just the way he used to scrap in college when his back was against a wall and a bully at his chest. "The hard way then?" He rolled his head on his neck ready to fight but he did so knowing he was hopelessly outnumbered.

He hadn't even thrown his first punch when pain exploded in his head and he slumped to his knees. His hands fell flat to the cold mud and his last thought was that these brothers, sons of a lawman and peacekeeper, did not believe in a fair fight.

He shouldn't have either…

FOR THE FIRST time in longer than she could remember, genuine fear clogged Rose's throat and the cold wind caused her eyes to water in a stream down her cheeks as she bent over Belle's head in a reckless gallop. Hoof beats sounded behind her and to her left so slowing down was not an option. If she could make the stables, she could sound an alarm and hope her father was willing to risk a few men to the dark to find Anthony.

This would mean she'd need to tell him the story, or at least some of it.

What really thumped in her mind and made her sick was that Smith had obviously no intention of holding up her end of the bargain at all. She should have trusted that Rose would return with Germaine and a good portion of the blunt her brothers owed. She'd been given seventy-two hours but had only used a few of those. Now she was out of time and out of options. Smith could take Germaine and run without the money. She may have realised it was never coming to her and given up hope of seeing a single coin, preferring a ransom instead.

Belle faltered but regained her step, veering left for the path that would take them back to the house. But it was too far left. The breathing of the horse chasing was close enough to be heard and in an instant, Rose was lifted off Belle's back, the vice at her stomach strong enough to knock the wind from her, which loosened her grips on the reins long enough for Belle to break free, the fear of another beast so close getting to her as she galloped off into the night, riderless but with direction.

Rose thrashed and kicked out and it was useless. She was thrown over the horse, the pommel only digging into the padding of her suit rather than her flesh but still she would have a bruise when, if, she ever was put down. A hand at her back kept her from being able to slide off, not that she could even if she wanted to. Her dress and suit were hooked on the pommel now. She was stuck. It was futile to try to fight from this position so she saved her strength and let her anger grow. Smith would regret this hasty move. Rose had money stashed at the castle. Gold and coins and goods. Not a lot but enough to be a good place to start the bargaining.

One day Rose knew she was likely to have to run from her father, from the estate, have a life of her own once she was old enough to be taken seriously by the world at large, so she'd started hiding coins and other items of worth for a rainy day. Smith could have been that rainy day. Rose would have given it all to her to be free of this mess.

But the other woman had gone and wrecked that now. Wrecked it for all of them. Rose had plenty of time to guess at the new plan. If it involved her father, Rose would be ransomed back to her family.

She snorted. Her father wouldn't pay a farthing to have her back. If the plan only involved Germaine, Smith didn't need her at all and could very well dispatch her and Michael while they sailed. Their bodies would never be found and Rose would be assumed a runaway. Germaine would be ransomed back to his family and Smith would be rich and free.

Damn. Rose hadn't thought of that. Smith had made it sound as though she only wanted Germaine aboard her ship to ensure her safe passage. It seemed as though Anthony was right when he'd called Rose an idiot. She truly was.

Naïveté was to be her downfall after all. She'd considered herself so smart and in control and yet she'd neglected to see this coming. She also couldn't for the life of her come up with a new plan.

Sooner than she'd thought, voices came to her in the dark. The men who'd stopped her and Anthony she had to presume? Rose's hanging hair made it hard to see much but then she spotted Anthony hanging over the saddle of a riderless horse, bound and gagged. She almost called out but kept her silence. They wouldn't bind a dead man and Smith needed him alive anyway.

A tightness grew in her scalp and a breath warmed her ear. "Sister, sister, sister, you have been busy."

Tension seized her. "Josiah?"

"Did you think you were the only horse in this race?" he responded, but he didn't give her time to answer. "You've messed things up for yourself quite nicely haven't you?"

Rose swallowed, measured her response. "I don't know what you mean."

"Out in the dark on your own with a man who doesn't even want to marry the likes of you. Very smart though to further dig the matrimonial hole. Did you let him ravish you? I s'pose you did. Best fuck you're going to get."

Rose thrashed again, striking out as hard and fast as she could but her brother only gripped her hair tighter and pulled harder. "Now, now, sister, better calm yourself before you get hurt. This will all be over soon."

"What do you mean over?" Was he going to hand her

and Anthony over to Smith? Did he think that would be enough to wipe his debt to her? Rose nearly scoffed.

"You'll see," he taunted.

At least he was smart enough not to share his plans with her. All Rose could do was hope he knew what he was doing because if he didn't, they would all be dead come morning.

CHAPTER TWENTY

COLD AND WET were the first notions to slide sluggishly into Anthony's brain as he struggled to remember what had happened and why he was having trouble opening his eyes. His head thumped miserably and there was a hardness at his back that was almost painful.

There was a warmth beneath his head though and were they fingers stroking his hair? Soft fingers? Was he still at the cabin with Rose? The fire must have gone out.

"Rose?" he said but his voice was croaky and he had to swallow a few times to work some moisture into his parched mouth.

"Sshh, I'm here," she said. "But they think you still asleep so stay still for a moment more."

Beyond his eyelids he thought it must be dark still and the coldness came from his wet clothes. "Where are we?"

"Josiah and Samuel have us locked in a stable."

"For what ends?"

Her sigh whispered over his cheek. "I don't know. I think he plans to hand us over to Smith but I can't figure out why. Without the money, she can't and won't leave."

Thoughts were getting easier to string together now and

it was an effort to stay still and quiet. "Could they have the money?"

Rose snorted softly. "I wouldn't think so. Smith is going to kill them both."

A little niggle itched in his mind. Why would the two brothers risk all for a confrontation with Smith if they only had two nearly worthless half-hostages? Rose could be ransomed back to her father but would he pay it? Anthony could be ransomed to his father but it would be months until Richard Germaine would get the message and come for his son. Months. None of it made sense. "Did your brothers not tell you anything?"

"Only that it would be over soon."

Dread prickled at his nape. "Where are we, Rose?"

"In the village. Somewhere near where Smith is currently waiting."

Hadn't her brother said something about Rose handing him over to Smith? Anthony opened his eyes and struggled to a sitting position. Made all the harder because his hands were tied behind his back rather than in front. He had to see her expression when he asked this particular question. "Tell me, Rose, had you already made your mind up to hand me to Smith before you lay naked in my arms?"

She didn't hide her surprise well, wasn't adept at schooling her features when put on the spot. Called out for her treachery. "What do you mean?"

Fury warmed him. "Don't play your silly games with me, Rose. Did you or did you not have a plan to hand me over to Smith? I want to know how sleeping with me plays into your scheming because it certainly wasn't because you are planning on becoming my wife."

Rose was flustered but she didn't look one bit guilty. "You don't understand. I need her to take me away from here. Far away."

"And I was thrown into the bargain? Did you offer me up on a platter or did Smith have to wrestle for me?"

"You're not going to be harmed, she promised. We're to be her hostages but she is going to leave us both in France, unharmed. Michael too, I think."

Bloody Michael. "What value does Michael have to Smith if you're there, Rose? You've tied a lovely little gift ribbon about the both of us and in Smith's mind, we're of use, but where does Michael factor in? Once he is of no value to her, she'll kill him."

Rose's lips set in a thin, stubborn line. "I don't believe she will kill any of us. She's not the bloodthirsty woman you've been led to believe she is."

"'*Been led to believe?*' Do you think my own sister almost being killed at Smith's command is 'being led to believe'?" Of all the foolish, naïve, ill-thought-out, most ridiculous notions. How did Rose fit them all in her head? Smuggling in her own backyard had closed her eyes to the real-life dangers awaiting her. Anthony would throttle Michael and her men for letting her believe there were no consequences for the games they played. "Smith has had men burned alive for debts unpaid. Her henchmen have pulled golden teeth right from the mouths of aristocratic sons while they screamed for their mothers before tossing their bodies in the

Thames. You have no idea what she is capable of dreaming up in punishment for those who cross her."

"You're being a little dramatic," Rose said, although her eyes betrayed her sudden and warranted wariness. "I've met the woman. She is all about the business and now, her baby. She wants what is owed her and safe passage across the Channel."

Lucky his hands were tied. He wanted so very badly to shake her. "And what if that isn't enough? What if she comes to the decision that the blunt owed by your brothers isn't enough to last her and decides to ransom us both back to our families as well? Yours doesn't pay because they already think you nothing more than a pebble in their shoe. Then you lose your value."

"We have an agreement. An accord. We shook hands and I have to believe she will behave with some honour."

Anthony tipped his chin back and laughed long and loud until the urge to bang his head against the timbers of the stable became too much to deny. He roared when it hurt more than it should have. He'd forgotten about being hit over the head.

"Would you hush for a moment, please? You don't know all there is to know about Smith. About Lucinda."

"Of course you're on a first-name basis with the woman."

"All my life I have been treated this way, as though I am simple, a woman, useless. I don't even get a say in my very own future, in the type of man I would marry, where I should live, what I should do with my days. Well, I am not stupid. I may have made a few questionable steps here but I am not an idiot. Lucinda promised you would not be harmed. I believe her. You don't have to but it seems neither of us have much choice in the matter anyway."

"So, what? Her honour means more than mine? I told you I could help with this but you'd rather just roll over and let others continue to decide what you shall do, who you shall be."

"Isn't that what you're doing by agreeing to marry me? You've let my father push you into this instead of standing up to him and saying no."

She had him there. But there was honour, and society's expectations. She knew nothing about any of that. "Did it ever occur to you that I am not upset by our impending nuptials? And that by saying no ruins both of us far more than a compromising fall in the dark?"

She scoffed and for the first time in his life he wanted to slap a woman. "You're saying you're happy to be forced into marriage with me?"

Anthony ground his teeth together and twisted his wrists to be free of the rope cutting off his circulation. "Not right this moment, no. Happy is not the word I would use."

"You know what I mean. Why would you want this? Why would you want to tie yourself to someone just like your sister?"

"You are not like Daniella."

"I crave adventure just like her. I don't want to marry and be curtailed, just like her. I want to be free, like any level-headed woman of my years would, just like her."

"You are not level-headed. A level-headed individual would not offer up her fiancé to a villain."

"You're straying from the point."

He spoke slowly and clearly so she would understand. "I had almost three long months to come to terms with what happened in the garden. To come to terms with who I would be marrying—you and your family. I accepted my fate because the choices aren't plentiful or attractive. If we survive this mess you've thrown us both into, we will be married, Rose."

Her lips didn't move much as she said, "Your honour is misplaced here."

"You don't get to talk about honour. You clearly know nothing about it and lack the necessary experience to take such a thing seriously. We have lain together, we will wed. I'll not have a bastard with my face on him enduring worse than I did from people who think they're better than you and me both."

ROSE RECOILED. NEVER had anyone spoken to her with such hatred filling their tone. She hadn't seen this side of Anthony Germaine and she didn't like it one bit. And, he was still missing her point. She wasn't going to marry him, bastard or no. By the time she might learn about a pregnancy, she would be long gone from here and building a life for herself as a young widow. He was right in that if a child did come from the hours of passion they'd shared, he or she would look like him as much as her. Would their child hate her for not marrying when she could have? For not legitimising their birth even to a hoyden and the son of a pirate? Society would not be kind either way.

Rose shook her head. She wouldn't have to worry about society because she would be far from it. "Come with me," she said, impulse once again driving her words before her brain had fully thought out the consequences.

"There is nowhere we could run to that you wouldn't be found. And what kind of life would that be? We have nothing between us. I have a home in the city you would find quite comfortable had you opened your eyes to the kind of life I could give you."

"As a Runner? A position gleaned from my father despite his hatred of you? A position he'd only give you so he could control you and ensure there was food on my table?"

Anthony surged to his knees and then his feet. He towered over her. "I deserve that position as much as the next man. I have the skills and I have the endurance, the focus, the ability to do some good."

"But he doesn't want you," she pointed out, getting to her own feet and facing him nose to nose.

Her words may have been designed to sting but he was used to those particular ones. Anthony was about to tell her exactly that when he lowered his gaze and took in the image of her tied hands. "Rose, you really are an idiot." He turned and shuffled backwards towards her. "Untie my hands."

She gave a little sniff. "I don't think I want to." He'd had murder in his eyes as he railed at her. His hair was matted at the back with blood and she actually worried that if she loosened his bonds, he might strangle her.

"Just do it, woman. Do it now."

She did as he said and worked at the lazy knot until it unravelled. Then she took a very large step back in the small cubicle, her feet crunching on hay.

"It doesn't matter that your father doesn't think me able, doesn't want me as a Runner, but do *you* want me, Rose?" he asked her. It was not what she was expecting.

"I don't understand."

"If we weren't compromised, if you weren't you and I wasn't me and we were free to pick who and what we wanted, would you want me? As a woman wants a man?" He stepped forward and she tried to move away but the wall at her back was solid, the man at her front determined and just as immovable.

He untied her hands and then took her fingers in his. She stared at where they were joined. As she'd sat with his head in her lap, running her hands through his hair and marvelling at lips that had kissed her so thoroughly, she'd had wanton thoughts about doing it again. With him. They were possibly in grave danger and definitely held against their will and all she could think of was his lips and his hands and his body. His mind was special too. He was smart and stable and she could do much worse if she was hunting a husband. Finally, she answered his question. "Yes. I do want you as a woman wants a man."

"And do you trust me, at all? Have I gained at least a measure of your trust?"

She nodded. "Yes."

"Then let me get us out of this and then we can decide what our future might look like. Then you can stay or you can run but at least I'll know I tried to convince you to accept me."

God, did he have to say it like that? Like a lost boy and she his only hope at a real life? She knew it not to be true. Not really. He could marry a fine woman and live happily ever after. Then his lips and hands and body would belong to someone else. Rose didn't like that idea much. They fit together.

Apart from the times he'd called her an idiot, he hadn't attempted to lock her in her room. And as much as he spoke about honour, he'd started this game of flesh between them when he'd come to her rooms while she bathed, when he'd cradled her breast and kissed her senseless. He'd started that. Awoken something inside of her.

"What do we do?" she asked him.

He gave her a nod and squeezed her fingers but then let go and considered the door to their temporary prison. "How many men were with your brothers?"

"I don't know. A dozen?"

"And they'd need most of those men with them to guard against Smith's crew. How many do you think she has? If you had to guess?"

"More than a dozen." She counted maybe fourteen when Smith had whistled for her hounds. There could have been more who didn't show their faces. She would certainly need more than that to crew her ship across the Channel. "Oh, God. The ship. We should find out where she is docked."

THE FALL INTO RUIN

Anthony shook his head. "We won't be needing it. We find Smith and arrest her, then your brothers can be brought to heel and taken to the magistrate. Or he can come to them. No one is going to make the ship before we have half of them in custody."

"You're going to have her hanged?" Rose's knees went a little weak. She would not let that happen. Lucinda was pregnant and the child was possibly of Rose's own blood.

He swung to her with his full attention. "She's guilty. There's no doubt the lengths she's gone to so far, or the lengths she will go to."

The horror must have shown all over her face. He grimaced but didn't rescind his words, instead he turned his attention back to the door.

Rose began stripping off her gown. She shimmied out of the padded suit and went to work on the fastenings.

"What are you doing?" Anthony hissed.

"I need to be able to run and move freely." Her fingernails were short so she used her teeth to loosen the laces that held the padded suit closed and tight, and then fashioned them into a belt around her too-loose dress. She then unbuttoned an internal pocket in the padding and took a dagger from the concealed compartment, secreting it into her boot before tossing the suit into the corner.

"I'm ready," she told him with a nod.

"You are not joining a fight."

Rose huffed and strengthened her stance. "I need to liberate Michael and…" She should have stopped there. "And get home before my absence is noted."

She had to stop treating him like a dolt, she realised when his lips thinned into a line and his hands lifted to his hips. "You will not warn Smith. You will not go anywhere near that woman again. I will rescue bloody Michael and you will find the authorities or the closest thing this town has to offer. There should at least be an officer of the court near the docks."

Rose took two steps towards the man who claimed she could have a life tied to him and poked him in the chest with her finger. Hard. "You do not own me yet, sir. We will do this together or I will go it alone."

CHAPTER TWENTY-ONE

ANTHONY COULD ONLY stare at his little hellion as fire flashed in her golden eyes, her finger attempting to stab a hole into his chest cavity. He might even wear a small bruise from her fury. He smiled. It was a mistake.

Her voice grew louder and louder with every word. "Do you think this is a joke, Sir Anthony Germaine—not a pirate, not a gentleman, not a Runner? You wouldn't know the first thing about—"

The door creaked open behind Anthony's back and they both froze, Rose mid-sentence.

"Oi," a voice hissed from the darkness beyond. "Do you two mind keeping it down in… Wait a minute!"

Anthony swung with all his might, his fist landing a solid, bone-crunching blow to the man's nose, or was it his cheek? It all happened so fast. First there was shock, and then his eyes were rolling into the back of his head as he fell.

It took only seconds to drag the unconscious guard into the stable and lock the door, with him inside. No one else was about but were they sleeping or had Josiah already gone to confront Smith? If Anthony had any luck left in the world at all, both villains would be together and neither would expect company. He guessed it to be almost dawn. The crunching of straw and the scuff of a boot on dirt had him turning on the spot, just in time to witness Rose skulking towards the street side door of where they were being held. He was no good with the direction since he himself had been unconscious on the way in.

He had no choice but to follow her. He wanted to draw attention to the fact he'd just felled a man with one blow. His hand didn't even hurt. His veins were abuzz with the need to do it again, a restless type of energy taking over. Not a pirate, no, but he was going to right a wrong here tonight.

He reached out a hand and gripped Rose's bicep in a tight hold only seconds before she would have stormed out into the night. Sleet fell but it wasn't heavy. It was cold though. "Wait," he commanded her.

She tried to shake him off but he held her steady. His voice was a whisper but he hoped it held a hint of warning, of danger. "Slowly, for God's sake, Rose. These aren't your cliffs or your home. You have no idea who is about."

Rose let him poke his head out first to determine if the street was clear. He gave her a nod and she shot off across the dirt and stone to an alleyway not far down. It was as dark as night. He couldn't see a bloody thing. He stopped to listen for her footfall but all he heard was the actual pirate curse she dropped into the pitch-black.

"You're going to slow me down," she complained.

He shuffled in the direction of her next curse word. She took his hand and resumed her steady pace until they emerged onto another street, this time the first rays of dawn peeked through the cloud and drizzling rain. Moisture had pooled in her hair in the form of tiny, delicate droplets and clung to her eyelids. Until she blinked and rubbed the back of her hand across her face much the way an urchin would wipe his nose. Her cheeks did flush right before she spoke. "The Cock's Wobble is two streets in that direction." She gestured with the same finger that had poked into his chest.

"Wait, the Cock's Wobble? A tavern? You went to a tavern, unchaperoned, to meet a villain, with only old men and boys at your back?"

"I was armed," she proclaimed. "And I had Michael."

He gritted his teeth and wondered if this was what he could expect from her for a lifetime. He had said he wouldn't curb her adventurous spirit and he'd meant that, but there would be no dockside taverns in her future, especially ones with cock in the name! "Of course, you had Michael." It was all he could say.

She glared at him and dropped his hand like she hadn't realised she still held it.

"I'll go to the tavern and look around. Josiah might not have even made it yet and now that he doesn't have the two of us to hand over, he might go back to the estate. We can deal with him there."

Rose nodded and said, "I suppose I'll run down to the docks and find someone to raise the alarm."

Her tone caught him off guard. Defeat filled her words. "It's the right thing to do, Rose. Smith is a criminal and she must be brought to justice. Don't let her fool you with her pretty face and delicate condition."

She nodded but bit her lip, her teeth pressing into the Cupid's bow. Anthony wrapped his arms around her and hugged her tight. "We can do this, Rose. Together. We'll get Michael back. I promise. We will prevail."

She nodded into his shoulder and squeezed him back. When he released her she lifted onto her toes and pressed her mouth to his. He poured as much of himself into the kiss as he could. He wanted to tell her all the things he was feeling, that there was hope that they would work this out. That there was a tomorrow to look forward to after today. But before he got the chance, she slipped away and was running down the street, blending into the shadows until he could no longer make out her form.

She had put her trust in him and he would show her he deserved it. He would capture Smith and she would be transported to London for her trial where she would be found guilty but she would not hang. Transportation was a far more likely outcome for a woman with child. If he thought she would hang, he might hesitate to take her down.

Anthony shook his head against that idea. The woman was responsible for a great many reprehensible deeds. She'd almost had his own sister killed, children too if Trelissick and the pirate Darius hadn't worked to save them all. Michael might already be dead if Smith found out he had very little value other than to Rose.

One booted foot in front of the other, Anthony moved as quickly and quietly as he could in the direction Rose had pointed him. He would do what was right and just. And then Clairmont would bow to public pressure and give him the position of Runner.

But for the first time in such a long time, the prickle of pride he was sure he would feel at the thought of being sworn to uphold the law didn't come. It didn't warm his chest or cause him to stand a little taller. All he saw in his mind was Rose's eyes and the way they would condemn him if Smith did hang…

OF ALL THE underhanded tactics Rose had ever employed, this one was the most deceitful by far. She threw a glance over her shoulder expecting the sounds of pursuit, but none followed. All was silent except for the beating of her heart as it thundered in her chest and struck a drum in her ears. She wasn't even sorry or fearful of being caught out. She worried about what might happen to Anthony if he stumbled upon the wrong street or any number of mishaps that could befall a man who couldn't see a thing in the dark.

She had the vision of a street rat, Michael always told her. Years of running about during the night had lent her the ability to see well the shapes of what one might bump into. But dawn was approaching and with it Anthony's coming realisation that she had sent him in the wrong direction. If he made the market where stallholders would be setting up for the morning trade, he could ask for the right direction and know she'd duped him.

A few hours. That's all she needed. One at least. As she came upon the tavern, she didn't approach via the front doors. She made her way to the back of the establishment and tried to peer through windows with layers of grime and soot blurring what was inside. Not one candle burned so far as she could tell.

As she sought a silent way in, she cursed a blue streak in her head. She'd said she would put her trust in him and this betrayal would sting. She did trust him to keep her safe; he was hard and yet gentle, safe and yet strong. With her. She just didn't trust him to walk the best course rather than the right one with Smith.

Finally a window that wasn't locked on the ground level slid upwards smoothly and she hoped it would hold once she had it open enough to slip through. She couldn't prop up the glass, hold her dress, protect herself and do it all without making a sound. A second pair of hands would have helped.

Holding her breath, she slowly removed her fingers from the frame and the blessed thing held in place. Probably the grime, she thought. Rose wiped her hands on her dress and then boosted her way inside the room. Her boots barely made a sound as she crouched in place, waiting for an alarm to be raised that an intruder had arrived. No such sound came. On a normal day of breaking into an establishment, she might close the window behind her but there wasn't time.

"Rose?" From the corner of the room came a whisper and it startled her into clapping a hand over her own mouth. Her muffled shriek of surprise turned into one of delight.

"Michael?" Fortune favoured her as she embraced her old friend. "How do you fare?" she asked in a whisper.

He didn't answer her question, just took her by the

shoulders and glared at her face in the glow of predawn through the open window. "What the hell are you doing here?"

She bristled. "I've come to rescue you."

His eyes widened. "You have her money?"

Rose shook her head. "I don't. But I've also come to warn her if she'll hear me. My brother and Germaine are here too. Josiah means to kill everyone to cover the trail of his misdemeanours and Germaine means to arrest her, which will also lead to her death. Either way, she needs to leave now. We all need to leave."

"Warn her?" Michael looked truly puzzled now. "Why would you warn her? She's a criminal."

"She is also a woman carrying a child," she pointed out. Did an innocent baby mean nothing to these men? "She can still get away. You go through the window and keep look out. I'll find Lucinda and get her moving. She must leave everything and return to her ship right now."

For a moment his eyes turned so hard and his fingers pinched into her arms until she had to bite her tongue against asking him to unhand her. But then his expression cleared and he turned to the door of this room he'd been held prisoner in.

"No," she whispered in a hiss. "You keep lookout and I'll find her. I'm lighter on my feet and can see better than you in the dark."

But Michael wouldn't hear her. He threw the door open and stomped down the corridor with all the grace, and noise, of a rhinoceros in charge. As he went, he banged doors and called, "Get up, we're moving. Right now."

Rose scurried after him, this time the confusion all hers. "Michael?" she called to his back.

But he didn't answer, merely took each stair two at a time until he reached the top. "Lucinda, get up, we need to leave. Right now."

By the time Rose reached him, he'd swung open the door to a bedroom lit by a single candle. Lucinda was dressed and perched on the edge of the bed struggling with her boots. "I heard."

She locked dark sleepy eyes with Rose's. "What are you doing here? Did you bring my money?"

Rose shook her head. "I was kidnapped by Josiah and— Wait just a moment." Spinning on the spot, she pinned Michael with a glare of her own. "Just what is going on here? Has she dazzled you too? Her prisoner?"

Michael grinned the same grin he'd been giving her for more than ten years but a prickling started at her nape and unease settled low in her belly. What he said next, she had not seen coming. "You really are very gullible, Rose. I was never a prisoner here. Lucinda is my sister. Another of Ashmoor's bastards."

Rose slumped to the wall at her back. "I don't understand. How? When? How?"

Lucinda called to them both, "Someone help me with these blasted boots. I cannot reach my feet."

Michael moved to kneel before the villain and gently helped her slide a foot into each dirty leather boot and then he laced them up for her. He'd done that for Rose once.

When they'd been drenched in a downpour and her fingers had been so stiff and numb she wasn't able to get her shoes off. How many times had Michael helped her? His friend? His confidante? Rose and he often joked they were all each other had in the world. There was no one else they would trust so fully with their own lives.

"You lied to me."

Michael looked up from his task. "An occasional necessity I'm afraid."

"And you?" Rose switched her gaze from her friend to his sister. "How long have you been waiting in the wings?"

Lucinda hauled herself from the edge of the cot with more of Michael's help and began throwing loose items in a canvas bag. "We've known about each other for some years."

Rose's mind was spinning like one of those little carved wooden toys you flicked between your forefinger and thumb. She cast back, sifting images and facts until she put at least one and one together to make two. "You were there in the gardens at my ball."

Lucinda tsked. "Bad news that night, wasn't it?"

"The note. You were the contact I was to pass Michael's note to?"

Neither one answered her but she took their silence as a yes. "Did you think I'd never find out?"

Michael shook his head. "I was rather hoping you wouldn't. At least not until we were under sail. But then you had to go and ask for passage. Do you really think you can just disappear, Rose? Lie about your identity for the rest of your life and spend all the time watching your back and keeping track of your stories?"

Rose scoffed and shuffled a little closer to the door that led to the landing. "Well you two have managed to pull the wool over the eyes of many people for many years. Does Ashmoor know about his daughter?"

They both laughed. "He knows about all of his bastards. He just doesn't care about any of us," Michael said.

Lucinda was in the process of awkwardly strapping a sword to her belly when she stopped and placed her hand to her middle. She stood like that for a moment and Michael's attention shifted and he went to her.

Rose didn't hesitate; she hit the stairs running, not paying any heed to the noise she made. She went back the way she came with the intention of hurling herself out the open window and onto the street. Anthony was right. She was an idiot.

A vice-like steel wrapped around her middle and lifted her off her feet, knocking the breath from her body and causing the room to swing wildly. She didn't bother with 'let me go' or 'unhand me'. She had walked into a trap of her own making and now she had nothing to leverage, no bargaining power. She had to hope that the mere fact she'd come with a warning would allow her some small mercy in the eyes of the villain. And the villain's bloody brother…

CHAPTER TWENTY-TWO

ANTHONY WAS GOING to murder her. Never mind marriage or building a life together because Rose would be dead. Strangled to death by his own two hands. He'd hit the marketplace at a run with no doubt in his mind his betrothed had sent him on a wild goose chase. There were no taverns here; he hadn't passed a one. He had passed fine establishments selling fripperies, gowns, a bookstore, a bakehouse and an apothecary.

He'd had to move slowly at first lest he trip and break his other ankle so by the time he reached the square and heard the commotion of stallholders setting up for the morning's trade, his blood was at boiling point. There was no point in asking for directions to the tavern now so he instead asked for the way of the docks. Not that he couldn't smell them, hear the birds squawking for fish heads and see the occasional mast between warehouses. He made his way a little faster as the sun began to rise behind the clouds. The drizzle had stopped but his mood was in hurricane mode.

He snuck down an alleyway in order to get his bearings once he could see water but a sound caused him to freeze. A scuff of a shoe? A rat? Suddenly, arms encased his and a hand wrapped around his face, right over his mouth.

He lashed out, began to struggle for his life. He lifted both feet and kicked hard towards the left and then the right but it seemed at least three men held him.

"It's me," was spoken into his ear at the same time the sharp point of a knife found his neck. "It's James."

Another man approached. *Hobson.* Trelissick's man and cut-throat if first impressions were to be believed, though he was introduced as an ex-soldier. Anthony placed his feet back on the ground and nodded and he was immediately released. How easy it would have been for them to cut his throat and leave him in the gutter if they'd been pirates or even thieves. He really wasn't as good at this as he'd thought.

Anthony wasn't sure whether he should embrace his brother-in-law or punch him in the nose. "What are you doing here?" His note couldn't have reached them already.

James beckoned him back into the shadows and said, "I was tasked with putting a team together to root out Smith once and for all. We were led here some days ago but there has been no traffic to or from the ship. All aboard have stayed aboard and none have approached."

"Perhaps they knew you were here?"

James flicked him an irritated grimace. "I rather think we're better at our jobs than that."

"Well, Smith isn't on the ship anyway. She's holed up at a tavern down the way…somewhere."

Hobson growled a curse, the same one Rose had used earlier, and then grabbed Anthony by the ratty shirtfront and slammed his back into the cold, hard wall behind them.

"Where is she? What do you know?"

Fury rose in him, the likes of which he'd never known. Not even the torture at school had made him feel lower than grown men constantly refusing to see he had worth. Any worth. Did Hobson think Anthony had sided with the fugitive? Thrown his lot in with the very people he despised the most? Anthony roared and charged, his shoulder in the man's gut pushing forward until Hobson lay on his back in the mud. He got one decent punch in before he was lifted free, his fist connecting with the man's cheek.

Hobson sat up, a little dazed and spat to the earth. "What the hell was that fer?"

Anthony shrugged off the men who once again held him. "Let. Me. Go."

James swung his attention from one man to the other. "Feel better?" he said.

Anthony straightened his shirt and ran a hand through his hair. "He could have just asked."

James picked up where Hobson had tried to go. "What are you doing here? I knew you were in the vicinity with your bride-to-be but what are you doing *here*?"

"I sent word to you, well, to the house—"

James swore long and loud. "If Daniella gets your note and not me, is she like to call for the carriage?"

"We don't have time to ponder if my heavily pregnant sister might come to join the fray. Not when we have a heavily pregnant Smith and a wild Clairmont to worry about."

That got everyone's attention. "She's with child?"

"According to Rose she is."

"Your bride?" James asked.

"Rose Clairmont and a stable lad from Ashmoor's estate have been smuggling for years here but that's not why Smith is cooling her heels. Rose's brothers fleeced her when she was forced to flee London and she won't, or can't, leave without the blunt."

"Wait," James said, his palm vertical in front of his chest. "Josiah and Samuel Clairmont? What have they to do with Smith at all?"

"They knew her in London, gambled at her tables. She introduced them into her fold, into her bed. She probably needed a scapegoat or someone who could be bribed easily if she were caught. A love-sick fool and an heir to a fortune would do her well but the sons of Clairmont would do even better."

"But they double-crossed her?" James guessed.

"Left her with child and took the coin and notes her clubs had amassed, the ones you didn't get to after that night." Anthony shuddered. He hated to talk of that night and he wasn't even there on account of his shattered ankle.

"She's after revenge," Hobson suggested.

Anthony shook his head. "Not by the sounds. I think she only wants her money and then intends to flee."

One of James's men stepped forward. "Then we let the navy deal with her in open water."

"No," Anthony told them all. "She will take hostages. Rose and I were to be those hostages but Josiah kidnapped us first, before we could…be taken." He wasn't going to tell these men his intended had planned to deliver him right to her.

James looked around as though he searched for something. "Where is Rose now? Where is Josiah?"

"I don't know where either of them are. Rose and I escaped the stable where we were held but then got separated. She's probably right this minute warning Smith in return for Michael's release."

"Michael?"

"Her friend," he spat. "Ashmoor's bastard who has been helping Rose with her smuggling." Or hiding behind her if he was caught, more like. "Smith took him yesterday." Was it only yesterday? So much had happened in such a short amount of time.

"What does Smith want with a bastard stable boy?"

Irritated, it was Anthony who cursed this time. "Michael was the bargain so Rose would come back with Smith's money. Rose and Michael are comrades; she wouldn't leave him behind."

James rubbed the bridge of his nose with a thumb and forefinger. "So your future bride has had a sit-down with London's most notorious criminal for an age, has herself been breaking several laws including smuggling, has been taking up with a stable lad, and all right under the nose of the man who is charged with keeping the law in London?"

"She has not taken up with a stable lad."

"I did my own investigation into Rose Clairmont," James told him. "She has been left alone out here for years. If what you're saying is true, you can't marry her."

He grit his teeth. "Rose Clairmont and I will be married." *If she didn't get herself killed first.*

Silence descended on the assembled men before James gave a single nod. There came a strange bird call from the direction of the shore front and everyone ducked and ran for the cover of the shadows. Anthony did the same. They crept along the side of a warehouse that reeked of rancid fish and brine, salt crunching underfoot the closer they got to the dock. A small party of around a dozen were making their determined way towards a rowboat. A flash of sun broke through the haze of cloud. *Rose!* Not dead yet then.

He was about to get closer when a hand closed around his arm. "Look," James said with a gesture in the opposite direction.

"Fuck," Anthony breathed. It was Josiah and his men, Samuel in tow. None of them looked to have bags of coin with them. They were well-armed though. Hired thugs who didn't care what the job was, as long as they were well compensated.

Smith's crew was also well armed, the lady herself, with her bulging middle even a full-length cloak couldn't hide, had a sword over her shoulder and a pistol in hand. Rose was about to get herself caught in the middle of a gunfight. When he looked closer, she appeared very pale. She was being held but was not bound. He thought she almost appeared frightened.

So far Anthony had tried to do it all by the letter of what was right and just, but the only times he got anywhere was when he just let loose, like knocking a man unconscious before he'd had time to blink. The only satisfaction he'd had was in letting go of what he wanted from life, letting go of the control he thought would make him the proper gentleman in the eyes of a society who'd never given him a chance, and simply given in to the moment. Those were the times that he'd felt a measure of power and he liked it.

With James's men at his back and villains in front though, how could he end it without putting Rose in even more danger than she already was?

This was not going to be a fair fight, of that he was sure.

JOSIAH PULLED UP at the same time Smith did and the two each eyed the other, taking in the men, the weapons, the chances and choices.

Smith spoke first. "How nice to see you, Josiah, Samuel. I presume you have my money?"

Josiah barked a laugh. "You should know by now that that money is long gone."

Smith swallowed, swore, gathered herself. "Then it's a good thing I have your sister isn't it?"

A smirk followed another short burst of laughter that bordered on the edge of hysteria. "It is a good thing you've found our Rose. She has an annoying habit of turning up where you least expect her." Josiah leaned slightly to make eye contact with Rose around the man at Smith's side. "Where's your beau, Rose? *Run* to get help?"

Rose bristled. Anthony was twice the man her brother could ever hope to be, Runner or not. She drew herself up and addressed Josiah in return across the distance. "I hope you get shot today, brother. I grow rather tired of your presence."

Josiah raised his weapon and pointed it in her general direction, which caused Smith's men to raise theirs in return. Perhaps it wasn't wise to bait her brother? Or perhaps it was.

Rose continued, attempting to step forward when a meaty hand closed about her shoulder to keep her where she was. "What's the plan now, Josiah? Much like me, you've nothing left to bargain with. Strange how everyone's plans hinge on the one man no one gives a thought to."

Josiah shrugged. "I don't need Germaine. Smith here is the one who can't get away without him."

Lucinda returned, "I have Rose to ensure no one retaliates once we are under sail."

Samuel threw in, "No one has to die here today. Lucinda, please, we can talk about this."

Lucinda swung her gun in his direction. "That's where you're wrong, lover. You could have prevented this. You could have been true to your word and prevented all of this."

The maniacal laughter rang out from Josiah once again. "Do you still honestly believe he would have married you? Father wouldn't have allowed it for one, and for two, how would we prove the origins of this get?" He gestured his pistol at Lucinda's belly. "It mightn't be Clairmont blood at all."

Rose was shocked to witness Samuel hold Lucinda's gaze and reply, "I wouldn't have cared if the babe was mine or not. I would have cared for you both."

"As your mistress? Your plaything until you grew tired of me, of us?" Lucinda spat. "No thank you to the both of you. I'll take my chances on my own."

Smith shuffled sideways towards the long jetty and Rose was jostled along too until Josiah roared, "STOP! No one is going anywhere."

Lucinda ignored him and kept moving, kept her pistol high and trained on Rose's siblings. "I am getting on my ship and I am leaving this place."

Josiah shook his head. "And how long until you come back? For vengeance or for coin? How long? This ends now."

A shot rang out and Rose immediately dropped into a crouch as others returned fire. The clash of steel on steel followed. Her fingers found the hilt of her dagger but before she could pull the knife from her boot, the hand was back on her shoulder and propelling her to take cover behind a large pallet of timber boxes. She twisted until the dagger was in her hand. Not great as far as weapons went but she could defend herself at least.

She peered around the side of the boxes to see Smith's men holding a line at the end of the jetty while Lucinda, Michael and three more men ran for the rowboat. Rose didn't waste any more time. She plunged her knife into the thigh of the man who held her and then pulled the blade free and got up to run. He reached out and grabbed her by the ankle, causing her to fall heavily on her side.

"Bitch," he called her before gaining his feet. Rose did not like the expression he wore. He withdrew his own blade from the belt at his waist and closed the distance. Rose retreated on her backside and hands but the man was quicker. Close fighting sounded from her right but she didn't dare take her eyes from her current adversary. Adjusting her sticky grip on the dagger's handle, she was about to thrust up into his leg again when the hilt of a sword clobbered him from behind. He fell forward, pinning Rose to the cold, wet ground.

She let out an oomph as she tried to kick him off her legs.

"Seems you might need a spot of assistance," was drawled from the crate's edge.

Rose scowled and hissed, "Help me up."

Anthony shook his head in defeat but he did use his boot to roll the oaf from her and took her hand to help her to her feet.

She got in the first word before he could. "Yes, I know I'm an idiot—you don't need to say it."

He shot her a grin. "The fact that you're even still alive is a wonder."

"And you," she replied, picking up the man's short sword in her bloodied hand and testing the weight.

"You don't need that, Rose. We are getting out of here. Trelissick can handle the arrests."

Rose peeked out again at the unfolding scene. Some men lay in pools of blood, some groaned, some still fought. Josiah was carving a path towards the jetty clearly still intent on murder. Or was it escape now that he knew he couldn't simply dispatch his troubles?

"We have to help Lucinda and Michael. Josiah will kill

THE FALL INTO RUIN

them both."

Anthony muttered, "Bloody Michael," under his breath but she heard.

"There's something I must tell you—"

He cut off her words with: "It can wait. We cannot let any of them make the ship."

Rose agreed and they skirted the edges of the fight, Anthony tucking Rose behind him, but no one paid them much attention at all.

Quietly but quickly they followed behind Josiah, Samuel nowhere in sight.

Josiah was intent on doing maximum harm and swung his sword.

Rose screamed, "Michael!"

The man turned with his sword raised and deflected what would have been a killing blow. When Josiah lunged at him again, Michael parried and managed to push Lucinda out of the way. "Go," he roared at her. "Get to the ship."

Anthony sprang into action but Rose held him back. "Please, help Michael. I will go after Lucinda."

CHAPTER TWENTY-THREE

ANTHONY WAS TORN between catching a wanted murderess and saving the life of Rose's friend. He should go after Lucinda. He should do the right thing.

The beseeching in Rose's golden-flecked eyes got the better of him and he gave her a brief nod. After all, the more dangerous foe right then was a madman, not a pregnant woman.

But Anthony didn't fight with swords. He'd done a little fencing over the years and was more often the loser than the winner. He was much better with his fists and was fast enough on his feet. The next time Josiah lunged at Michael, Anthony swung his leg and kicked the man in the thigh. He stepped back in time to keep his head rather than have it cleaved from his neck as Josiah roared.

Michael came at him again and again but Anthony couldn't get close enough to do any real damage. He lunged with the sword, hoping to wound, and sliced through Josiah's hip. Rose's brother turned with surprise on his face, dropping to his knees on the rough timbers of the jetty with a howl of pain. A dagger slid from his boot to clatter at his side.

Josiah wiped blood from his side. "You stabbed me in the back," he said.

"Aye," Anthony said, holding the point of his sword to the man's chin. "And you'd have done the same to me, to Rose, to any one of us."

Leaning heavily on his sword to stay upright, Josiah nodded.

Anthony addressed the other man present. "Rose has gone after Smith. You guard this filth and I'll go after her."

Michael shook his head. "Your sword skills are atrocious. You stay; I'll get Rose."

He wanted to protest. Rose was his to save. His to prove his worth to. But Michael was right. He was a much dirtier fighter and was stealthier with the sword. He nodded. "Keep her safe."

Josiah began to laugh again.

Anthony sighed. "Everything is quite hilarious to you today," he said.

"You actually have feelings for Rose. You've known her less than a week."

"You don't get to talk about your sister. You gave up that right when you kidnapped her and planned to kill her."

Josiah just kept on chuckling. He was more than cracked. He needed to be in an institution. Anthony used his foot to slide the dagger closer to his own hand rather than risk Josiah picking it up.

"Throw away your sword," Anthony told him.

"Throw away yours," came the reply.

"You've lost. Can't you see it?"

Sobering in an instant, Josiah said, "You're the one who doesn't see it. I'd rather die than be arrested by the likes of you. A nobody. You spout on about honour but you didn't arrest Rose. Didn't turn her in to Father. You could have prevented her being here but you didn't. Why is that?"

Anthony thought about it. "I didn't have the entire story."

"You felt sorry for her," Josiah said with a spit over the edge of the jetty to the ocean below.

"She has spirit, your sister."

"She is a blight to this family."

Anthony smiled and hoped Josiah felt the chill. "And yet here you are, fucking a murderer and then stealing all her money. Was it your idea or Samuel's?"

"Samuel doesn't have original ideas."

"You've both disgraced your father's name. Rose's scandal will pale compared to what will happen when word of this reaches the capital. Your parents will need to move countries to escape the shame, and for what? Was it the thrill? The danger of being caught?" Anthony had to keep him talking until James or one of his men came to take the brother into custody but he worried about Rose. He couldn't see far enough up the jetty to know what was going on. He swung his gaze back towards the fight still going on behind.

He shouldn't have. His sword was hit from the bottom, which created a pendulum action and it was all Josiah needed to surge to his feet and fight in earnest.

"Never look away from your enemy," Josiah roared. "You're pathetic!"

Anthony blocked a blow that was aimed to once again take his head clean off. He held the sword high to keep blocking but Josiah had mania on his side and Anthony wasn't a swordsman. Each blow vibrated down his arm. He ducked and twisted to gain more ground, picking up the dagger as he did. Josiah did not relent. He just kept coming. Anthony raised his sword to block another blow and Josiah's blade slid down his until they were hilt to hilt, eye to eye. Instinct took over and he swung his free arm wide and then plunged the smaller blade into Josiah's neck.

Shock registered as he coughed, gurgled, coughed again. He tried to say something but only blood poured from his mouth. He removed the dagger but still the man couldn't talk. There was so much blood. Anthony lifted a leg and kicked the man, sending him over the edge of the jetty, his sword still clenched in hand, his eyes wide with surprise. He hit the surface of the water with a splash and in only seconds he had sunk beneath.

Anthony doubled over and breathed great heaving breaths of salty sea air. The heavy tread of boots sounded and he spun, his sword high again in one hand, the bloodied dagger in the other. "Hobson?"

James's man looked him up and down. "Any of that yer blood?"

Anthony shook his head.

"And Smith? She got away again?"

Wrenching his neck in the direction Rose and Michael had run, he didn't wait. He took off, his grip on the sword tenuous. "Find James," he called over his shoulder. He was sweating and hadn't even realised it. His pulse thundered and as the cold wind picked up, he realised his face was wet but it wasn't raining. Not yet.

It had felt as though an age had passed while he argued and fought with Josiah but it can't have been too long because Rose, Lucinda and Michael were still on the jetty ahead. The villain had her arm around Michael's neck but they moved slowly, Rose at their side.

"Stop," Anthony called to them. The three of Smith's men turned at the sound, as did Smith herself. "It's over. You don't have the men to sail or to fight. Give it up."

Lucinda let out a panting breath and said, "Never."

Michael let the woman go and swung his arm around Rose's neck, the point of a dagger at her throat. "Throw down your weapons, Germaine," he called. "Or Rose dies."

What the devil?

From where he stood, he watched as Rose rolled her eyes and said, "Michael, don't be ridiculous."

"This is keeping her safe?" Anthony said. What had he missed?

"She's coming with us and so are you. Throw down your weapons."

"But you're not going to kill her because she's your friend. Isn't she?"

This time Rose spoke. "Michael and Lucinda are brother and sister."

He sputtered as he switched his gaze from one and then to the other. They had the same black hair but didn't look like siblings other than that. "I don't believe it."

"Both are Ashmoor's bastards," she revealed, but then Michael held the knife closer.

"Shut up now, Rose."

Fury pierced his surprise as though bursting a bubble. His eyes sought Rose's. "You knew about this?"

"I just found out this morning and I did try to tell you but you didn't give me the chance."

"Of all the… Rose, this is something you could have tried harder to mention." He would never have let Michael go after her knowing this. And why hadn't Rose tried to get away? No one had been holding her before he got there.

She still wanted to leave with them. His blood boiled anew. He glared at Michael. "You will let her go."

"I will slice her pretty neck wide open right here if you don't throw down your goddamned sword!"

Smith dropped to her knees and let out the most terrible keening sound all the while holding her belly, her eyes squeezed shut against the pain. Michael was finally torn between holding Rose and going to his sister's aid. He gestured to two of the men with his fist still holding the knife, away from Rose's throat for now. "Pick her up, damn it. Luce? Is the baby coming?"

Smith was breathing deep and replied, "How the fuck should I know? I've never done this before."

If they waited there long enough, Hobson and James would come for them but each moment Michael held the blade to Rose's throat was a moment too long. There was an urgency here. To get Smith to the ship. To get away. But they hadn't even enough men to row the boat to the ship.

Once he realised they weren't getting away, he could kill Rose. On his own there was no way to disarm her men, arrest Smith and punch Michael in the face. Anthony could only save Rose or take down Smith. One or the other. Smith held the key to unlocking his career as a Runner, restoring his honour and his name. But Rose was his to protect too. Despite her ridiculous belief in her own skills, she could not get out of this on her own. She honestly thought Smith and Michael would just let her go? When they didn't get their money and they had nothing to live off?

Anthony dropped his sword with a clatter. "Why don't you see to your sister, Michael? She doesn't sound very good."

Smith's head snapped up. "I'll be just fine but I appreciate your concern." She climbed to her feet and shook off her men as they helped her. "We're wasting time here."

Anthony juggled his own dagger in his hand and when Michael moved from Rose's back to collect his sword, he let the dagger fly. Anthony leaped forward, threw an arm around Rose's middle and they both went over the side of the jetty.

CHAPTER TWENTY-FOUR

T HE WATER WAS frigid as it closed over her and she hadn't taken a breath since his arm had knocked the air from her lungs. By the time Rose gained the surface, she was spluttering and coughing, saltwater coating her tongue and burning her throat. "What did you do?" she railed at Anthony when his head popped up from the water.

"I just saved your skin, Rose."

The jetty was too high to clamber up onto and the nearest ladder was a fair swim. By the time she made it the action above should be over. Footsteps thundered on the boards and as he tread water, the rowboat in the distance bobbed. Damn it. They were getting away.

"You've ruined everything," she said, starting her swim.

He followed. Once she had her feet on the rungs, he spoke. "They would have killed you and you know it. You must know it."

She didn't utter another word until she was on her feet on the jetty, her dress in a shambles as water sluiced off of her. Her hair clung to her cheeks and neck and her teeth chattered. Anthony had two hands on the top of the ladder and was about to step over when she rushed him and tried to push him back into the cold sea. He held fast until she stepped back again.

"Are you done?" he asked her.

Rose looked towards the end of the long jetty but even if she was the fastest person on earth, she was too late. "You have no idea what you've done," she told him, her voice soft, small even.

"I would do it again in a heartbeat," he told her.

"You don't understand. My father has these plans. Even if I wanted to marry you, he won't let it happen. Not to you."

"We can talk about this later, Rose. Let's get you dried off and someplace warm."

A stranger was waiting for them as they stepped from the timbers to the ground. The fight was over. Bodies were being stacked up without ceremony. The living were loaded into the back of a wagon, their hands and feet tied. Samuel was amongst them. His head was down but she was not mistaken.

The stranger stepped forward and clasped hands with Anthony. "I'm glad you are still alive. There's no telling what Daniella would do if I let something happen to you," he said.

Anthony tensed at first but then laughed. "And I you," came his reply. "What will happen to Smith now?"

"We'll send word to the navy and hope they intercept her. We don't think she has enough men to sail but we've underestimated her time and again and she still gets the better of us all." There was a short pause and then the man asked, "How did she get away again? We had her."

Anthony sighed but Rose spoke first to save his dignity, his honour. "That's my fault."

The stranger took her in and Rose knew she must look a fright. It's not every day you fought for your life and then got tossed into the ocean for your troubles. He wore a gentle smile as he said, "You must be Rose Clairmont then?"

She nodded.

"Welcome to the family." He exchanged a solemn look with Anthony and then walked away to help with the prisoners.

"I don't think he likes me," Rose said, her eyes burning and her throat clogging up. *Welcome to the family* could only mean he was James Trelissick and he'd spoken too soon.

Anthony came to stand in front of her and wrapped his arms around her as she began to sob against his wet shirt-front, stained with blood and God knew what else. "It's going to be all right, Rose. You'll see."

She shook her forehead back and forth across his chest and her voice was muffled when she said, "It's not going to be all right." She hiccupped and mumbled, "I'm not to be married to you."

"I know that isn't what you wanted but you have to see it's a good option." He didn't have to add, *I'm a good option.* She could hear it in his voice.

Why did it all have to go so wrong? She should have been on the decks of a ship right now as it sailed far away from England and he was to be by her side. They could have talked and got to know one another, enjoyed each other's company before deciding if they should wed or if she should disappear in France and become someone new. She was to have time and choices. He'd taken that from her but her resentment wasn't with him. Not really. He was doing what was right by her. Or what he thought was right.

"You've blown your chances to be a Runner well and truly," she pointed out.

"I don't want it anymore," he said as they began to walk to a nearby crested carriage.

She sobbed, miserable. "You're just saying that to save your dignity."

"No," he rushed to assure her. He leaned into the carriage and pulled out a soft blanket. Much the same as when he'd undressed her in the cabin. He wrapped the clean, soft wool around her shoulders and used the fabric to pull her closer. "I don't want to be a Runner anymore because I don't want to have anything to do with your father or your family." He chuckled softly. "There's no chance he'd have me now anyway."

Rose drew in a deep breath. "There's something I haven't told you."

He also inhaled. "There's something I need to tell you also."

"I want to go first," she blurted. He was right that she could have warned him about Michael and she hadn't for her own selfish reasons. Now those reasons were dust on the wind. "My father has promised me to a man named Harcourt. He'll arrive in two days to take me to Gretna."

Anthony stilled. "Do you know him? This man?"

Rose shook her head and sniffed. "I believe him to be as

old as a dinosaur and very possibly a killer of his first three wives."

"What do you want to do?" he asked.

She met his gaze with hers. "What do you mean?"

"I'm asking you, Rose. What do you want to do next? Marry this stranger? Hie off to Gretna with him and give yourself over to the fate you've dreaded worse than death?"

"If we go back to Hell's Gate, that is what will happen."

Anthony smiled and shrugged. "So, we don't go back to Hell's Gate."

Confusion over his statement and also the smile angered her. Was he making fun of her? "The ship has sailed without us. Smith has left. Where else would we go?"

Anthony looked behind him at the carriage. "I may not have much to my name, which is worth even less than my worldly possessions, but I'll take care of you. If you marry me instead, you'll never have to face your father again. You'll never know a cold shoulder or an unkind word."

Rose gestured wildly at what went on around them. "This scandal will be even worse than the garden incident. There will be no getting out of this mess. You'll be a social pariah, worse than you are now."

He smiled again and she wanted to hit him. How could he be so positive at a time when nothing had gone right? He said, "Did you know my sister sold her virginity at an auction, in London, with lords in attendance? One of those lords tried to buy her. She survived. Her reputation survived. Yours will too, after a time, and mine can't possibly sink any lower."

"You don't know what you're saying. My father will kill you before he lets you take me away."

He sobered. "There is something I have to tell you. It's about Josiah."

Rose's heart skipped a beat in her chest. Did he get away as well? She looked towards the horizon where Smith's ship was sailing off into the day and hoped Josiah hadn't caught up with her.

"No," Anthony said and brought her hands into his. "He's dead. Josiah. I killed him."

Rose would not mourn a brother who'd treated her so poorly. A brother who could have killed his own sister and a woman who may have been carrying his child. She searched Anthony's gaze, looking for answers in the green depths. "That's probably for the best."

He frowned. "You're not upset?"

"Are you?"

"No. He would have killed me if I hadn't defended my-self."

"There's no way my father will name you a Runner now. Not a chance."

"I told you, Rose, I don't want it. I'll find another job, another way."

"But it's all you've ever wanted." He'd said so himself. His honour, his family name, his dignity. He'd give it all up for her?

"The truth is, I've wanted it for so long that I didn't see what it was doing to me. I think it was sucking the life from me. It certainly was making me soft. I actually begged your father. Begged him."

Rose chuckled. "So you'll become a pirate then? Like your father?"

Anthony laughed. "Definitely not that. I'll find something in between. How does that sound?"

"It sounds as though you might be a worthy choice after all," she told him, rising to her tiptoes and touching her cold lips to his. When she pulled away, she said, "But we can't marry without my father's permission and he'll never give it."

This time when Anthony grinned, he did resemble a lawbreaker. "I supposed we'll need to steal a few horses and make haste to Scotland."

Rose tipped her head back and laughed. He'd gone from upholding the law to breaking it in such a short amount of time. Perhaps it was she who would have difficulty keeping up with him?

EPILOGUE

ROSE ELMIRA GERMAINE used the servants' entrance to the kitchen of the modest townhouse a few streets back from the wealthiest in London. She toed off boots caked with mud and left them to stand next to the hearth where they would be cleaned, polished and set to rights. Not much could be done about her hem and Molly would be upset that Rose had ruined yet another day dress.

She left Ned to eat his fill, the cook cursing and shaking a fist about meal times but giving him a warm smile anyway and a bowl of hearty soup to tide him over.

Tiptoeing through the house, she gave it her best effort not to disturb the stuffy butler so she could surprise her husband. Surprise him she did.

Anthony sat at his desk in his study with stacks of paper before him, ledgers and maps and pieces of string cut to length and waiting for the next destination to be revealed. When the door closed with a click, he looked up from his work, tired, but the glint in his eye meant he was getting somewhere.

"How was your afternoon, my love?" he asked her, a ritual of sorts.

Rose beamed and paced the room. Her words rushed out and nothing could stem them. "Did you know there's a house on Mayfair that looks perfectly respectable from the outside but is less than respectable on the inside?"

His answering smile didn't slip but the glint in his eye turned into a gleam. He gave a her a nod. "How is Madam Belange?"

"Oh, she's lovely. We had tea and she answered so many of my questions."

This did change the expression on his face. "You took tea with a brothel owner on Mayfair? On a Tuesday afternoon in broad daylight?"

Rose nodded. "And she sent me to see a man on the river where the youngest son of the Douglas clan might fence his mother's jewels before visiting such an establishment."

Anthony had to clear his throat before he answered. Rose liked to rattle him like this. She rather thought he enjoyed it as much as she. He merely said, "The lad has expensive taste."

In the month since they'd returned from their elopement and an extended honeymoon she hadn't expected, they'd opened an office together, the idea coming to her husband late one night after many wines and a dinner with retired pirates. With Trelissick's endorsement, Anthony was an investigator of private matters and Rose too. Only, she was supposed to question people and then turn her information over to her husband to do the actual running to ground. She didn't. So far she'd solved three matters. He was far too busy chasing down Smith with Trelissick. The crown wanted her and were paying quite well to follow all leads they received.

"How goes your afternoon?" Rose countered. "You look as though you have fit another piece of the puzzle."

Rose came to stand next to him at the desk, leaning over his notes and map. There was a new mark over the Caribbean.

"I can't believe she sent you a letter," he said.

Her attention was diverted when he spun her so the backs of her thighs rested against the solid timber. "What did you learn at the brothel, Rose?"

Her cheeks warmed and she had to remember to keep eye contact lest he think her lying. He'd taught her that. "I only asked about the missing jewels and the Douglas lad. I am still a lady."

Her husband made a sound like *pfft* through his lips before lifting the hem of her mud caked gown. "Breeches," he muttered. "I really am beginning to hate the inventor of these blasted things."

"All right, almost a lady," she conceded. When he went to work on the laces at her waist, she said, "My gown is ruined and you can't just lift my skirts whenever it takes your fancy."

He gave her a lazy shrug and dropped her hem, only to turn her just as quickly until she was bent over the desk, her cheek to the map somewhere over the Americas. "You won't mind if I ruin it a little further, will you, wife?"

The winged creatures that lived inside her took flight as they did when he treated her like this. Her skirts were flicked up and over her back and her loosened breeches were yanked down.

He stroked her.

She groaned and pushed back against him.

He may claim no link to being a pirate like his father once was but he knew how to behave as one when they were alone. She worked to loosen one ankle when he gave her bottom a sharp slap.

Rose stilled. His words reached her. "Did you hear a noise like that on Mayfair, Rose? Or was it sharper? Louder?"

She raised her head and caught a glimpse of his expression over her shoulder. His green eyes were glazed and his expression was intent, heated, hungry. "You've been there." It wasn't a question so much as an accusation.

"Perhaps."

And he showed her something new, bent over his desk, her ankles trapped in the breeches she insisted on wearing despite his protests. They would both receive dirty looks from the butler when they would eventually emerge.

A slip of paper floated to the floor when a ledger was pushed to the carpets.

Dearest Rose,

I wanted to apologise for all of that nasty business at the docks. I don't think you would have been harmed, M is rather fond of you after all, but probably a good thing your Germaine rescued you. The journey was interminable and I added a screaming child to it. Tell Josiah he has his eyes. Tell your brothers I won't be back. You can

be rest assured I won't be coming anywhere near Eng-
land ever again.

   I have all that I need.

Best of wishes,
L

The End

Want more? Check out Darius and Eliza's story in
The Slide into Ruin!

Join Tule Publishing's newsletter for more great reads and
weekly deals!

Author's Note

One of the hardest parts of writing a romance set in such an intriguing time in history is naming all the characters! The most avid Regency buffs might have wondered why the Earl of Clairmont's surname is also Clairmont. Hell's Gate is obviously a fictional castle standing on almost inhospitable terrain and has been in place for hundreds of years, as has the family name and seat. Just like Princess Diana's father, the Earl of Spencer, if the title is old enough or new enough, the title and family name would be the same. Rose just seemed like a Clairmont despite not wanting to be a part of the family. We are who we are and while we can choose friends and lovers, we cannot choose our family…

I promise this won't be a trend in my books and if you want to reach out to me, feel free to hunt me down on the socials or my website contact—www.bronwynstuart.com.

You can find all of the Daughters of Disgrace books at tulepublishing.com/authors/bronwyn-stuart and where good books are sold!

If you enjoyed *The Fall into Ruin,*
you'll love the other books in....

THE DAUGHTERS OF DISGRACE SERIES

Book 1: *The Road to Ruin*

Book 2: *The Slide into Ruin*

Book 3: *The Fall into Ruin*

Available now at your favorite online retailer!

ABOUT THE AUTHOR

Bronwyn Stuart is a multi-published, award-winning author of both contemporary and historical romantic fiction. Her latest Regency series, Daughters of Disgrace, will be released July 2020 by Tule Publishing. She and her shoe collection share a house in the Adelaide Hills with her husband, kids, dogs and cat. She's a sucker for a love story and a bad boy.

You can find out more at www.bronwynstuart.com

Thank you for reading

THE FALL INTO RUIN

If you enjoyed this book, you can find more from all our great authors at TulePublishing.com, or from your favorite online retailer.

TULE
PUBLISHING

Made in United States
Orlando, FL
08 March 2024